Lys
an
a l——gy, —————sm career in which she had to write way too many
sad endings, she decided to return to the stories that guaranteed a
happy ever after. Once described as 'funny, adorable, and a wee-bit
heartbreaking,' Lyssa's books feature women who always get the
last word, men who aren't afraid to cry, and dogs. Lots of dogs.
Lyssa writes full time from her home in Michigan, where she lives
with her sports writer husband, her wickedly funny daughter, and a
spoiled Maltese who likes to be rocked to sleep like a baby. When
she's not writing, she's cooking or driving her daughter around from
one sporting event to the next. Or rocking the dog.

Connect online with Lyssa:
lyssakayadams.com/newsletter
Twitter: @LyssaKayAdams
Instagram: @lyssakayadams
Facebook: /lyssakayadams

Praise for *The Bromance Book Club*:

'A you're-gonna-burn-dinner book because you will not want to put
it down. Laugh out loud with tons of heart, this is an absolutely
adorable must read'

Avery Flynn, *USA Today* bestselling author

'A delight! . . . I raced to finish this book, but still never wanted it
to end!'

Alexa Martin, author of *Intercepted*

'A delightful, fast-paced read with the perfect mix of laugh-out-
loud and swoony moments – every town should have a Bromance
Book Club'

Evie Dunmore, author of *Bringing Down the Duke*

'It is the reading aloud in this story that ultimately wins my heart,
and shows   ned from
romance'

ing Fraser

By Lyssa Kay Adams

The Bromance Book Club

Undercover Bromance

UNDERCOVER
Bromance

LYSSA KAY ADAMS

HEADLINE
ETERNAL

Published by arrangement with Berkley,
an imprint of Penguin Publishing Group, a division of
Penguin Random House LLC. First published in the United States in 2020

First published in Great Britain in 2020
by HEADLINE ETERNAL
An imprint of HEADLINE PUBLISHING GROUP

1

Cataloguing in Publication Data is available from the British Library

ISBN 978 1 4722 7165 5

Offset in 10.18/15.43pt Sabon LT Std by Jouve (UK), Milton Keynes

Printed and bound in Great Britain by Clays Ltd, Elcograf S.p.A.

Headline's policy is to use papers that are natural, renewable and recyclable
products and made from wood grown in well-managed forests and other
controlled sources. The logging and manufacturing processes are expected
to conform to the environmental regulations of the country of origin.

HEADLINE PUBLISHING GROUP
An Hachette UK Company
Carmelite House
50 Victoria Embankment
London EC4Y 0DZ

www.headlineeternal.com
www.headline.co.uk
www.hachette.co.uk

To Mom
Thanks for raising me to be a strong woman
and for teaching me that there really isn't any other kind.

ACKNOWLEDGMENTS

Not gonna lie. This book nearly killed me, and I wouldn't have survived without the help of my patient agent, Tara Gelsomino (you were right, Tara; this book was, indeed, very ambitious), and my creative, reassuring editor, Kristine Swartz. Thank you for putting up with the panic attacks and helping me bring Mack and Liv's story to life. Thank you, also, to the entire Berkley team. Bridget O'Toole and Jessica Brock, you are the best at what you do. I am forever in your debt for answering all my questions about marketing and publicity. And I would be a total jerk if I didn't shout a loud THANK YOU to the copyeditors who catch important details, including interesting tidbits about chicken genitals.

All my love and thanks to my writing squad—Meika, Christina, Victoria, and Alyssa—and my hilarious Binderhaus crew. As always, you keep me sane.

Thank you to my family. I love you all so much. You make it possible for me to live this dream. I do what I do for you.

Lastly, thank you to survivors. I believe you. Always. #MeToo.

(I refuse to thank, however, the real Randy the Rooster. You're an asshole, Randy. Leave the damn hens alone.)

CHAPTER ONE

Braden Mack pulled his Porsche SUV into an empty spot at the back of the dark parking lot and waited for the signal. Facing him from two rows down, a Suburban idled with its lights on.

A moment passed. Then two.

Finally, the Suburban flashed its high beams twice.

It was time.

He turned off the engine, silenced his cell phone, and shoved it in the pocket of his leather jacket. As he exited his car, the men in the other vehicle did the same. One by one, their hulking frames unfolded from the Suburban, their breaths forming little puffs around their faces. Mack met them halfway between the two cars.

"You're late," said Del Hicks, one of Mack's closest friends.

"I had to save a marriage."

"Another lonely wife?" That was from Derek Wilson, a local businessman.

"Men never learn."

"Which is why we're here, right?" said Malcolm James, his

voice deep and Zen-like behind the thick beard that hung nearly to his collarbone.

"Right." Mack sized up each man, measuring guts and commitment. "Anyone who wants out, say it now, because the minute we start this, there's no going back."

"I'm in," Derek said.

"Yeah, man." Del pounded one gloved hand into the other. "Let's do this."

"What the fuck are we doing again?" whined Gavin Scott, one of the newest members of the group, his shoulders hunched against the wind. "Besides freezing our balls off?"

Mack turned and looked at the building. A bright-red sign lit up the bustling sidewalk that ran the length of the strip mall. MUSIC CITY BOOKS. For three years, their book club had hidden in the shadows. Read in secret. Met behind closed doors. There were ten of them in all—professional athletes and city officials, tech geniuses and business owners. And, in the case of Mack, the owner of several Nashville bars and nightclubs. All drawn together by a shared love of books that had made them better men, better lovers, better husbands.

Except for Mack on that last one. He was currently one of the last single guys in the group. "What are we doing?" he repeated, looking at the guys. "We're going to buy some goddamned romance novels in public."

He planted his hands on his hips and waited for the dramatic response. Maybe some cinematic music or something, or a loud cheer from the guys. But all he got in response was a resounding fart from the fifth member of their group, a hockey player whom everyone just called the Russian and who had an unfortunate intolerance for dairy products.

The Russian clutched his stomach. "I have to find the bathroom."

Mack shook his head. "Let's go."

The Russian took off first with a slightly lopsided gait. The rest of them followed, with Mack in the lead. They waited at the edge of the parking lot for a line of cars to pass before jogging to the sidewalk. The Russian disappeared inside without a backward glance, his steps growing quicker every few feet. Things were getting diccy there. That bathroom had no idea what it was in for. RIP to the bookstore's plumbing.

Mack took a deep breath, hand on the door handle. He looked once again at the rest of the guys. "Okay. Here are the rules. Everyone has to buy at least one book for the rest of the club to consider for our next read. No hiding the covers. And if anyone asks, you are not buying it as a present. You're buying it for yourself. Any questions?"

"What if someone recognizes us?" Gavin grumbled. Of all the guys, he was probably the most famous and recognizable right now. As a player for the Nashville Major League Baseball team, the Legends, he'd skyrocketed to national fame last year when he nailed a walk-off grand-slam homer in a playoff game.

"Who cares if we're recognized?" said Malcom, another famous face. He was the running back for the Nashville NFL team. "We spend a lot of time talking about the unfairness of how our toxic masculine society forces us to be ashamed of embracing romance novels. Yet we buy our books in secret. It's time we practice what we preach."

"Couldn't have said it better myself," Mack said, standing tall.

"Of course not," Gavin snorted. "Malcolm has a genius IQ, dumbass."

Mack flipped him off.

Gavin returned the gesture.

Del sighed and opened the door. "I'll go first."

They attracted attention as soon as they walked in, but Mack doubted it was because anyone recognized any of them. How often did a group of hulking, good-looking men walk into a bookstore together? They were like an offensive line for the Literary League of Tennessee.

"Where's the romance section?" Del asked quietly.

Mack shook his head, eyes searching the signs that hung from the ceiling. "I don't see it."

"We're going to have to ask for help," Malcolm said.

Gavin cursed and tugged the brim of his cap lower to hide his face.

They approached the information desk, and a woman in an *I Read Banned Books* T-shirt looked up from her computer screen. "Can I help you?"

"Can you tell me where the romance section is?" Malcolm asked.

She squinted. "Like marriage and self-help?"

"No," Mack said, sidling up next to Malcolm. He propped one hand on the desk and leaned toward her with a smile. "We mean romance novels."

"You guys are looking for the romance novel section," she said, skepticism hanging on every word.

"We sure are." Mack winked.

The woman's cheeks flushed under his attention. "I've never had men ask for romance novels."

Mack leaned closer and lowered his voice to a level somewhere between seductive and conspiratorial. Her blush deepened. "There are a lot of us," he murmured.

She pointed toward the back of the store. "Last shelves on the right."

Malcolm led them through the store. Gavin made a disgusted noise. "Is there anyone you don't flirt with?" he asked Mack.

Mack shrugged. "Not my fault if I'm born with natural charm."

They stopped at a single aisle in the back with a meager selection of paperbacks. Just one wall had been set aside for romance. "This is a disgrace," Malcolm said, shaking his head.

Gavin glanced around nervously. "I wouldn't mind if we were still shopping online."

"Have some pride," Mack said, turning his head to read the spines of the books.

The Russian returned. "Good bathroom here. Very clean."

The Russian could identify the best public bathrooms in every major city in the United States. If he ever retired from hockey, he could create an app ranking them and make more money than he ever did as a player.

Mack found his favorite author and pulled *The Protector*, her newest book, off the shelf. A romantic suspense about a Secret Service agent and the president's daughter. He loved a little danger with his romance, and he especially loved an enemies-to-lovers story. There was just something satisfying about two people discovering that what makes them fight is also the thing that makes them perfect for each other.

"Are we meeting Friday night?" Gavin asked, glancing at a book with a red spine. "The game doesn't get out until probably seven, so Del and I can't meet until late."

"It'll have to be Saturday," Mack said, cracking open his book to read the first page. "I have a date with Gretchen Friday night."

A knot of tension unfurled in his gut. Tomorrow night would officially be three months with Gretchen, a local attorney he'd met at a party, and he wasn't sparing any expense to make it special for her. He'd pulled every string he had to make an impossible-to-get reservation at Savoy, one of Nashville's swankiest restaurants, which was owned by a celebrity TV chef. And if all went well, he planned to do the thing he'd never done before—have the talk. The *let's be exclusive* talk.

The silence behind him was suddenly too obvious to be a coincidence. He turned around and found the guys having a silent conservation with raised eyebrows and hand gestures. Del dug into his wallet and shoved a twenty-dollar bill at the Russian.

"What the fuck is that? What are you doing?"

They jumped with matching expressions of guilt. "He owed me money," the Russian said, shoving the twenty in his pocket.

"Bullshit. What are you guys talking about?"

The Russian's shoulders drooped like a puppy who'd just been scolded for pissing on the carpet.

"He won the bet."

Mack's eyebrows furrowed. "What bet?"

"That you would choose a romantic suspense," Del said quickly.

Mack folded his arms over his chest, tucking the book under his armpit. "You expect me to believe that you made a bet about what kind of book I would choose?"

The Russian whistled and looked around. Del smacked him upside the back of the head.

"For fuck's sake." Gavin sighed. "They have a running bet over how long until you dump Gretchen."

Mack blinked. "Are you fucking kidding me right now?"

"It was his idea," the Russian said, pointing at Del.

Del didn't deny it. Instead, he shrugged. "I've lost a lot of money, but I'm impressed that you've stuck with her this long. This has to be a record or something."

Mack gaped, trying not to be insulted, but what the fuck? Sure, he probably deserved his reputation as a one-and-done bachelor, the kind of guy with a different woman on his arm every weekend. He'd just never met anyone he could imagine settling down with. And despite what most people thought of him, he did want to settle down. But his own friend was betting against him? If that wasn't a kick in the balls, he didn't know what was.

Mack pointed at Del. "I'll have you know, douchebag, that I've *stuck with her* this long because I like her. She's beautiful, smart, and ambitious."

"And totally wrong for you," Malcolm interrupted, entering the conversation for the first time. He'd been studying the shelves during most of the exchange but now turned around with four books tucked in his massive hands.

"Excuse me?" Mack sputtered. "How is she totally wrong for me?"

"Because all the women you date are wrong for you," Gavin snorted.

Mack sputtered again before responding. "Dude, you've known me for less than six months."

"Yeah, and in that time you've dated six different women. Amazing women. All smart, talented, gorgeous. *Perfect*."

"And that's a problem?" He sounded defensive, which made him feel defensive. Dammit, he *was* defensive. They were supposed to be buying books, not analyzing his love life.

Gavin shrugged. "You tell me. You dumped them all."

"Because it didn't work out with them," Mack said in a growl.

"And it's different with Gretchen?"

"Yes," Mack said.

"How?" Malcolm asked.

Mack had no response to that. It was different with Gretchen because, because . . . dammit, because he was ready for it to be different. Wasn't that enough? He was tired of watching his friends live happily ever after while he fruitlessly searched for the future Mrs. Mack—someone he could spoil, grow old with, and cherish forever. He was the founder of the damn book club but the only one who'd never experienced the real thing. So, yeah, he was working extra hard this time to stick with it because, dammit, he wanted his own happily ever after.

Gavin held up his hands in a truce. "Look, all we're saying is that for all your talk about being the expert, it seems like you miss the most important lesson of these books."

"Which is?" His tone now edged toward petulance, but he didn't like being lectured about the lessons of the manuals—which was what they all called romance novels—by the newest member of the club.

"There's a big difference between romancing someone and loving someone."

Mack rolled his eyes. "Easy for you to say. You fell in love at first sight with the perfect woman."

Gavin sobered. "My wife isn't perfect. She's just perfect for me. And there's been nothing easy about our marriage."

Tension once again tugged at Mack's gut, this time from guilt. Gavin and his wife, Thea, had nearly divorced six months ago before the book club stepped in to help Gavin get her back.

But rather than apologize for being an asshole, he dug in. "I'm going to prove you wrong," he seethed.

Mack yanked his wallet from his back pocket, heart pounding with the arrogance of something to prove. He shoved a hundred-dollar bill at Del.

"Five-to-one odds that after tomorrow night, I officially have a girlfriend."

CHAPTER TWO

"You look beautiful tonight."

Mack reached across the table for Gretchen's slim fingers. She smiled as he brushed his thumb across her knuckles. The earrings he'd given her last week for her birthday hung from her delicate earlobes and sparkled in the candlelight.

"Thank you," she said. "You certainly say it enough to make me feel beautiful."

"New dress?"

She laughed and looked down at herself. "Um, no. I got this at Macy's a couple of years ago. Clearance rack."

"It's beautiful."

She tugged her hand back. "Thank you. Again."

Gretchen tore her gaze from his and looked around at the restaurant. Their VIP table in the loft gave them a full view of the urban-chic decor. Wrought-iron chandeliers hung from the high ceilings, and exposed-brick walls gave it an unfinished feel. But when paired with the dark woodwork and the ornate gold, it also had an old-world opulence to it.

"I always wondered what it looked like in here," Gretchen said.

"What do you think?"

"It's, um . . ." She winced as if reluctant to criticize. "It's a little over the top."

"So is Royce."

"You know him?"

Mack adjusted his sport coat as he sat back in his chair. "We've met several times. Charity golf tournaments and that sort of thing. We tend to run in the same circles as business owners."

"Ah. Of course." She squinted. "I don't really run in those circles, you know."

"You run in more important circles." Gretchen was a public defender specializing in immigration cases.

Their waiter approached the table with a bottle of chilled Dom Perignon. Mack had ordered it when he'd made the reservation, along with the signature dessert—the Sultan cupcake. It was so elaborate and expensive, it had to be ordered in advance. He couldn't wait for Gretchen to see it.

"Champagne?" Gretchen asked as the waiter popped the cork.

"We're celebrating," Mack said with a wink.

The waiter poured two tall flutes and then left the bottle in a bucket of ice next to the table before saying he'd be back in a few minutes to go over the specials for the night.

"Sure," Gretchen said, accepting her glass. "So what's the occasion?"

Mack raised his glass. "I closed the deal today on the new building," he said. "But more importantly, here's to us. Three months. And hopefully many more."

Her smile didn't quite reach her eyes when she clinked her glass with his. He thought at first that he was imagining it, but she looked away when she took a drink.

"Everything okay?"

She swallowed and nodded. "This is wonderful."

"So are you."

There it was again. The *not quite a smile* smile. Mack set down his glass and reached again for her hand. "Are you sure you're okay?"

"I'm fine. I'm just . . . To be honest, I feel a little guilty being at a place like this."

"Why?"

"My clients can barely afford boxed macaroni and cheese for their children."

"Doesn't mean I can't spoil you, does it?"

"I don't need to be spoiled, Mack."

"But you deserve to be." He tried again with the wink and the smile. This time it worked. Her fingers relaxed in his.

"Thank you. You definitely know how to wine and dine a woman."

"I aim to please." He gave her fingers a final squeeze and let go. "Now I hope you're hungry. Because I have a surprise for you later."

Gretchen drank from her champagne and looked at her watch.

"I swear to God, why not just light a thousand bucks on fire?"

Liv Papandreas stepped back from the stainless-steel counter to study her latest culinary masterpiece with a disgusted shake of her head. As a pastry chef at Savoy, it shouldn't surprise her anymore what the one percent would waste their money on, but sadly, it did. And she had known the minute her boss put the gold-infused cupcake on the menu that the city's richest celebrities and show-offs would order it in droves just because they could.

Well, that, and so they could pose for an Instagram-worthy photo with Royce Preston, celebrity chef, television host, and the dickhead who signed Liv's paychecks.

Every week, millions of fans tuned in to his reality show, *Kitchen Boss*, for a dose of his smooth-talking charm. Little did they know that his smooth-talking charm was as fake as his hair. When the cameras were off, he was a belligerent douchebag who stole most of his recipes from his own staff. Liv had somehow managed to survive an entire year in his kitchen, mostly because she had a stubborn disdain for wealthy posers. Who could've guessed that a teenage career in breaking rules and antagonizing authority figures would actually help her someday?

Rumor had it that tonight's cupcake schmuck was some nightclub owner. Liv wouldn't know. Nightclubs weren't really her thing. Because people. People weren't really her thing either.

Suddenly, her fellow prison inmate—er, pastry chef—Riya Singh clapped her on the back. "You don't think your talents are worth a thousand dollars?"

"I think my talents are worth a lot more. I just don't think a single freaking cupcake is. Every single person who orders one of these should be forced to immediately write a check for the downtown food bank."

"Starting with Royce."

Yeah, right. Men like Royce didn't give money to charity. They hoarded it, flaunted it. Bribed their kids' way into elite colleges with it. And he was about to make a helluva lot more of it. In one month, the first official *Kitchen Boss* cookbook would be published—a cookbook full of recipes he'd ripped off. One of Liv's was in there—a twist on baklava using pomegranates and natural honey.

"I still don't understand why you don't just quit and take your sister up on her offer," Riya said. "You could be free of this place forever if you wanted. The rest of us have to stay because we don't have any other choice."

Liv's sister, Thea, had offered at least a dozen times to give Liv the money to open her own business. Thea was married to a Major League Baseball player who made a major league salary. But the thing no one seemed to understand, including Thea herself, was that Liv didn't want to succeed because of someone else's money. If that were the case, she'd just call her rich father and finally accept his endless offers to buy his way back into her life. She didn't want his guilt money, though.

Anyway, Liv had worked too hard and overcome too much to take the easy way out now. She had the drive and talent to succeed on her own, and she was going to. If she could last one more year here, she could write her own ticket in the cutthroat culinary profession, because everyone knew that if you could survive Royce, you could handle anything. Every single day was a fight, but Liv had worked too damn hard to risk her career now by spiking the man's breakfast smoothie with rat poison.

Not that she'd, like, thought about that or anything.

Jessica Summers, a young hostess who'd started just a month ago, crept over to the counter, biting her lip. "Is that it?" she asked breathlessly, staring at the cupcake.

"Yep," Liv said.

"I haven't worked a shift yet when someone ordered it. You can really eat the gold?" She bent down to study it, eyes wide. "What does it even taste like?"

"Ostentatious greed."

Jessica looked up. "Is that good?"

"Rich people think so."

The swinging doors to the kitchen slammed open. Everyone held their breath as Royce stormed in. He wore his standard uniform—a tailored suit, crisp white shirt with the top three buttons undone to reveal a smattering of chest hair, and a leather necklace that he claimed was a gift from some indigenous tribe but Liv would bet cold hard cash was actually a cheap trinket from a shop downtown.

"Olivia," Royce barked, because he refused to use her nickname like everyone else. It was some kind of weird power-play thing.

Jessica gulped, cheeks red and eyes closed, as Royce approached them. Poor girl. She wasn't going to last long if she couldn't even handle the bark of his voice. You just had to know how to bark back.

"Is it going to be ready on time?" Royce growled.

"Have I ever been late with one?"

He turned a bright shade of red. His eyes gave her the once-over, and he shook his head. "Clean yourself up before we take that out there."

Yeah. Not only did she have to make these gold-encrusted monstrosities, she also had to trail behind his holiness to deliver them to the customer. Royce was all about the show. Liv glanced down at herself. Chocolate was smeared across her coat. Hazard of the job. Royce snapped his fingers at Riya. "Give her your coat. Now. Come on."

A clean coat was suddenly thrust in her line of vision. Liv shot an apologetic look at her friend as she unbuttoned her soiled coat and traded it.

"Get back to work," he ordered Riya.

He stormed off again, and Jessica let out the breath she'd been holding. Liv could've sworn she saw tears in the girl's eyes. Yeah, she was *so* not going to last. *Mental note: Help Jessica find another job before she has a nervous breakdown.*

Or before Liv really did spike his smoothie with rat poison.

Liv carefully lifted the tray holding the cupcake and met Royce by the doors. She tried not to openly roll her eyes when he told her not to fucking drop it.

As if she ever had.

The instant they entered the restaurant, Royce transformed into the easygoing guy everyone knew and loved from the show. An excited whisper followed in his wake, and he ate it up. He was all hearty waves and sideways peace signs. Phone cameras captured his every move, and behind him, Liv pretended to be proud of the gilded concoction she carried. She held the tray high in her right hand and pasted a smile on her face to hide the fact that she was silently wishing Royce would burst into flames. She followed him toward the VIP section of the restaurant, where a red velvet rope separated the chosen ones from the lesser mortals. Liv waited for Royce to approach the table first, of course. This was his show. From ten feet away in the dim lighting, Liv could make out the forms of two people at the table—a man with broad shoulders beneath a sport coat and a woman with glossy hair and smart eyes. Whoever this dude was, he was laying it on thick for his date. Their plates revealed the remnants of steak, lobster, and truffle pâté.

"Friends," Royce said in his best TV show voice. "May I present to you the Sultan."

The man turned in his seat and—oh crap. Liv knew him.

What was his name? Mike? No. Mack. Brad Mack? *Braden.* Braden Mack. He was a friend of her brother-in-law, Gavin. He was the dude who'd dragged Gavin into some weird, secret romance novel book club for men to help Gavin convince Thea not to divorce him. But, more important, he was the jerk who had eaten her Chinese food leftovers the first time they met. She'd been looking forward to those leftovers. What kind of person ate someone else's lo mein? The same kind who saw no problem spending a thousand bucks on a cupcake, apparently.

The man stood and extended his hand. "Royce. Good to see you again."

Of course. Of course he knew her boss. Because a guy who would waste a normal person's entire paycheck on a single dinner out would definitely run in the same circles as Royce Preston.

Royce shook Mack's hand and did the manly back-pounding half-hug thing. "I had no idea you were here tonight. I'll have to have a word with our hostess about that."

Oh no. Poor Jessica. Maybe Liv would have time to warn her before he chewed her to pieces.

"This is Gretchen Winthrop," Mack said, gesturing gallantly to his date. "She's an attorney."

"An attorney, huh?"

The woman lifted her hand for Royce to shake. Instead, he pulled it to his lips and kissed her knuckles. "Beautiful *and* smart," Royce said. "It's a pleasure."

Liv puked in her mouth.

The woman gently pulled her hand away. "Likewise."

Except she didn't really seem sincere in that. Liv liked her immediately. She was too smart for these guys.

"How's business?" Royce asked as Mack returned to his seat.

"Great," Mack said. "Just signed the papers on a new building in the old industrial area."

"That was you?"

"That was me."

"I had my eye on those buildings."

Mack spread his hands out in a fake apology. "Sorry. I'm leaning toward a restaurant this time."

"Ah, you're expanding your empire," Royce said. "Good man. Let's talk and see if we can work together on some things."

It was the kind of noncommittal, *we're all in this together* bullshit Royce dished out to all the other rich men who walked into Savoy. But he wouldn't follow through. Royce didn't share the wealth or the limelight with anyone.

"I'm sorry to interrupt," Gretchen suddenly said. "But I feel bad that she's been standing there this entire time just holding that thing. Can she at least set it down?"

Royce shot Liv a deceptively blank stare that simmered with rage. His left eyebrow twitched almost imperceptibly. But then he broke into a broad grin. "Of course. Olivia, if you would."

Liv strode forward, eyes everywhere but on Mack, and lowered the tray so the cupcake was eye-level with Gretchen. She tilted her face away from Mack, but he probably wouldn't recognize her anyway. Her snug chef's hat hid her curly hair, and she doubted Mack had studied her face long enough while eating her noodles for him to remember it now.

"The Sultan is our signature dessert, featuring a mixture of chocolates from twelve different countries," Royce continued.

"With a champagne-jelly filling and edible gold adornments, it's served with a twenty-four-carat-gold spoon and a scoop of the finest Ugandan vanilla bean ice cream."

"Wow," Gretchen said with just enough snark for Liv to decide they should be BFFs. "I'm almost afraid to eat it."

"How about a picture?" Royce said, walking behind Gretchen's chair to pose.

Just once, Liv would love to see someone say no to a photo.

And wonder of wonders, today would be that day.

"Oh, that's—no, I'm fine," Gretchen said, and somewhere in the world, angels began to sing. If only Liv were telepathic, because her brain was screaming *YOU ARE MY BEST FRIEND*.

Royce's eyebrow twitched again. It was bad enough that a woman had said no to a picture. But to do so in front of a staff member. Oh, the raging would be loud tonight. But definitely worth it.

Liv quietly cleared her throat and was just about to set the cupcake on the table when—

"Hey, I know you." Mack leaned forward, studying her face. "You're Thea's sister."

Without waiting for her to confirm or deny, Mack nodded at his date. "This is amazing. I had no idea she worked here. I've told you about Gavin, right? This is his sister-in-law."

"It's nice to meet you," Gretchen said. "I'd shake your hand, but obviously your hands are full. This looks delicious by the way. Thank you."

Liv smiled. "Nice to meet you."

Royce cleared his throat. Oh, shit. She'd said words, hadn't she? That was bad. She was going to pay for that later.

"I swear, I didn't know you worked here," Mack said, still

clueless. "Gavin only said that you worked at a restaurant downtown."

"Olivia has worked for me for several months," Royce said, not to be left out.

"A year," Liv corrected quietly. Royce cleared his throat again. Quietly. Firmly. *You are so dead*-ly.

Mack suddenly stood. "We should get a picture. I'll send it to Gavin."

Liv darted a glance at Royce, whose forced smile suggested he was not happy about being overshadowed. He didn't share the camera lens with anyone.

"I appreciate the gesture," Liv said steadily. "But I prefer to stay behind the scenes."

"No way," Mack said. "You should get credit for your work."

Liv imagined the top of Royce's head literally blowing off, along with his toupee, but he was too much of a showman to do anything besides smile and say, "Absolutely. Olivia, please."

She was going to pay for this later. It didn't matter that she'd done nothing to encourage this. Royce wouldn't see it that way.

"Wait," Mack said. "Do you prefer Liv or Olivia? I've only ever heard Gavin call you Liv."

"Liv, actually. But Royce calls me Olivia."

"Why?"

Liv looked up. "Yeah, Royce. Why?"

Royce's fake smile was so cold that it practically hummed "Ice Ice Baby."

Mack shrugged and handed his phone across the table to Royce. Liv's mouth fell open. He was . . . he was asking *Royce* to take the picture? No one did that to Royce. No one. *OMG, do not smile. Do not smile.* If she smiled, she would end up *in* the cupcake, not serving it.

Royce nodded, still smiling, but Liv knew that smile. It hid a boiling fury that Royce would certainly unleash later in a torrent of flying spittle and *I've met dead slabs of lamb smarter than you* outbursts. But what the hell was Liv supposed to do? Hit Mack over the head with her tray and run away?

Actually, that was a tempting idea.

Mack rounded the table and stood next to Liv. He slung an arm around her shoulders and—

The tray wobbled in her hands. She tried to correct, tried to steady it with her other hand, but her reflexes were too late.

Time slowed to the blurry speed of a horror movie as the cupcake slid to the edge of the tray. It balanced there for a moment, teetered like a car in a movie that stops just in time before plunging over the edge of a cliff.

It was just long enough for her entire career to flash before her eyes. Long enough for her to imagine all the ways she was going to kill Braden Mack for this. Long enough for a single word to drag along the length of her tongue. "Fuuucck . . ."

Then gravity did its thing.

And the cupcake landed in Gretchen's lap.

"Oh my God, I'm so sorry." Liv dropped to her knees next to Gretchen's chair.

"It's okay," Gretchen told Liv. She held her hands aloft, fingers coated with frosting.

"This is my fault," Mack said. "I knocked the tray out of her hands."

"Olivia, go to the kitchen," Royce barked. "We will have another one made for you."

"That's not necessary," Gretchen said, lifting the cupcake from her chocolate-stained lap to her plate.

"Can I help clean it up?" Liv asked. "Please. Let me—"

Royce cut her off. "Obviously your entire meal is on us tonight."

Liv groaned.

"And please allow me to cover the cost of cleaning your dress."

"Truly, that's not necessary," Gretchen said. "This was an accident."

"This is my fault," Mack said again.

"My staff is trained to handle anything," Royce said. "Clearly that failed tonight. We will make this right."

"There's nothing to make right," Gretchen said smoothly. "Accidents happen."

"We will send someone over to help clean up the mess immediately."

"I'm so sorry," Liv said once again to Gretchen.

"That will be all, Olivia."

Liv turned another homicidal glare in Mack's direction before retrieving her tray. Then she spun on her heel and quickstepped toward the kitchen without so much as a backward glance. Liv figured she had roughly a ninety-second head start on Royce. Maybe it would be enough time for him to calm down.

Liv headed straight for the employee locker room and tore off her hat. She sank onto a bench of front of her locker as Riya rushed in.

"What happened?" Riya asked, unbuttoning the chef's coat Liv had given her.

"You're not going to want to be around me."

"Oh shit, why?"

"I dropped it!"

Riya winced. "Oh, Liv."

The slamming of the swinging doors outside made them both jump. "OLIVIA."

Liv braced herself. She stood tall as Royce stormed into the locker room. He shook from head to toe, and his face was as red as a lobster in a pot.

"You," he said, pointing at Riya. "Out."

Riya squeezed Liv's arm in sympathy before leaving.

Royce wagged a finger in Liv's face. "My office. Twenty minutes."

Then he turned and stormed back out, shouting as he did, "Find me Jessica!"

Shitshitshit.

Mack had nearly followed Liv to apologize again, but then he remembered Gretchen. He turned around and found her wiping her hands on her napkin.

"Are you okay?" he asked, crouching down next to her chair.

"I had a cupcake dropped on me, Braden. I wasn't shot."

"No, but this isn't how I wanted tonight to turn out."

"I'm a little more worried about how this night is going to turn out for your friend Liv."

"She's not my friend."

Gretchen responded to that with furrowed eyebrows. Mack rushed to clarify. "I mean, I barely know her. But yes, of course I hope she doesn't get in trouble for this."

Gretchen braced her hands on the arms of her chair and started to stand. "I'm going to run to the restroom to get cleaned up."

"Right. Of course." Mack stood and held out his hand to her to help her rise.

The extent of the damage to her dress became clear when she stepped away from the table. A dark-brown splotch marred the delicate green silk. He knew enough about fine fabrics to know the dress was a lost cause.

He shrugged out of his sport coat. "Do you want this to cover it up?"

She smiled but shook her head. "I think that would just make it a little more obvious."

Mack watched her walk away and then sat back down. Great. Just fucking great. Things had been going perfectly until that moment.

Two busboys dressed all in black arrived with plastic tubs and wet rags. With quiet apologies for the mess, they began picking up the remnants of the cupcake from the floor and Gretchen's chair.

Mack stepped out of their way and softly cleared his throat. "Do you, uh, do you know if the woman who made the cupcake— is she getting in trouble for this?"

The two young men shared a nervous glance and had an unspoken conversation. One of them shrugged then and shook his head. "We don't know anything about that."

When they left, Mack dropped a couple of twenties on the table. Just because they were getting their dinner for free didn't mean the staff should be shafted their tips.

Gretchen returned to the table a few minutes later. A wet spot had replaced the chocolate frosting.

"Are you ready to go?" Mack asked. "I was thinking I could drive you home to change and—"

"Mack," she said, calmly cutting him off. "How much did that cupcake cost?"

Ah shit. That was a loaded question if he'd ever heard one. "Why do you ask?"

"Because a woman in the bathroom told me the Sultan costs a thousand dollars. Is that true?"

Mack felt like he was about to enter a minefield. He tested the ground with the tip of his toe. "I wanted you to have the full Savoy experience."

Gretchen started fanning her face as if she was going to pass out. "Oh my God," she breathed. "You were going to spend a thousand dollars on a *cupcake*?"

"Everyone I've talked to said it's worth it."

"No cupcake is worth a thousand dollars!"

He cracked a smile and tried to ignore the glances of other diners. "I guess it's a good thing we didn't have to pay for it, then, right?"

Oops. He'd found a mine. Gretchen gathered her purse, and there was a finality to her movements that made him sweat.

He stood with her. "I'm sorry if it was too much. I just wanted everything to be perfect tonight."

She shook her head. "I need to go."

He trailed after her as she walked away from the table in the opposite direction. This time she was most definitely leaving.

"Gretchen, wait." He caught up with her on the stairs. "Do you want to go home and change?"

She smiled but shook her head. "I think I'll call an Uber."

Mack marched ahead to open the door for her. Then he followed her outside. "Let me drive you home. I don't want tonight to end like this."

She turned around and placed a hand on his arm. "I'm going to be honest with you."

Yikes. That didn't sound good. It sounded like the sort of thing someone said before they dumped you. He wouldn't know, though, because he'd never been dumped.

"I've had a lot of fun."

"So have I."

"But I feel like I don't really know you very well," she finished.

That threw him for a loop. He opened and closed his mouth twice before responding. "Me? No way. I'm Mack. I'm an open book."

"You're not, actually."

"What do you want to know?"

Gretchen shrugged. "I mean, I know about your businesses, your cars, but I don't know anything about *you*. We spend so much time talking about me, but when I ask anything about your life other than the surface stuff, you clam up."

"No, I don't. I just want to learn more about you."

"You had more meaningful interaction with *Liv* in the five minutes she stood there with that cupcake than you and I have had in three months."

He was busy processing that statement when she glanced down at her phone. "My driver is almost here."

"I read romance novels," he blurted.

Gretchen's looked up. She blinked twice. "You . . . you read romance novels."

"I do. I'm part of a book club with other men who all secretly read romance novels."

"Um, okay."

"You said you wanted to know something about me. That's something."

She lifted her eyebrows. "It certainly is. And it also explains a few things."

"What do you mean?"

"The fancy dinners, the expensive wines, the nonstop flower deliveries." She tucked her purse under her arm.

"What about them?"

"They're perfect."

"And perfect is bad?" Jesus, why was everyone so opposed to perfect all of a sudden?

"It is if it doesn't mean anything." She looked at the street in search of her car.

"Gretchen, wait. What makes you think they don't mean anything?"

She turned. "Look, it all makes sense now. The sex was amazing, and I'll be honest, it's one of the reasons I stuck around. Because, wow, every time. I felt like you must have read a textbook on female pleasure."

He did. Everything he knew about sex, about how to please a woman, he'd learned from reading. No one had ever complained before. He prided himself on making sure no woman ever left his arms unsatisfied. "How the hell is that bad?"

The car pulled up and she opened the back door and turned around. "Because no woman wants to feel like she's just been sexed up according to an instruction manual. Eventually she wants it to feel real."

Mack planted his hands on his head. This was not happening.

"You know how to romance a woman, Mack. But I'm not sure you know how to *be* with a woman."

She slid into the car without giving him a chance to respond.

As if he could respond. Because she'd basically said exactly the same thing Gavin had said yesterday.

Mack watched the taillights of the car merge with traffic.

What the hell had just happened?

Del just made five hundred fucking dollars. That's what just happened.

CHAPTER THREE

"If I don't come out alive, I want you to have this."

Liv handed Riya her favorite whisk. Her friend accepted it without all the bullshit platitudes someone might be tempted to offer in a situation like this, and Liv loved her for it. Everyone knew what it meant when Royce summoned you to his office. Even if she came out with her job intact, she was now officially on Royce's shit list. Which meant that either way, her life was about to become a swirling turd pond. She'd get stuck with the worst shifts (as if there were a good one at Savoy), the worst tasks, and the worst verbal abuse. All her hard work, all the bullshit she'd endured for a year, was going to count for nothing.

Because of Braden Mack.

Liv felt her lip curl. It probably wasn't fair to blame him, but none of this would have happened if he hadn't ordered the stupid cupcake. He deserved to take the blame for *something*.

Riya gave Liv a quick hug. "Good luck."

"You know it won't help."

"No, but it feels rude to say *I'm glad it's you and not me*. No offense."

"None taken." Liv would feel the same if their situations were reversed. It was every man for himself at Savoy, even among friends.

Liv took the elevator to the third floor, where the administrative offices were located. The doors opened at the end of a long, dark hallway—an omen if she'd ever seen one. Most of the administrative staff had already left hours ago, and their cubicles now glowed an eerie shade of blue from their computer monitors. Liv had only been up here twice in the entire year she'd worked at Savoy. The first time had been when she was hired and had to fill out a bunch of employment paperwork and sign a nondisclosure agreement. Which had seemed like bullshit at the time, but now she understood why. The only way Royce was able to protect his perfect image was by ensuring that no one would talk after they left.

The second time she'd been up here was for a mandatory sensitivity training for all kitchen staff, which had been an hour-long test of her self-restraint. Had these people ever heard Royce in the kitchen? The human resources staff was either totally oblivious or completely hypocritical.

Royce's office was at the end of the hallway. It took up the entire length of the floor and overlooked the bustling street below. The other two times she'd been up here, she'd been able to see inside through a wall of floor-to-ceiling windows that she suspected Royce had installed just to show off his luxurious digs and make the cubicle losers feel like shit. Tonight, however, the blinds had been lowered on every window.

Liv dragged her feet closer. She just needed to get this over with. Whatever awaited her inside, she could deal with it. The office door was mostly closed but for a small crack that let out a sliver of light. Liv raised her hand to knock, but the low murmur of voices inside brought her fist to a halt inches from the door.

"Please, Royce. I'm sorry. I didn't know I was supposed to tell you that he was here."

For fuck's sake. He was still berating poor Jessica?

"You like this job?" he asked.

"Y-yes."

"And you'd like to keep it?"

"Yes, but not like this. Please."

Cold sweat dampened her armpits. What was going on in there? Liv slid to the left of the door so she wouldn't be seen through the crack and cranked her head to press her ear toward the opening.

"I need to get back to work," Jessica said.

"Your shift is over, honey."

"But I still have some things I need to do."

"You're a hostess. What's there left to do?"

"I-I have to log my time card in and—"

"If you want to keep your job, you know what you have to do."

Rage turned Liv's stomach to pure acid as indecision grabbed hold of her racing thoughts. There was no way she could walk away. Liv would never forgive herself if she left that poor girl in there to deal with this alone, but confronting Royce would definitely mean the end of her career. He wouldn't just fire her. He would make sure she never worked in the industry again.

"Royce, wait," Jessica suddenly pleaded.

Liv held her breath. What was going on in there? Who was she kidding? She knew exactly what was going on in there, and Royce sounded way too practiced at it.

"I could help your career," Royce said in that snakelike voice. Liv's stomach churned as she imagined what he meant.

"Please, Royce. I need to go."

"You're not interested in learning . . . new things?"

"I just want to do my job."

"I think you want more than that."

There was a rustling sound. A shuffle of feet on carpet. A whisper she couldn't hear.

"Please stop," Jessica suddenly begged.

Liv had heard enough. She threw open the door just in time to see Royce slam his mouth down on Jessica's.

"Get your slimy, disgusting hands off her, you asshole."

Jessica wrenched away from him with a gasp. She stumbled back so quickly that she collided with the edge of his desk and knocked over the framed picture of his wife. Royce whipped around and—

"OH MY GOD, PUT IT AWAY."

Liv slapped her hands over her eyes as her retinas burned with an image she'd never unsee. Royce's pants undone, his shriveled penis flapping like a raw piece of scrod.

"Oh my God. I saw it. I saw it. I'm going need therapy." She peeled her hands away and looked at Jessica. "Just go. Get out now. I heard everything, and I will help you make a report."

Jessica's eyes began a rapid blink. "I—a report?"

Royce took his time tucking in his dick and zipping his pants. "This is none of your business, Olivia. I suggest you back out of the office and come back when I told you to."

"I did come here when you told me to. Luckily for Jessica, you obviously can't tell time." Liv looked at Jessica. "Human Resources has an emergency after-hours line." Liv narrowed her eyes at Royce.

"He won't get away with this. Though something tells me he already has many times."

Royce approached in a slow, menacing way. "I suggest you leave now."

"Not a fucking chance, asshole. How many women have you done this to?"

"Watch yourself, Olivia," he sneered.

"Let's go, Jessica," Liv said, backing toward the door.

"No."

The refusal was so quiet, so reluctant that both Liv and Royce did a double take. *"What?"*

"It's—it's nothing," Jessica stammered, straightening her shirt. "You misunderstood. It's all a misunderstanding. I-I walked in on him when he was, um—"

"Coming out of the bathroom," Royce finished.

"There's nothing to report," Jessica said in a fragile voice.

Disbelief slammed into Liv and stole her breath. "Are you serious?"

"It's fine. Please—"

"Jessica, I heard everything. Jesus God, I saw everything. He's sexually harassing you. He can't do that to you."

"No, it's fine. I'm fine. Please just leave it alone."

"He won't stop! Who knows how many women he's done this to before or will after you?"

"You're done," Royce hissed. "I was going to let you beg me tonight to keep your job after your little fuckup earlier, because despite your shitty attitude, you're a helluva pastry chef, but this is it. You're done. You're fired."

"No," Jessica said. "Royce, please."

Royce stalked around to the other side of his desk, picked up the receiver to his phone, and hit a button. "Get in here."

"Please, Royce," Jessica said beseechingly, grabbing his forearm. He yanked away from her so hard that she stumbled again.

She looked at Liv. "I'm sorry. I didn't mean for this to happen."

"It's not your fault, Jessica."

"I need this job," she pleaded. "I'm sorry. You can't tell anyone."

Royce slammed the phone down. "Shut up, Jessica."

With a gulp, she backed away from him.

Royce glared at Liv. "You'll never work in this business again, Olivia. You hear me? You're finished!"

"You've made that threat a lot, haven't you?"

"I don't have to make threats. I just make promises."

"So do I. And I promise that if you touch her again, you'll be pissing blood for the rest of your life."

Royce's face flashed beet red, and Liv had the sudden image of a volcano about to spew its lava. Ew. No. She didn't want to think about Royce spewing anything.

He suddenly nodded at someone or something behind her. "Get her out of here."

"Sorry about this, Liv." A clammy hand wrapped around her elbow. Geoff, one of the security guards.

Liv yanked her arm free. "Do you know what he's doing in here?"

"I just do what I'm told," Geoff said, pulling on her arm again.

"Of course. Just like a real man."

Liv spun around—and nearly face-planted into the massive chest of Royce's other security guard, Sam. She lifted her gaze from his thick neck to his pockmarked cheeks until it collided with his ice-blue eyes.

Liv had always assumed the tank-size goons were mostly for show, because nothing said *I'm a big, important man* like bodyguards. But apparently Royce also used them to intimidate the newly fired. Like now.

Sam wrapped a beefy hand around her upper arm. "Let's go."

Liv snatched her arm free. "Touch me again and you lose a testicle."

"Make sure you watch her clean out her locker," Royce said. "If she tries to steal anything, call the cops."

Liv whipped around. "That's rich coming from a guy whose about to release a cookbook full of other people's recipes."

Royce's eyes bulged so far out of his head Liv feared he was having a seizure. "Get her the fuck out of my sight!"

Sam pulled her out of the office.

"You're not very attached to your balls, are you?" Liv snapped, once again trying to pull from his grasp. This time he simply held on tighter.

At the end of the hallway, Geoff held open the elevator doors, his face ashen as he stared everywhere but at Liv. Sam had less shame. He all but tossed Liv inside.

She rubbed her arm where he'd grabbed her. "How much does he pay you to cover for him?"

They ignored her and instead took up matching wide-legged poses in front of her as if they were afraid she'd bolt as soon as they reached the ground floor.

"Do you know what I just saw in there? What he was doing to her?"

The elevator beeped as they reached the second floor.

"You work for a *predator*. Who knows what the hell he's doing to her in there!"

With a soft shake and the groan of metal on metal, the elevator reached the ground floor. The doors slid open, and the sudden silence in the kitchen was as pronounced as the blare of a live band at the Grand Ole Opry. Sam and Geoff stepped sideways to hold the doors open and allow her to exit.

In her year of employment there, Liv had watched a half dozen other employees make this particular walk of shame, and now that it was her turn, she felt guilty for all the times she'd behaved exactly as her fellow prisoners did now. The averted gazes. The *there but for the grace of God* exhale as she passed. The stink of nervous flop sweat. Liv had smelled the odor often enough in her time there, and now she was the one who stank.

Or maybe it was the goons. They reeked of strong-armed intimidation and also maybe a salami sandwich. Which was a surprise because Liv had always assumed that Royce kept them locked in the basement with nothing but protein powder to snort in between bench pressing each other and snarling incoherently.

Riya was the only one who risked the malodorous contagion by daring to speak to her. "I'm sorry," she said, hugging Liv.

"I'll survive," Liv said, giving her a tight squeeze. She pressed her lips close to Riya's ears and lowered her voice. "Be careful."

"What do you mean?"

Sam gave a none-too-gentle shove against her shoulder. "Let's go."

"We'll talk soon," Liv said to Riya. Her friend nodded, brown eyes pinched in concern, and Liv was struck with a sudden sickening thought. What if Riya was next on Royce's list of victims? What if she'd already been the target of his harassment? Liv glanced quickly around the kitchen at all the faces so obviously turned away from her. How many women in that room had he abused? How many were hiding a dark secret like Jessica's?

And worst of all, how many women was Liv leaving behind to face Royce alone?

Liv stomped to the locker room, Sam and Geoff close behind. Two women were huddled in a corner of the locker room, talking in low, hushed tones when they walked in. The women immediately shut up and scurried out, their eyes glued to the tile floor. One might have even covered her nose.

"You may retrieve your personal belongings, but everything else stays here," Sam said. "You are also reminded that you signed a nondisclosure agreement when you began working here."

Geoff cleared his throat. "A copy of your NDA can be provided to you should you need one."

Liv tapped her temple. "No need. Got it all saved up here. What happens at Savoy stays at Savoy, right?"

"Any violation of this agreement will result in civil litigation," Sam said.

"You should be careful. Those are big words for you," Liv said, shoving toiletries in her duffel bag. She held up her deodorant. "Either one of you want this? It's clinical strength."

Sam barely blinked. "Any personal items left in your locker will be disposed of."

Liv shrugged and dropped the deodorant in her bag. "I was trying to be discreet, but I guess I need to be more direct. You stink."

Sam raised an eyebrow over his ice-blue eyes. Geoff turned his head toward his armpit.

"Probably the steroids. That shit will mess you up." Liv shut her locker and hoisted her bag over her shoulder. "It's been fun, boys. Now why don't you both fuck off and die?"

Five minutes later, she stormed into the night. Her bag banged against her thigh with every angry step that took her from the brightly lit alley behind Savoy to the corner. Her car was in a parking garage two blocks away because Royce was too cheap to provide his employees with on-site parking. There was more than enough room behind the building, but oh no. Only Royce got to park there. So instead she and every other person who worked for him faced a nightly game of dodge-the-douchebags on Broadway. At least she could leave this bullshit behind. Her next job was going to be as far away from Honky Tonk Row as possible.

The sour taste of panic stung the back of her throat. Her next job . . . Wait. Would there be a next job? Holy shit, this was really happening. She'd been fired. Her mind raced with a thousand thoughts connected by a single underlying question. *What the hell do I do know?*

Call the cops? He'd *assaulted* Jessica. She'd asked him to stop. Begged him. And he'd kissed her anyway. Rage returned and turned Liv's blood to liquid fire. Her fingers gripped the strap of her bag so hard that the fake leather squeaked in protest. Men like Royce Preston thought they could get away with anything, didn't they? And why? Because they *did* get away with it. They got off on the power.

She needed to talk to someone, but she couldn't. And not just because of the NDA but because Jessica didn't want anyone to know. What the hell was she supposed to tell people about why she was fired? Everyone was going to think she couldn't hack it, that she was just another flameout in the burning hellfire of Royce's kitchen. After everything she'd endured and worked for, her career would now bear the permanent stain of this.

Of course, that didn't matter compared to what Jessica was

going through. Why wouldn't Jessica let her report him? Why would she even want to stay working for an abusive asshole?

She stopped at the corner to wait for the light to change. Fucking men.

"Liv?"

She turned around at the sound of her name.

Of course.

Braden-Fucking-Mack.

"What the hell do you want?"

Of all the things he expected Liv to say when he saw her at the corner, it hadn't been that. He'd been heading back to his club because it was only a few blocks away and because the thought of going home to his empty house was too depressing to consider, and then he saw her. Hoofing up the street like her bag was on fire.

The light changed with a beep, and Liv whipped back around to cross the street. She didn't even wait for him to answer her question.

"Liv, wait." He jogged to catch up with her.

She glared over her shoulder in the crosswalk. "Are you following me?"

"No. I'm going to my club. What are you doing?"

"Going home."

Dread was a sour taste in his mouth. "What happened?"

Liv looked around. "Where's your date? Did you stuff her in your trunk or something?"

"She went home."

"Lucky her."

They'd reached the other sidewalk by now, and she obviously had no intention of slowing to talk to him.

"Liv, wait. Come on." He grabbed her arm.

She whipped around swinging. "Do. Not. Touch. Me."

Mack held up his hands, truce-like. "I'm sorry. Jesus, just wait. Talk to me. What happened?"

She scoffed. "What do you think happened?"

"Oh, shit. You got fired? Just now?"

"No, yesterday. I just decided to come in and work today for free because I knew you were going to be there and wanted to make something extra special to throw in your date's lap."

He probably deserved the sarcasm. She turned again and started walking.

"Liv, wait." He was saying that a lot tonight. "Jesus, let me do something. Come to my club. I'll get you a drink."

"No thanks. You've done enough."

Gavin was going to kill him over this. "At least let me walk you to your car."

"Why?"

"It's not safe this late at night for you to walk to your car alone."

Liv stopped in the middle of the street and faced him head-on. "Are you kidding me right now?" It was clearly a rhetorical question, because she plowed ahead. "I don't need you. I've been walking into that parking garage by myself for a year now. So why don't you run along and do whatever it is you do when you're not spending a thousand dollars on a stupid cupcake."

"Liv, I'm sorry."

She whipped around again, and this time it hit him. He could fix this.

"Wait."

She groaned. "What?"

He jogged to get in front of her and started walking backward. He'd be lucky if he didn't wipe out. "I'll hire you."

Liv stopped so fast that her bag fell off her shoulder. There was a pause, and then she tipped her head back and laughed.

"What's so funny?"

"I am not going to work for you." She hoisted her bag back onto her shoulder. "Get out of my way."

He slid left when she slid right.

"Liv, I feel terrible about this. Please—"

She shoved him sideways, and for the second time that night, he watched a woman storm away from him.

CHAPTER FOUR

The last thing Mack wanted to do the next morning was face the guys at a damn book club meeting, especially at Gavin's house. But if he didn't show up, they'd just hound him with text messages and obscene gifs. There was no avoiding it. So just before noon, he parked in front of Gavin's house, grabbed his book and the pizza box, and trudged up the porch steps to bang on the front door.

A boisterous bark from inside greeted him seconds before the door swung open. Gavin's wife, Thea, smiled and held back their dog, a golden retriever named Butter Ball.

"Hey," she breathed. "Come in."

Mack held back for a split second, studying her face for any signs that she was going to pound him for what happened with Liv last night. When no signs of violence emerged, he bent and brushed his lips across her cheek. "Hey, Thea. Thanks for having us."

"Of course. The guys are all out back."

"Where are the girls?" Gavin and Thea had twin daughters, Ava and Amelia, who had recently turned four.

"Napping, thank God," Thea laughed. "They almost never do anymore, but Gavin wore them out this morning teaching them how to hit a curve ball."

The picture that painted—of domestic bliss and family—brought a pang to his chest that soured his mood even further. Gretchen could have been the one he shared that with. He was sure of it.

Mack carried his pizza through the living room to a set of French doors leading to Gavin's backyard. They opened to a covered brick patio, which is where he found them—Malcolm, Del, Derek, Gavin, and the Russian.

Gavin looked over his shoulder at the sound of the door. "Dude, you're late," he said over a mouthful of what looked like a grilled chicken sandwich. During the season, he tended to eat as healthy as possible. Which also pissed Mack off. Because he wanted to indulge in some fucking pizza and beer.

Mack dropped the pizza box on the patio table and plunged his hand into the pocket of his shorts. He withdrew the five hundred dollars he owed Del and shoved it at him.

Del wiped a napkin across his face. "What's this?" he asked, wary and curious at once.

"What do you think it is? You won the fucking bet."

The guys got quiet for a moment.

Del gathered the money. "So . . . you and Gretchen?"

"Congratulations," Mack grumbled. "I think I got dumped last night. Happy?"

Malcolm cleared his throat. "You *think* you got dumped?"

"I swear I'm not making fun of you," Gavin said slowly, "but how does one not know if he got dumped or not?"

Mack tossed his hands in the air. "Because I've never fucking been dumped before, okay?"

This time, the silence was followed by a burst of collective guffaws that vibrated windows and shook the table. Gavin laughed so hard he fell forward onto his arm on the table.

"Yeah, real fucking funny, assholes," Mack said, yanking a chair away from the table so he could slump into it.

Del clapped a hand on his shoulder. "I'm sorry, man, but damn. Welcome to the real world, Mack. How's it feel?"

"Like shit, thank you very much."

"What happened?"

"I don't know. One minute things were fine, and the next, Liv dropped the stupid cupcake, and then Gretchen was backing away from me with some lame excuse—"

"W-w-wait," Gavin interrupted, his stammer revealing his sudden tension. "What did you just say about Liv? What does she have to do with any of this?"

Oh shit. That's why Thea hadn't mentioned anything about it when he'd arrived. She and Gavin didn't know. *Shit.* Mack swallowed hard and looked around the room. "She, uh, she didn't tell you guys?"

"No," Gavin said. "She didn't. And you have about thirty seconds to start from the beginning, or getting dumped is going to be the least of your worries."

Mack gulped. "She, uh . . . she got fired last night."

Mack had faced some intimidating people in his life, but Thea Scott would go down as one of the scariest. She stood barely five three and weighed less than one of his legs, but if she so much as twitched right now, he'd shit himself.

Gavin had dragged him inside the house to tell her what happened. He gulped again. "I swear to God, Thea, that's all I know."

How the hell was Mack supposed to know that Liv wouldn't have told her own sister by now that she'd been fired last night? It was almost one o'clock for fuck's sake. He looked at the other guys for help, but they all suddenly found something super interesting in the carpet or on the walls or in the backyard. Lotta fucking help they were.

"She said she's on her way here?" Gavin asked his wife cautiously.

Thea nodded, arms crossed and jaw clenched.

"Uncle Mack, come play with us!" Ava and Amelia ran into the room trailed by Butter Ball. Ava threw her arms around Mack's legs. He hoisted her upside down in the air and tossed her over his shoulder. Ava shrieked in delight. Amelia hopped up and down, screaming, "Me next, me next!"

Thank God for kids. "Wanna jump on the trampoline?"

Both girls exclaimed, "Yeah!"

"Uncle Mack is grounded," Thea said. "Why don't you see if one of the other guys will go outside with you."

The guys couldn't move fast enough. They raced en masse toward the back door and collided all at once. Malcolm shoved Derek out of the way. Derek fell to his knees. Del wrestled his hand onto the door handle. The Russian batted it away and managed to throw the door open. All four men fell out in a heap of cowardice. Someone yelled he was bleeding and someone else responded to just run.

"Start from the beginning," Thea said as soon as the girls had run out back.

"I saw her at Savoy. I might have gotten her in trouble with her boss, and then later—"

Gavin held up a hand. "Might have gotten her in trouble with her boss? What the hell does that mean?"

"I ordered that thousand-dollar cupcake—"

Thea made a choking sound. Mack shrugged. "I was trying to impress Gretchen."

"Which obviously backfired," Gavin said.

Mack flipped him off.

"Continue," Thea seethed.

"Anyway, I guess she has to deliver the damn thing as part of the package, and so I recognized her, and I said, 'Hey, I know you,' and she said, 'No, you don't,' and I was like, 'Yeah, you're Gavin's sister-in-law,' and I called her Liv, but Royce calls her Olivia—"

"For fuck's sake," Gavin growled. "Does this story have an end?"

"She dropped it," he blurted.

Thea choked again. "She dropped the cupcake?"

"In Gretchen's lap."

"Oh my God," Thea breathed. She even swayed a little.

"She was *working*, Mack," Gavin said. "Couldn't you have just left her alone?"

"Was I supposed to ignore her? How fucking rude would that be?"

"Maybe she'd still be employed if you had!"

There was a knock at the front door followed immediately by Butter's rapid bark. Thea held up her hand to silence them. Mack swallowed hard and tried to calm his breathing. Shitshitshit. Liv was here, and she was gonna be so pissed at him. More pissed than even last night. And he was pretty sure the only person scarier than

Thea when she was pissed was Liv, and he was even more sure that he'd only gotten a small taste of Liv's capacity for pissed-offed-ness last night.

Thea crossed the living room to the hallway that led to their front door. Butter barked and bounced alongside her, oblivious to the fact that a ticking time bomb waited on the porch.

Gavin looked at him, dragged his finger across his throat, and mouthed, *You're dead.*

It was followed moments later by a now-familiar voice.

"You asshole. You couldn't wait to share the good news?" Liv stomped through the small entryway of her sister's house and nearly ran into Mack around the corner. She'd been working on her résumé all morning, trying to figure out just how to tell Thea what had happened, when the phone had rung and her sister had screeched, "*You got fired?!*"

Mack threw his hands in the air. "Why the hell didn't you tell them?"

Liv shoved a finger in his chest. "Because my sister has a tendency to freak out about things, and I was trying to figure out how to break it to them. But thanks to you—"

Thea was right behind her. "Hey, I do not freak out about things."

Gavin and Liv shared a none-too-subtle *yeah right* look.

"Well, why wouldn't I freak out if I have to find out from Mack that you got fired last night?"

Liv turned around. "I was going to tell you today."

Thea crossed her arms. "When?"

Liv matched her pose. "After I finished my chores."

Behind her, Mack whispered to Gavin, "Chores?"

"She sort of lives on a farm," Gavin whispered back.

"I can't believe you didn't tell me last night, though," Thea said. "Why didn't you call me?"

"Because I was still in shock last night."

"So you just went home?" Thea asked it with the same level of incredulity as if Liv had announced that she'd decided to streak naked down Broadway.

"Yes. I went home, studied my bank account, and threw darts at a picture of Royce's face. What else does someone do when they get fired?"

Mack stepped into her space. "You left out the part where you turned me down when I offered you a job."

Liv whipped around. "Oh my God, is there anything else you want to tell them that is totally none of your business?"

"What?" Thea exclaimed. "What's he talking about? Can someone please tell me what the hell happened last night?"

Her sister's outburst had a silencing effect on the entire house. Even Butter dropped to the floor with a whimper. Liv sucked in a breath, glared one last time at Mack, and lowered her voice.

"Can I just talk to you alone, please?" she asked Thea.

"We'll be outside," Gavin said. The sound of their feet hurrying toward the back door had a cartoonish effect.

Liv followed Thea into the kitchen and sat down at one of the tall chairs lining the granite island. She watched silently as her sister stormed to the fridge and withdrew the ingredients for what looked like maybe an omelet.

"What're you doing?" Liv asked, following her sister's trek to the stove as eggs, milk, and cheese threatened to spill out of her arms.

"Making you something to eat."

"I'm not hungry."

"Well I need something to do to keep from screaming."

"Could you make me pancakes instead, then?"

Thea slammed down the ingredients and glared over her shoulder. So that was a *no* for pancakes.

Thea dragged a skillet out of a cupboard, plunked it onto the stove, and whipped on the burner beneath it. She aggressively cracked an egg against the edge of the counter and dumped the goo into the skillet.

"I still can't believe you didn't tell me this last night," she snapped, taking it out on another egg.

"I didn't want to worry you."

"It's my job to worry about you."

Here we go . . .

Liv held back a bone-weary sigh. At twenty six, Thea was only a year older than Liv, but it might has well have been twenty. Their parents divorced in a messy split when Liv was nine, and eventually they were forced to live with their grandmother for a while. Thea had taken on the role of big sister and mom, and even now as adults, she had a hard time relinquishing the role. Not that Liv was going to complain. If not for Thea's support, she'd probably still be a loser with no goals, no future, and no culinary degree. So no, she wasn't going to complain about Thea's overprotectiveness right now.

Thea attacked the eggs with a vicious stir. "So I hope this means you're going to finally let me give you some money?"

Liv made a *yeah right* noise. "Nope."

"You are so stubborn."

"She said as she unnecessarily beat the shit out of some eggs,"

Liv deadpanned. "You know the key to scrambled eggs is low heat and a gentle folding motion, right?"

Thea glared over her shoulder. "Do not lecture me about cooking right now."

"Then don't lecture me about money."

"You don't have any money."

"Not true. I have enough saved up to last for a couple of months."

Thea turned off the stove and unceremoniously dumped the eggs onto a waiting plate. Then she turned and plunked the plate in front of Liv. A glass of orange juice followed.

"Do I get a fork?"

Thea practically threw one at her.

Liv ducked. "What're you mad at me for?"

"I'm not mad at you. I'm worried. And I get angry and tense when I'm worried."

Liv poised her fork over the eggs. "Yeah, I know."

Thea sat down next to her. "So what are you going to do?"

"What else? Find another job." *And make sure that fucker pays.*

Liv's friend, Alexis, owned her own café. "Maybe Alexis needs some help in the meantime."

"Thea, I'm fine. Don't worry about it. I'll figure everything out, okay?"

"I've heard that before."

Her words were like a knife to an old wound. "I'm not the fuckup I used to be, Thea. Give me some credit."

Thea reeled back. "I have *never* called you a fuckup." Thea had just enough sincerity in her voice to make Liv feel guilty.

It was true. Thea had never said those words to Liv. She was just projecting. Liv had called herself a fuckup enough times in her life that it became a self-fulfilling prophecy. But she thought she was beyond those days. Now here she was—unemployed and carrying a heavy secret that she had no idea how to deal with.

"Please just let me help you," Thea said, leaning forward again. "Let me pay off your loans, or—"

"No."

"Gavin and I have more money than we know what to do with, and you're family."

"Stop, Thea. I'm not taking money from you."

Thea tossed her arms in the air with a frustrated sound. "Why? What is wrong with accepting my help?"

"Because that's all I've done my entire life!" Liv blurted. She instantly regretted it. Thea got that look on her face—that half mom, half best friend look that had always been the defining balancing act of their relationship.

"Look, I will find another job," Liv said quickly before Thea could launch into one of her sisterly lectures. "I don't know when or where." *Or if Royce will try to ruin me.* "But I will find something."

Thea bit her lip. "What about working for Mack?"

Liv snorted. "Uh, no."

"Why not?"

Liv shoveled in another bite and chased it down with orange juice. "I worked in a bar for three years during school. I don't want to do it again."

"But this would just be temporary until you can find another pastry chef job."

"No."

Thea opened her mouth as if to argue further but then apparently thought better of it. Instead, she turned her ire onto Royce. "I can't believe that jerk. After everything you've put up with, the hours you've worked, the holidays you've missed, the abuse you've had to endure. Just like that, you're done because of one mistake?"

Not exactly. Liv didn't say it or correct Thea's misunderstanding. Liv didn't know what she was going to do, but she did know one thing: she was not going to tell her sister the whole story about how and why she got fired. Telling her the truth meant getting her involved, and Liv was not going to drag her sister into this mess. Liv had already been the cause of too much trouble for Thea throughout their lives. The past two years had been the only ones when she hadn't been a major burden on her sister. There was no way she was going to turn back the clock now.

The slide of the French doors in the living room brought their conversation to a quick, blessed end. Ava and Amelia ran into the kitchen, pigtails swinging in unison.

"Aunt Livvie!" Ava yelled, throwing herself against Liv's legs.

Liv crouched down and gathered them into a tight hug. They smelled like the outdoors and strawberry shampoo.

"Can you play with us?" Amelia asked.

"You know what? I actually have to get going—"

"What?" Thea said. "Where are you going?"

"—but I promise I will be back soon to play, okay?"

The girls nodded and pulled away. Liv stood just as Gavin and Mack shuffled nervously into the kitchen. Their eyes darted between Liv and Thea as if asking permission to enter.

She needed to get out of there before the interrogation started again.

"My offer stands, Liv," Mack said, sober in a way she wouldn't have expected from him.

"I appreciate it. Really. But I'll find something," she said. She looked at Thea then. "And I can't take your money. This is something I need to figure out on my own."

"No, you don't," Thea said.

"Then can you just accept that I want to?"

Thea's face softened with understanding—an expression Liv had only ever seen on one other person in her life. If not for Thea and Gran Gran, Liv would have been lost.

Liv closed the distance to Thea and wrapped her in a tight hug. "Trust me," she whispered. "I'll be okay."

Thea gave her a squeeze and lowered her voice. "I do trust you."

Liv escaped before Thea could see how much those words meant to her. And how desperately she wanted to live up to them.

CHAPTER FIVE

The next morning, Liv's landlord, Rosie, tucked a hen named Gladys under one arm and planted her free hand on her other hip. "I was burning my bra forty years ago over shit like this, and it's still happening."

Liv reached into the nesting box and felt around until her fingers found two more eggs. She put them in the basket and shut the lid.

"You did the right thing," Rosie said. "You couldn't let him do that to that poor girl."

"Too bad that poor girl won't stand up for herself." Liv yanked open the door to the root cellar where Rosie stored eggs, vegetables, and chicken supplies. "How could she not want to report this? Doesn't she know he's going to just keep doing it?"

"Most women don't report it."

"Which I don't understand."

"I suppose until you've been in their shoes, you can't."

Rosie set down Gladys to join the twenty other hens scratching around in the freshly overturned flower beds. She kicked her foot out to knock back Randy the Rooster, who was on a mission to impregnate as many hens as possible in his lifetime. Liv didn't know why Rosie didn't either get rid of him or put him in a soup pot. Probably because his one redeeming quality was that he hated men as much as Rosie and chased off everything with a penis that tried to enter the farm.

That's probably why Liv stayed there too. She'd answered Rosie's ad two years ago for someone to live in her garage apartment and help out around her organic farm, which hadn't actually been Liv's thing, but she couldn't afford to live downtown, and she didn't want to intrude on her sister's family life.

The day she'd moved in, Liv had found a beaten-up copy of the original *Our Bodies, Ourselves* sitting on the bedside table like a hotel might set out the Bible. She'd fallen in love with the place and Rosie immediately.

Liv moved the basket of eggs to her other hand and started back toward the farmhouse. Her breath formed white puffs around her face in the chilly morning air. Even in Tennessee, it could get cold on an April morning. Rosie lived on twenty acres a half hour outside the city in what had once been nothing but farmland but now skirted the edges of strip malls and suburban chain stores.

Rosie shook her head and started muttering again as she walked out of the cellar. "Still can't believe we're fighting this shit. Marched my ass off in the seventies so your generation wouldn't have to deal with pricks like that."

Liv followed Rosie into the main house through the back door. It led to a mudroom with an ancient washer and dryer set, a pile of rubber boots covered in chicken poop and other farm gunk, and a line of hooks where they hung up their coats and hats. Rosie had knit each of them. She was on a knitting streak lately. Said she needed a hobby to keep from losing her mind over the news. Every hen now had a sweater to wear when the weather got really cold. Which wasn't as crazy as it sounded. Rosie subscribed to a backyard chicken magazine, and hen sweaters were a thing among the crazy-chicken-lady set.

Rosie kept muttering to herself as she made her way into the kitchen to start breakfast. Liv helped cook whenever she was home, though Rosie always told her she didn't have to. *I pay you to tend to the animals and the garden, not cook.* Liv didn't know how to tell her—or maybe was just too embarrassed to tell her—that she liked it. Cooking with Rosie reminded her of the years she and Thea had lived with their grandma. Gran Gran's kitchen was where she'd discovered her love of cooking. Some of her best memories were of Gran Gran, Thea, and her making dinner together as Gran Gran told stories and imparted sage bits of wisdom. Those years were the only time in her life when she'd felt like she and Thea had a real family.

The bang of the back door interrupted her, followed by a loud belch. Moments later, Earl Hopkins wandered in.

Hop, as he went by, was a part-time farmhand who was madly in love with Rosie, and either Rosie had no idea or maybe she just didn't care, because no two people could be more opposite. He was a Vietnam veteran who liked to drink beer and rant about the liberal media, and she was an avowed hippy who'd once protested the war and now watched Rachel Maddow at top volume every night.

"Start a fire, will ya?" Rosie said, pretending not to watch Hop's butt as he walked into the living room and squatted in front of the fireplace.

"Quit ordering me around," he griped.

"If you don't like it, you're welcome to find breakfast somewhere else."

"I'm probably better off. You're going to poison me one of these days."

Liv scooped the onions into a neat pile and then dumped the peelings into a bowl that Rosie would take out to the goats later. They wouldn't be thrilled, but they'd eat it. They'd eat anything. Cabbage day was definitely their favorite. Wait, no, second-favorite. The best day was when Rosie made them fresh biscuits.

Jesus, this was her life now. She knew the eating habits of chickens and goats. Liv groaned and dropped her forehead to the island and banged it twice.

"What'd I miss?" Hop asked, wheezing slightly as he came back into the kitchen.

"Livvie got fired last night."

Hop patted her on the shoulder. "Finally told him where he could stick his spatula, huh?"

Liv laughed. "I wish."

Rosie spun away from the sink, knife pointed like a weapon. "I'll tell you what happened. She caught him sexually harassing a young college girl, and he fired her for it. Just like a typical man."

"Spoken like a typical feminist," Hop snorted.

Liv sighed heavily and shook her head. This fight was going to be a long one. She removed the knife from Rosie's hand. "I'll finish the potatoes."

Rosie swatted her hand away. "You go on up to your room and relax. I'll bring you some food when it's ready."

Liv considered protesting, but Rosie and Hop had settled into a hearty argument. She was too exhausted to play referee. She slipped out the back door and headed toward the garage. A staircase in the back of the building led to her apartment, which was cozy but small. The door opened into an eat-in kitchen that faced a small living room. A single hallway led to her bedroom on one side and the bathroom on the other. It smelled faintly of dust from the garage below, but she could usually mask it with a couple of well-placed candles.

Liv sat down at her small kitchen table and turned on her laptop. She'd lied when she'd told Thea she'd already done this, and she had officially put this off too long. She needed to crunch some numbers. She logged into her bank account and did some quick math.

After ten minutes of holding her breath, Liv realized she had enough in savings to last three months without a paycheck. Would it take that long to find another job? Would she be able to find another job? And if she did, would it be in Nashville? She didn't want to leave. Thea and Gavin and their twins were there. And Rosie was basically a grandmother to her.

What if Royce really did try to ruin her in the restaurant scene? Now that she'd seen him in action, he knew she was a threat to him, so he probably would make good on his threat to make sure she never got another job. A man who would sexually harass an employee would think nothing of ruining someone's career to protect his dirty little secret.

If it even was much of a secret. How many women had he done this to? How many women had he harassed or fired to cover it up? How many people had helped him?

Part of her wanted to scream *it's not fair*! But nothing in her life had been very fair, and whining about it hadn't ever done much for her.

Maybe she was being stupid. Maybe she should just give in and take Thea up on her offer and open her own damn restaurant and be thankful that her sister was willing to get her started. But money had a way of changing things between people. It had a way of corrupting. She didn't want that hanging between her and her sister. Thea was too important to her.

When Rosie knocked on the door, Liv jumped up and let her in. Rosie walked in balancing a tray. "Brought you an omelet and some toast."

Liv stretched her arms over her head. "Thank you. You didn't have to do that."

Rosie set it on the table and then pointed a finger at Liv. "Now you listen to me. I know you, so I know you're sitting here worried about how you're going to pay your rent and all that shit, so just stop. I don't care about that."

"Rosie, I can't live here rent-free."

"You can if I say you can."

Liv swallowed against a surge of emotion.

"All I want you to do is decide what you're going to do about that bastard and to protect that girl," Rosie said.

"I don't think she wants my protection."

"Then you'll just have to convince her, won't you?"

Liv wandered to the window to stare at the farmland outside. "I don't know what to do."

"Get her out of there, Livvie. Whatever it takes, just get her out of there."

CHAPTER SIX

Two days later, Liv pulled her Jeep into an open parking space along the curb in front of the ToeBeans Cat Café, the coffee shop and bakery owned by her friend Alexis.

Alexis was the only person on Earth who hated Royce as much as Liv, which was probably why they'd bonded so quickly during the brief time when they'd worked at Savoy together.

Alexis had been there for almost two years when Liv started, but she'd left within a couple of months to care for her sick mom. She and Liv remained friends, though, and after her mom passed away, Liv helped her pursue her lifelong dream of opening her own place—a dream they both shared.

Judging by the line of people waiting to order when Liv walked in, business was good. Of course, it was Tuesday, and Tuesdays were always busy for Alexis, because that was the day when a local cat rescue brought in cats and kittens who were looking for homes. Alexis had a soft spot for lost things and lonely creatures.

Which was another reason she was the only logical person for

Liv to turn to for help. She'd never turn Jessica away. If Alexis agreed to hire her, then Jessica would have no reason to stay at Savoy.

Liv sidestepped the back of the line. Alexis spotted her and lifted her hand in an enthusiastic wave, sending the knot of curls on top of her head into a bouncy dance. She spread her fingers wide and mouthed, *Five minutes?*

Liv pointed to the swinging door that led the kitchen. Alexis nodded and returned her attention to the customer in front of her. The small kitchen was bright and clean, with white subway tiles along the walls and open shelves displaying plates and bowls in rainbow colors. A single cook maneuvered feverishly between a grill and a stainless-steel counter where he assembled plates of sandwiches, salads, and pastries. He barely spared Liv a glance when she walked in. She understood. When the heat was literally on in the kitchen, there was no time for politeness.

Liv ducked out of his way and wandered to the back, where a tray of fresh scones was cooling on top of a range. They smelled like a cozy Saturday morning and a warm blanket. Liv's stomach grumbled instinctively.

"Lemon and lavender," Alexis explained, coming up behind her. "I'm not sure if the flavor is right yet, though. Will you taste one and let me know what you think?"

Liv picked one up and took a bite. The pastry melted on her tongue. "It's perfect," she breathed, wiping a crumb off her lip.

Alexis smiled in relief. "You're sure? This is my fourth attempt."

Liv took another bite and nodded. "Definitely put this on the menu."

"If they have your stamp of approval, then it's done." Alexis untied her apron and hung it on a hook by the tiny office in the back corner. "Can you sit for a few minutes? Are you on your way to work or something? How's Riya? You have to tell me about the plans for the cookbook release. Is Royce driving everyone crazy?"

Liv tried to keep up with Alexis's typically frenetic rapid-fire questions as her friend opened the door to her office.

"Come on in—Beefcake, no!" An orange cat the size of a small toddler tried to escape through the narrow opening of the door. Liv shoved her leg in the way just in time to block him and earned a glare that said Beefcake would definitely try to kill her later. Another cat—a tabby named Howler—darted beneath Alexis's desk before peeking back out with his own evil glare.

"I keep them in my office on Tuesdays," Alexis explained, gesturing for Liv to sit down. She shut the door. "They hate the strange cats."

Howler and Beefcake were rescues who lived in the café fulltime to charm the patrons in between adoption events and, apparently, to plot murdery stuff at night.

Alexis dropped into the creaky chair behind her desk. She let out a dramatic sigh and let her head fall back against the top of the chair. "My entire body hurts. I'm only thirty. How can I hurt this much at thirty?"

"Because you're on your feet all day and never sleep."

"You know me too well." Alexis lifted her head and narrowed her eyes. "Something's wrong. What is it?"

Liv swallowed away the sour taste of nerves and guilt. Alexis was a new business owner, probably barely turning a profit. She hated to put her on the spot, but she had to get Jessica away from Royce. "I need to ask you for a favor."

"Of course. Anything."

"I need you to hire someone."

Alexis tilted her head. "Like, someone specific?"

"Yes."

"Okay," Alexis said slowly. "Who?"

"A young woman named Jessica. She works at Savoy."

Alexis's face went blank for the briefest of moments. But with a rapid blink, the moment passed. "And you need me to hire her because . . . ?"

Liv let out a long breath. "Something sort of happened."

Alexis sat up straighter. "What kind of something?"

Five minutes later, the entire story hung in the air between them like a rancid smell, the kind that would whip in from the back-alley dumpsters whenever the busboys would go out for a smoke on a hot night. Alexis's expression was the same too—pinched and nauseated.

A deep swallow tightened the cords of Alexis's throat. "What are you . . . what are you going to do?"

Liv shrugged. "Whatever I can to help Jessica and stop Royce."

Alexis did the rapid-blink thing again. "What do you mean, stop Royce?"

"Stop him from doing this again. There's no way Jessica is the only woman he has done this to, but she's going to be the last."

Alexis shot to her feet and threw open the door. Beefcake and Howler saw their chance to escape, but Alexis either didn't notice or didn't care when they skittered between her legs into freedom. Liv hovered in the doorway of the office, mouth agape as she watched Alexis grab a bottle of bourbon and two glasses. Alexis wasn't much of a drinker. Never had been. But when she returned to the office, poured a single shot, and threw it back, Liv felt the dual smack of shock and realization. "You're not surprised to hear this, are you?"

Alexis filled both glasses this time and handed one to Liv. "Royce has always had a reputation."

"A *reputation*?"

Alexis stared at the second shot but then pushed it away.

"You *knew* he was like this?"

Alexis sat down again.

"And it never occurred to you to tell me?"

Alexis winced. "I wish I could hire Jessica, but I can't. I'm sorry. I'm barely squeaking by as it is with the staff I already have."

"She probably doesn't get paid very much as it is. Maybe she could just start—"

"I can't, Liv. I'm sorry." Her sharp tone left no room for argument.

Liv wanted to be pissed, but had no right to be. It was a long shot from the start. "It's okay. I shouldn't have put you on the spot."

"What about you?" Alexis asked.

"I'll find something."

"The Parkway Hotel is looking for kitchen staff. I know the head chef there. I could call him tomorrow."

Liv nodded absently. "That'd be great. Thanks."

"How are you for money in the meantime?"

If anyone else had asked the question, Liv would have bristled at the bluntness, but this was Alexis. Practical and steadfast. A wise old aunt in the body of a thirty-year-old. "I have enough in savings for a few months."

"I'm sure Rosie will give you a break on rent and bills."

"She already does."

Alexis reached across her desk and squeezed Liv's arm. "I'm sorry, Liv. I know how disappointing this must be for you after how hard you've worked."

"I'll survive." It was the story of her life. She'd learned quickly as a child how to adapt to new circumstances. You learned a lot of lessons when you grew up with two warring parents who were too busy trying to one-up each other to notice that with every argument, every custody hearing, every petty slight, they were yanking the rug out from beneath their daughters' feet. She'd survived worse. She would survive this.

"Maybe this is a sign," Alexis said after a pause.

"Of?"

"You've proven yourself. You're talented and ambitious. Why don't you just take a loan from your sister and—"

Liv felt her jaw tighten. "No."

"Why not?"

"Just because I know rich people doesn't mean I can treat them like an ATM. Money ruins relationships. Trust me, I know."

Alexis winced. "I'm sorry. You're right. I don't understand what that's like."

Dammit. Liv shook her head. "I shouldn't have snapped at you. I'm sorry. I know you're just trying to help. I'm just—" She let out a frustrated noise, interrupting her words. "Nothing pisses me off more than injustice."

"I know. That's why I love you. But I need you to promise me something."

Liv lifted her eyebrows.

Alexis's eyes darkened. "Be careful. Royce is more powerful than you know."

"I'm not afraid of Royce Preston. He's a bumbling idiot. He literally got caught because he can't tell time."

Alexis ignored the joke. "He'll destroy you."

"Not if I destroy him first."

"You really believe you can, don't you?"

"What I believe is that I don't have a choice. I can't walk away knowing what he's doing and has probably done a hundred times before. I can't let someone else walk into that kitchen knowing he's a predator. If I have to bring down his entire stupid empire, I will."

Alexis stood and peered down at Liv through beseeching eyes. "Please don't do anything rash. I know what you're like, and—"

"What does that mean?"

"It means you sometimes act without thinking."

Liv allowed herself a moment of wounded pride before sputtering, "Am I supposed to stand by and let him get away with this?"

"Just promise me you'll think about the consequences before you go after Royce."

Liv stood so she was eye to eye with Alexis. "I'm going to stop him from hurting other women. Those are the only consequences I care about."

"They shouldn't be. Other people could get hurt. Think of how many people could lose their jobs if you bring down his empire."

Liv shook her head, disappointment and confusion a strange cocktail in her veins. "I don't get this. I figured you of all people would be on my side."

"I *am* on your side."

"It doesn't sound like it."

"I just don't want you to get hurt."

"I'm more worried about Jessica."

Alexis's sigh carried weary resignation. "What exactly are you planning to do?"

"I don't know. But I'll think of something."

Alexis worried her lower lip with her teeth. "Will you keep me posted?"

"I will."

A young woman in a ToeBeans T-shirt knocked on the door and stuck her head in. "Beefcake just stole someone's muffin and tried to pee on a kitten."

"I'll go," Liv said quickly. "You should probably deal with that."

Alexis's smile seemed forced as she rounded her small desk for a quick hug. "I'll keep my eyes open for jobs," she said with a squeeze.

Liv ducked out the back way and walked around the block to her car. But rather than drive away, she sat in the front seat for several long minutes, staring at nothing as she worked out her next move. *You sometimes act without thinking.* Maybe Alexis hadn't meant to, but that one had struck a tender spot. Liv had worked her ass off to overcome the transgressions of her wild youth. And though her precious Gran Gran hadn't lived long enough to see Liv finish culinary school, Liv liked to imagine that the old lady was still up there somewhere feeling proud that she'd managed to set Liv on a better path before it was too late. Liv wouldn't have gotten her shit together in time to graduate from high school without Gran Gran's help. And Thea's, of course.

But could someone ever really feel like they'd made up for the mistakes of their past? Would Liv? Could she ever do enough to be worth all the trouble?

Liv shoved the key in the ignition and waited for a break in traffic to pull out. She wouldn't go down without a fight. Royce couldn't get away with this. But before she could deal with him, she had to get Jessica out of there. And if Alexis couldn't hire her, Liv knew at least one person who could.

Braden-Fucking-Mack.

*   *   *

Temple Club was supposedly one of Nashville's swankiest dance clubs, but in the middle of the afternoon, it was just a dark, empty tomb with the odor of stale beer and lost hope that hung over every bar on the strip. Liv's boots clunked across the distressed wooden floor when she walked in.

"We open at four," a woman at the bar said without even looking up. She had a jagged purple haircut and an attitude that Liv would've admired in other circumstances.

Liv approached the bar. "I'm Liv. I'm looking for Mack."

"He's not here." The woman still hadn't looked at her.

"Where is he?" Liv asked, parking herself on a barstool.

The woman looked up, one pierced eyebrow arched over vibrant green eyeshadow. "Not here and none of your business."

"See, it is kind of my business because I need to talk to him."

"You and every other woman in Nashville. Take a number."

Liv faked a gag. "Stop. I have a sensitive stomach."

The woman suddenly grinned. "What'd you say your name was?"

"Tell him it's *Olivia*."

The woman picked up a phone and punched a couple of buttons. A moment passed before she spoke. "It's Sonia. There's some woman here named Olivia who says—"

There was a pause, a quick *okay*, and then Sonia hung up. "He'll be here in twenty minutes. You can wait in his office."

Liv slid off her stool to follow Sonia down a hallway behind the bar.

"So who are you?" Sonia asked, looking back over her shoulder.

"Huh?"

"Mack doesn't do this—let random women sit in his office. So you must be someone."

"He got me fired last weekend. I'm here for revenge."

"Can I watch?"

"I'll even let you help."

Sonia opened the door to a back office and waved her arm for Liv to go inside. Liv sank into Mack's desk chair and kicked her feet up on the surprisingly tidy surface.

Sonia grinned. "His file cabinet is color-coded. Sometimes when I'm mad at him, I mix them all up."

Liv laid her hand over her heart. "Can we be best friends?"

"Yep."

As soon as Sonia left, Liv leaned back in the chair and studied the office. The decor was spare but professional. A couple of file cabinets lined one wall beneath a framed black-and-white photo of what was probably Temple before it became Temple. The only personal touch in the room was a line of photos tacked to a fabric pinboard beneath the prefab cabinets that matched the desk.

She tried and failed several times to avoid staring at them, so she finally just gave up and studied them. They were obviously family. They all looked like Mack—dark hair, big smiles, same eyes.

"Comfortable?"

Liv danced her feet along the desk to swivel the chair around. Mack stood in the doorway wearing jeans and a black button-down with the sleeves rolled up. He leaned against the wood frame with his arms crossed, smiling like a man who knew he was good-looking and was used to getting his way because of it.

Liv rolled her eyes. "You practice that pose in the mirror?"

He winked. "Every day."

"Your office is clean."

"You sound surprised."

"I figured you the type for an overflowing trash can and dirty coffee cups."

"Then you figured wrong." He pulled away from the door and walked inside, pointing at the photos. "That's my family."

She shrugged.

"You're not even curious?"

"Not really," she lied.

He moved closer to her and started rattling off names. "That's my brother, Liam. His wife, Allison. Their two kids. They're pretty much the cutest kids on the planet." He pointed to the last picture. "And that's my mom."

Liv would've known that even if Mack hadn't pointed it out. He had the same dark hair, golden-brown eyes, and long lashes as the woman in the picture. Not that Liv had spent any time studying Mack's eyes or the length of his lashes. They were just obvious, like the plumes of a peacock. A person could admire the beauty of the bird while hating its aggressive mating behavior.

Liv crossed her legs at the ankles. "Your manager thought I was some girl you're stringing along."

He chuckled. "She has no filter."

"I know. I like her."

Mack sat down in the chair on the other side of the desk. "So do I. She's been with me since I opened my first club."

"Poor thing."

"I've gotten used to the attitude."

"I was talking about *her*."

He winked again. "Give it time. You'll start to like me. Everyone does."

"Only if you have Chinese food to replace the leftovers you ate."

"Damn, you still salty about that?"

"I take food very seriously."

"Gavin said I could eat them," he defended.

"They weren't his to give away."

"Is that why you don't like me? Because I ate your lo mein?"

"No. I don't like you because you spend more on hair products than I do."

"It takes a lot of work to look this good, honey."

"Exactly. No woman could ever compete with that. I bet you have a mirror in every room of your house and practice smiling into them."

"Don't you?"

She snorted.

"So you seriously don't like me?"

She gave him another side-eye. "You say that like it actually surprises you."

At his silence, she stared, incredulous. "It does surprise you."

He shrugged. "Everybody likes me." He hooked an ankle over the opposite knee. "I take it you changed your mind about the job?"

Liv dropped her feet to the floor. "Yes, but not for me."

He squinted, sending a spray of minuscule crinkles around his eyes. "Not sure I follow."

"If you really have openings—"

"I do."

"—then I need you to hire a girl named Jessica. She's a hostess at Savoy, and I need to get her out."

"Why?"

"Because I do. That should be enough."

He shrugged again. "It's not."

"Well, I can't tell you why. But you said you wanted to fix this." She pointed at him. "Those were your exact words, and this is how you can fix it."

"How does hiring someone else fix *your* getting fired?"

"I'm not asking you to fix that. I'm asking you to help a young woman get out of a bad situation."

It might have just been her imagination, but Liv could've sworn that a vein popped along his jaw. "What kind of bad situation?"

"I can't tell you that."

"Then I can't help you."

She gave him a blank stare. "It's a bad situation."

Mack stood abruptly, walked to the door, and swung it shut. When he turned back, he adopted a bouncer's stance and a stern expression. "How bad?"

"Really, really bad."

"Does this have something to do with you getting fired?"

"Does that matter?"

"It does if you want me to hire this girl."

"You have openings. I know someone who needs a job. The details shouldn't make a difference."

"Humor me."

It took her five minutes to get the entire story out, but it took all of one for Mack's blood pressure to rise and his vision to blur. He couldn't speak. Could barely breathe. He jerked his hands through his hair and forced himself to sit down in the chair opposite his desk.

That sonuvabitch. He was going to destroy him. He was going to tear the motherfucker apart.

"Did he—" Mack had trouble getting the words past the thick swell of *I will fuck someone up* that was blocking his vocal chords. "Did he ever do that to you?"

"No," Liv said, hesitating for a split second. "But I don't think this was the first time he's done it. He was way too confident about it and way too unconcerned about being caught."

"We have to do something," Mack rasped.

Liv gave him a look. "*We* aren't going to do anything."

"He can't get away with this."

"I don't plan on letting him, but the only thing I need you to do is to hire Jessica."

He needed water. Rage was turning his throat to sandpaper.

Liv stood up. "I'll be in touch. And if you could please not tell Gavin or Thea about any of this until I figure out how to do it, that would be great."

She walked toward the door, threw it open, and breezed through. Holy shit. How many times was this woman going to walk out on him?

Mack leaped up and followed her. "Whoa, whoa, whoa. Hold up. Where are you going?"

Sonia, who was sitting at her cubicle outside his office, swiveled in her chair and watched the drama with unabashed amusement. Yeah, yeah, so he'd never literally chased after a woman before. Big fucking deal.

Mack gripped Liv's elbow and tugged her back to keep their conversation private. Liv sighed, exasperation written across her face. "What?"

"What the hell did that mean?"

"Which part?"

"The part about making the bastard pay."

She gave him a *duh* look. "It means what it means. I'm going to expose him and ruin the bastard."

"By yourself?"

Liv shrugged. "Why not?"

"You can't do this by yourself. If he really does have a history of this, then he knows how to hide it. How exactly do you think you're going to expose him? You can't just go to the media and tell them what you saw and heard."

"That's not my plan, but thanks for treating me like an idiot."

"What is your plan, then?"

"I haven't figured that out yet, but I will. Anything else?"

"Yeah," Mack said, feeling his equilibrium return for the first time. Because, of *this*, he was absolutely certain. Men who abused women deserved to pay. He didn't care what it took. If Royce Preston was preying on women, Mack was going to stop him. "I want in."

Liv snorted. "You want in."

"I'm going to try not to be insulted by that noise, but yes. If Preston is a predator, I want him exposed too."

Liv gave him a look that screamed skepticism and distrust. She folded her arms over her chest and leaned on one hip. "You sure about that? Because I saw you with him that night at Savoy. All buddy-buddy, *let's get together.* You guys are pals. You expect me to believe you didn't know about this?"

"No, I didn't know about this. Jesus." Mack dragged his hands over his hair. Was that really what she thought of him? That he would cover for a sexual harasser?

"Well, someone had to know. Men like him always have enablers."

"Well, I wasn't one of them. I barely know the man."

"And what if you had heard that? Would you have done anything?"

"Yes, goddammit. I would have."

Liv tilted her head and studied him as if trying to decide whether she believed him. He noticed for the first time how much she looked like her sister. They had the same eyes. The same coloring. But Liv had a wariness about her he'd never seen in Thea. She looked like someone who desperately wanted to trust people but didn't know how.

And he suddenly desperately wanted her to trust him. "You know you can't do this alone, Liv. Don't be stubborn."

"You want to help? Fine. Give Jessica a job. I need to get her out of there."

"Done. I'll hire her today. How do I contact her?"

Liv blinked. "I—I don't know."

"You don't know?" He matched her skeptical tone from earlier.

"It's not like we were friends," she said, spreading her hands wide. "I don't have her phone number, her social media is all set to private, and it's not like I can go talk to her at work."

Mack thumbed the screen of his phone. "What's her last name?"

"Summers."

Mack typed the name into a Google search bar and added "Nashville" to filter out the results.

Liv squinted. "Are you being serious right now?"

"Yes, I'm serious."

"You're going to offer her a job."

"I just said that, didn't I?"

His Google search turned up about two million results. Liv let out a heavy breath and shook her head. "You really think I didn't try that already?"

When he didn't respond, she rolled her eyes so hard he could almost hear it. "I'll let you know when *I* get in touch with her," she said.

This time, when she walked away, Mack let her. Because even if Liv didn't know how to find the girl, Mack knew someone who could.

Mack shoved his phone back in his pocket and dug out his keys. He passed Sonia at her cubicle. She looked up. "What the hell was that all about?"

He ducked the question. "I'll explain later."

Sonia shrugged and said something sarcastic under her breath. Mack walked through the kitchen and out the back entrance into the alley behind the bar where he'd parked his car.

He drove across town quickly, making a phone call as he went.

It was just before four when he pulled into the meeting spot— a three-story brick rectangle with the name Dagnabit's painted in fading green letters on front above the door. It looked like the kind of place where the whiskey was cheap and the cooks didn't wash their hands. Which made it the perfect place for meetings like this.

Mack walked up the weedy, cracked sidewalk and pulled open the door. It creaked as if offended. Inside the lights were dim and the TV was loud. The place was nearly empty except for a pair of biker dudes who leaned heavily on the bar over half-finished pints of beer, their eyes glued to the baseball game on the TV. Neither glanced his way. Two seats away from them sat a man with stringy hair and a phlegmy cough who looked like he was one minute away from losing his shit and screaming about the CIA.

Mack chose a spot safely in the middle and ordered a beer.

Five minutes later, the door creaked again, and Noah Logan walked in. He had his hands shoved in the pockets of a beaten-up leather jacket and a skullcap tugged low across his forehead. By all outward appearances, he was your average, everyday computer IT specialist. Mack suspected it was a cover for some kind of super–secret agent thing. No one could be that smart and deceptively well built without working for the government on the down low. Mack had hired him several years ago to help set up his network security but realized rather quickly that Noah's skills went far beyond the standard, and he'd been essential in helping Mack with another sensitive project that had earned him a permanent spot on Mack's most-trusted list.

"Dude," Noah said, claiming the stool next to Mack. "What's the big emergency?"

"I need you to do something for me."

"Yeah, I figured."

Mack dropped a five on the counter and stood. "Let's take a walk."

"We just fucking got here," Noah complained.

Ten minutes later, he was no longer complaining. Noah slowed his steps and shook his head. "Holy shit," he breathed. "I knew there was something sleazy about that guy. What do you want me to do?"

"To start? I just need you to find Jessica for me. Liv can't approach her at Savoy, obviously. See if you can find out where she'll be when she's not at work or home."

"What else?"

"I need to find out how many women he has done this to."

Noah looked skeptical. "I'll see what I can find, but I need to know right up front how deep you want me to look."

"How deep can you look?"

Noah's face went eerily calm. "Pretty fucking deep."

"Send me a bill," Mack said, walking away. "Quietly."

"No charge," Noah called behind him.

Mack spun around. "What?"

Noah seemed to grow several inches in height. "Fuckers like Royce Preston deserve whatever they have coming to them. This one is pro bono."

CHAPTER SEVEN

Sunset turned the horizon orange Wednesday night as Mack exited the freeway and followed the GPS directions out of the city. Gavin hadn't been kidding. Liv lived on a farm. And not the hipster co-op kind either. This was a *farm* farm, with pastures and sheep—wait, no, those were goats—and a massive red barn surrounded by other smaller outbuildings. And smack in the middle, atop a small hill, was a soaring white clapboard house with a stone fence that looked like it had been erected sometime during Reconstruction.

Mack turned into the gravel driveway, drove under a canopy of trees, and slowed to a stop by a detached garage. A staircase wrapped around one side of the building and led to what he assumed was an upstairs of some kind. A single window overlooked the driveway.

Mack parked next to a dusty Ford pickup and behind a black Jeep with a faded, peeling bumper sticker that read, "A Woman Needs a Man like a Fish Needs a Bicycle." Yeah, he was definitely in the right place.

But what the hell? Why did Liv live here?

Mack killed the engine, opened his door, and reached for the bag of Chinese takeout he'd brought as a peace offering. He'd barely slept last night. There was no way he was going to sit on the sidelines while Liv took on Royce by herself. He just had to convince her to let him help.

He slid from the driver's seat . . . and that's when he was attacked.

The beast came out of nowhere. Mack heard an angry squawk, saw a puff of black-and-red feathers, and felt a chunk of his shin rip beneath his jeans before he could even register what the hell was happening. The beast flew several feet in the air and kicked its legs out. Talons tore into his skin again. Mack threw himself back into the front seat and slammed the door shut just in time, but the beast simply attacked his car with a screeching cry of vengeance.

Then, suddenly a savior appeared at the top of the garage stairs. She wore floppy rubber boots and carried a broom in one hand.

"You lost?" she yelled.

A clunk against his door made him wince. The fucking thing was going to scratch his car. Mack banged his fist against his window. "What the fuck is that thing?"

Liv held a hand to her ear in the universal *I can't hear you* gesture.

Mack rolled down his window. "What the hell is that?" he yelled.

She snorted. "It's a rooster, dumbass."

"It's fucking possessed!"

She shrugged. "Roosters are extremely territorial."

"It attacked me!"

"They're also excellent judges of character."

"Get rid of it so I can get out. We need to talk."

"If you're trying to incentivize me, you have failed."

He held the bag of Chinese food out the window. "Pork lo mein and wonton soup."

One eyebrow rose. "From where?"

Christ on a cracker. "Jade Dynasty."

"Fine." Liv clomped down the stairs and turned the broom on the bird. "Get. Go on."

The bird puffed up his feathers and went after the broom. Liv swore at him and swept him all the way to the fence line before locking him inside a chain-link gate.

She returned then to the driver's side. "There. You're totally safe. Now hand over my food."

Mack held the bag out the window. Liv snatched it from his fingers, peeked inside, shut it again. "Thanks. You can leave now."

"Nope." He opened the door. "We have stuff to talk about."

"No, we don't."

"I'm going to help you with Royce."

"I'm pretty sure I made myself clear yesterday."

Mack got out and shut the door. "If you didn't want me to help bring him down, you shouldn't have told me what he was doing."

"God, you're like an annoying chin hair that grows back no matter how many times you pluck it. You rip the bastard out, and then *ploop*, two days later, there it is again."

"As fascinating as I find it to learn that you struggle with chin hairs, we have more important things to talk about."

"Like how those shoes look like they cost more than my car?"

"You're going to give me fashion advice? You look like the before picture of a makeover segment."

"This man bothering you, Livvie?" A man with a barrel chest and a bad knee ambled toward them from one of the outbuildings, wiping his hands on a grease-stained towel. His buzzed hair and steely eyes spoke of a life spent in positions of authority. A limp said he was past his prime.

"Your boyfriend?" Mack whispered.

Liv glared up at Mack before answering the man. "Very much," she said. "Can you make him go away?"

Mack strode forward, hand extended. Behind them, Liv snorted. "Don't. You might mess up your manicure."

"Braden Mack," he said.

The man accepted the handshake with a stronger-than-necessary grip. "Earl Hopkins."

"We call him Hop," Liv said, joining them. She nodded toward Mack. "And I call *him* Chin Hair."

Hop sized him up. "Ever serve?"

"Time or in the military?"

"Either."

"Nope."

Hop snorted and looked Mack up and down once more, stopping with a smirk at the bloody, ripped shin of his jeans. He glanced at Liv, eyebrow raised. "Randy get him?"

Liv smiled.

Hop nodded. "Rooster's good for something, at least."

"You named it *Randy*?"

Liv rolled her eyes. "It's okay, Hop. Tell Rosie I'll be in in a few minutes to help finish dinner."

Hop nodded at Mack. "He eating with us?"

Liv and Mack spoke at the same time.

"No."

"I'd love to."

Liv glared at him. "You're *not* staying for dinner."

"What're we having?"

"Whatever you're allergic to."

Hop gave another snort and wandered toward the main house. "Quite a life you've got here, Liv."

"Feel free to leave anytime."

"Come on, seriously. Why the hell do you live here?"

She stomped up the same path that Hop had taken without answering.

"Perhaps you didn't notice," Mack said, scrambling to catch up. "But I'm *bleeding*."

"You'll survive."

"Who knows what kinds of diseases that thing has?"

"You're right. You should leave and head straight to the emergency room and tell them exactly what happened."

He was ready with a quick retort, but it died on his lips because ten feet away, on the other side of the fence, Randy jumped on the back of a hen and—"What the hell is he doing to that chicken?"

"Didn't spend much time in the country as a kid, did you?"

"Sure. Spent a whole day at a one-room schoolhouse where we shoved a stick into a rotten apple and called it a doll. There was never a murderous rooster in any of our lessons."

Randy jumped off the hen's back. "Jesus. That was fast."

"The male of every species is trash."

"I'm not. I'm one of the good guys."

Liv snorted as she opened the back door. She let the screen go, and it damn near smacked in him the face.

"Thanks," he said, ducking in just in time. He followed her into a mudroom and down a short hallway that led into a spacious farmhouse kitchen where a woman with a long gray braid stood at the stove, stirring something that smelled awesome in a large red pot.

"I found a stray," Liv said, heading for the fridge. "Randy got him."

The woman turned around, wiping her hands on a dish towel. "And who might you be?"

Mack flashed his signature grin and held out his hand. "Braden Mack, ma'am. Pleasure to meet you."

He threw in a wink for good measure, and the woman smiled as she shook his hand. "Well, it sure is pleasure to meet you too."

"Seriously?" Liv said, putting her Chinese food in the fridge. "Even you?"

"Sorry to intrude at dinnertime, Ms. . . ." He let the sentence hang.

"Call me Rosie," she said, waving her hand at the formality. "And it's not an intrusion at all. We have plenty. We're having pot roast."

Mack patted his stomach and winked again. "My favorite."

Liv made a gagging noise, which earned her a scathing look from Rosie.

"Liv, where are your manners?" Rosie chided, nodding toward the hallway. "Go help him clean that cut."

Liv let out a sigh like a kid who'd just been told to watch her little brothers while the grown-ups played cards. "Fine. Come on."

Mack followed her to a small downstairs bathroom. He sat down on the edge of the white porcelain tub and stretched his legs out. They spanned the entire distance between the bathtub and the pedestal sink, where Liv was wetting a wash cloth.

She turned around with a bottle of something sinister-looking. "Roll up your pant leg," she said, crouching in front of him.

He fought the dirty urge to comment on the convenience of her position. Instead, he bent at the waist and pulled his jeans up to reveal an inch-long cut on his shin. Blood matted the dark hair and trickled down in a little river toward his shoe.

Liv scoffed and looked up with a curl of her lips. "*This* is what you've been carrying on about?"

"Look how much blood there is."

"It's a scratch. God, be a man."

"That," he said, pointing in her face, "is the second sexist comment you've made since I got here."

"What was the first?"

"When you made fun of my manicure."

Her eyes went round. "If you throw your money away on manicures, you deserve to be ridiculed."

"I don't get manicures, but so what if I did? Men can get manicures if they want."

"Never said they couldn't. I think anyone who wastes money on manicures should be ridiculed."

It was an interesting tidbit that Mack filed away for further examination later. For now, he'd just change the subject. "What's up with Hop? He a cop?"

"Retired state detective and a Vietnam vet. I wouldn't fuck with him if I were you."

"He doesn't seem like Rosie's type."

"Oh, they're not together." She laughed, and it was the first genuine sound of affection he'd ever heard her make. He kind of liked it. "He helps out here, and I'm pretty sure he's been in love with her since high school, but no, they're not together."

She poured cold liquid onto his cut, and Mack yelped. "Jesus, what the hell are you doing?"

"Cleaning the wound."

"With what? Hydrochloric acid?"

"Peroxide, pansy-ass."

"There you go again, questioning my manhood. I'll have you know that it is a scientific fact that men have a lower threshold for pain—Jesus Christ!" She'd poured another capful of the vile liquid on his wound. "Was that really necessary?"

"Absolutely." She stood. "I needed to test your scientific theory. Turns out you're right."

"It stings," he pouted.

"Here," she said, handing him a square bandage. "Come out when you're done, or better yet, don't."

Mack let that one slide. He taped the bandage over his wound, washed his hands, and then walked back into the kitchen. Liv was setting the table in the attached dining room.

"Want some help?" he asked.

Rosie answered. "You just sit and make yourself comfortable. Liv, get him something to drink."

He sat down in one of the open chairs with a grin.

"What do you want?" Liv practically growled.

"Water is just fine." He winked at her, and she bared her teeth.

Hop wandered in then, hair wet and clothes fresh as if he'd just showered. "I'm having a beer," he said pointedly as if to say *that's what real men do.*

"Well, if you are, then so am I."

Hop nudged Liv away from the fridge, grabbed two bottles of Budweiser, and sat down opposite Mack.

"Where are you from?" Hop asked, shoving a bottle across the table.

"Des Moines."

Liv looked up quickly from the island, where she was sorting silverware. "Really?"

"Yeah, why?"

She shrugged. "You don't seem like the Iowa type."

"Family?" Hop prodded.

Mack stiffened, which did not go unnoticed by Hop. The man lifted a single eyebrow.

"My mom still lives in Des Moines, but she's moving here soon. I'm buying her a house."

"And your father?" Hop asked, eagle-eyed.

"Dead," Mack gave the familiar lie.

"I didn't know that," Liv said, and he glanced over at the softness in her tone. "I'm sorry."

Mack shrugged to cover the shame. He felt guilty about her sympathy but not enough to tell her the truth. The truth was worse. "It was a long time ago."

Ten minutes later, dinner was served. Liv sat in one of the chairs across from him, and Rosie and Hop claimed the other two ends.

"Gorgeous place you got here, Rosie," Mack said.

Liv rolled her eyes and shoved the bread basket into his hands.

"Been in my family since 1870," Rosie said. "Both my grand-father and my mother were born right upstairs."

"No kidding?" Mack said. "And where were you born?"

"A coven in the woods," Hop said.

"You can eat out with the goats if you want," Rosie told him.

"Don't mind her," Hop told Mack. "She's just pissed the Equal Rights Amendment was never adopted."

"One more state. That's all we needed."

Mack was beginning to understand why Liv lived here. This was pure entertainment.

"So you and Livvie are dating?" Rosie asked.

Water sprayed from Liv's mouth. "God no."

"That's too bad. It's been a long time since Liv had a man."

"Rosie," Liv whined.

Mack grinned again. "Is that right?"

Liv sat up straight. "I don't want a man. I don't have time for a man. They're needy, clingy, and never keep their promises."

Mack whistled. "Damn, girl. Who hurt you?"

"The patriarchy," she deadpanned.

"So what brings you by, then?" Hop said.

"I'm trying to help her."

Liv shoved a bite of food into her mouth. "I don't need his help."

"What's this about?" Rosie asked.

"Mack here thinks he's Superman and wants to swoop in and save the damsel in distress."

"And *Olivia* here"—a booted foot nailed him in the shin under the table—"thinks she can take someone like Royce Preston down all by herself. I'm trying to convince her that she's going to need help."

"He might be right, Liv," Rosie said.

"I can handle this," Liv said, with a pointed glare in his direction.

Rosie shook her head, lips tight. "I can't believe we're still fighting this shit."

Hop sighed. "Here we go again."

Rosie pointed her fork at Hop. "You men need to get after your own. We've been fighting this shit too long."

Hop held up his hands. "What're you yelling at me for? I didn't do it. I've never sexually harassed a woman in my life."

"Oh, don't you pull that *not all men* crap with me. The reason men like Royce Preston get away with it is because every other man in the world enables them."

"How'd I become the bad guy?"

Mack cleared his throat. "I believe what Rosie is trying to say is that bad guys get away with it because the good guys look the other way."

He met Liv's surprised gaze and shrugged.

Hop shook his head. "Bad guys have always existed and always will."

"Only because good guys let them."

"Now listen here," Hop said, getting all blustery, "I was putting dirtbags who hurt women in prison when you were still in diapers. So don't come in here and lecture me, son."

Rosie slammed down her fork. "And this is my table, Hop, so you'd better be politer to my guests if you want to keep sitting at it."

Liv kicked him again under the table.

Mack held up his hands. "I apologize. I was rude."

"You were no such thing," Rosie said. "He needed to hear that."

Hop muttered under his breath and returned to his food. Rosie put on a bright smile. "So your mom is moving to Nashville?"

"She is." He smiled. "She's actually flying out next weekend to look at houses. She'd love a place like this, but I'm trying to convince her to get something closer to my house."

"Oh, how fun. You should bring her by and let her see the farm."

Liv sat up straight. "What?"

"That sounds amazing, Rosie." Mack winked. "I just might do that."

"We'd love to have her."

Dinner continued with a steady stream of mindless chatter about the farm, but every few seconds, Mack caught Liv shooting daggers at him across the table. When they were finally finished eating, he thanked Rosie for the delicious meal and offered to help clean up.

"You two go on," Rosie said. "Hop will help me."

Hop grumbled something impolite, and Mack didn't want to wait around to see how Rosie responded. He stood. "Liv, shall we?"

Liv puffed out another one of those long-suffering sighs. She led him outside and back to his car. She stopped by the driver's door and folded her arms across her chest.

"What's up with your shitty mood all the time?" he teased, because he was quickly finding that teasing her was one of life's great pleasures.

"Hmm, let's see." She cocked a hip and pretended to think. "I worked my ass off to be a pastry chef, and now I'm back to searching for a job."

"I offered you a job."

"My old boss is out there sexually harassing women—"

"Which I offered to help you do something about."

"And Jessica hasn't returned any of my messages."

He grinned and leaned closer. "Which I have an answer for."

"Excuse me?"

"I just thought you'd be interested to know that I know where to find her."

Her mouth dropped open.

Mack twirled his keys around his finger. "Meet me at Temple tomorrow at three. We'll go together."

"I don't like the *together* part of that sentence."

Mack winked. "You keep fighting it, Liv. But you're going to start to like me."

He could practically hear the eye roll.

"Afraid my charm will start to get under your skin if you spend too much time with me?"

She sighed. "Fine. I'll be there at three."

He climbed behind the wheel and shut his door. She stood in the driveway and watched him leave.

It was a petty thought, but he smiled with the realization that he'd finally been the one to walk away from her.

CHAPTER EIGHT

The next afternoon, Mack heard the clunk-clunk of his manager's chunky-heeled boots making a loud beeline for his office as soon as he arrived.

Sonia produced far more noise than seemed possible for a woman who stood barely five feet tall and couldn't have weighed more than a hundred pounds soaking wet. But Sonia walked like she lived—pissed off and deliberate. Which sounded like someone else he was getting to know. She and Liv were either going to start a girl gang or kill each other.

Sonia appeared in the doorway, hands on her hips. "What are you doing here so early?"

Mack lifted his chin to indicate he wanted her to come inside. "Shut the door. I need to talk to you."

She whined. "Is this going to take long? Because Joe fucked up the bourbon order, so unless you're here to save my ass, I don't have time for a chat."

"You do remember that I'm your boss, right?"

"Yeah, for all the good it does me. You made any progress on hiring a new bartender yet?"

Mack crossed his arms, feeling smug and looking forward to proving it. "I just might have, actually."

Sonia paused before asking skeptically, "What kind of progress?"

"I know someone who needs a job."

"Great. When can he start?"

"She."

"When can she start?"

"Well, I haven't actually convinced her to take the job yet. Or even asked her if she wants it."

Sonia grunted. "I don't have time for this."

Mack nodded again at the chair in front of his desk. "I really do need to talk to you, though."

His serious tone raised the maturity level in the room. Sonia shut the door and sat down. "This sounds serious."

"It is," he said. "I need this to stay between us."

The maturity didn't last long. "Oh God, you got someone pregnant."

"What? For fuck's sake. No."

"Good. Because I am not ready to be an aunt or anything, and Lord knows I am no one's idea of a godmother."

"Can you stop talking for a minute?"

She sank against the chair. "I'm all ears."

"I mean it, Sonia. You can't speak a word of this to anyone."

"Fuck you. When have I ever—"

He held up his hands. "Okay, okay. I just—this is serious."

"Then what the hell is taking so long? Spit it out."

He picked up a pen and twirled it. "You know Royce Preston, right?"

She fake gagged.

"I take it that's a *yes*."

"I only know *of* him. Why?" She groaned and tilted her head. "Don't tell me you're thinking of going into business with him or something. I swear to God, I'll quit. Like, right fucking now."

"Mind if I finish what I was saying?"

"You better, because I will not let you sell your soul like that."

He leaned back in his chair. "Just out of curiosity, why?"

Sonia shrugged. "I don't know. There's something about him that makes my vagina want to send out a cease-and-desist email."

"Interesting visual."

Sonia pointed at her crotch. "The vag doesn't lie."

Given the context of their conversation, it seemed especially inappropriate to be talking about her vag for any reason. "Have you ever heard any actual stories of him, you know . . ."

She squinted. "What?"

"You know."

"Chaining teenage girls up in his basement? Selling Beanie Babies on eBay? You're going to have to be more specific."

"Sexual harassment."

Sonia's eyes narrowed further. "What is going on?"

"I just heard a rumor."

"About sexual harassment?"

"Along those lines, yeah."

"Wouldn't surprise me."

Well it had surprised *him*, and that bothered him. How had he missed it? He'd known Royce for, what, five years? And though they weren't friends by any definition, they ran in the same circles. Played in charity golf tournaments together. Attended the same Chamber of Commerce parties. Rubbed elbows at sporting events.

In all that time, he'd never once seen anything that had given him a sexual harasser vibe. Yet Sonia had picked up on it without even knowing the guy. Were women just born with a radar for that kind of thing? Or did they just develop it through life the hard way?

"Oh shit," Sonia suddenly breathed.

He blinked out of his thoughts. "What?"

"You're going to do something, aren't you?"

"No."

"Yes, you are. I know that look."

"What look?"

"The Superman look."

"What the hell does that mean?"

"That you're about to grab a white horse and race in to save the damsel in distress."

Okay, that was the second fucking time in as many days someone had accused him of thinking he was some kind of hero, and it was officially pissing him off. "Don't you think someone should do something if there's an asshole out there sexually harassing women?"

"So you *are* thinking of doing something."

He slammed his pen down. "Yes, dammit, I am."

She stood. "Then count me in."

"What?"

"I hate that motherfucker, and that was before I knew I actually had a reason to. So I want in on whatever you plan to do."

"I don't have a plan. But we might need to hire someone else."

"For what?"

He lifted a shoulder. "I don't know yet. We'll make up a job if we have to."

She cocked her eyebrow again. "Damsel in distress?"

He flipped her off. She returned the gesture and then turned to leave.

"Sonia."

She spun around. "What?" She said it with her characteristic whine.

"The conversation we just had—"

"I won't tell anyone."

"No, that's not what I mean. The whole vag thing. Did that make you uncomfortable?"

"I'm the one who said it."

He nodded absently. "I know. I just, sometimes you and I . . . we say things."

"We're friends, Mack. There's a difference."

"You're sure? I need you to tell me if I've ever done or said anything that has made you uncomfortable, because that was never my intent. I mean, I know intent doesn't matter, impact does, but—"

"Mack," she said, her voice as somber as he'd ever heard it. "You are nothing like Royce Preston. You're probably the best guy I know, and if you ever tell anyone I said that, I will hurt you."

He nodded. "Deal."

"Want me to shut this when I leave?"

He nodded again.

She saluted and walked out. Mack stared at her empty chair for a moment. *You are probably the best guy I know.* So why did he feel like such a shit? He swiveled in his chair to avoid both the question and the answer.

He grabbed his phone and dialed his mom's number. She answered at the last minute, out of breath. "Hey, just a second, okay?"

Her voice was muffled as she apparently pulled the phone away from her ear to speak to someone. He made out the words, "They're beautiful. Thank you so much."

"Who was that?" he asked when she came back on the line.

"A florist."

Mack's own radar went on alert. "Who sent you flowers?"

"I don't know. I haven't looked at the card."

She was being cagey. He hated it when she was cagey. "Why don't you look and tell me."

"You know, Braden, I appreciate how much you look out for me, but just because I'm your mother doesn't mean I'm not entitled to some privacy."

He bristled under the admonishment and the use of his first name. His family were the only people who used it. "Did you get the plane ticket?"

"Yes. Thank you, honey."

"I'll send you several more listings that my real estate guy found that I think you'll like."

"Sounds . . . great. How many?"

"Six I think."

"I'm sure they're . . . great."

She was being cagey again. "What's wrong, Mom?"

"Nothing. Why do you ask?"

"You sound weird."

"Just tired. Listen, I gotta run. Call you tomorrow?"

"Um, okay. Check your email for the listings."

"Yep. Love you, sweetie."

And she hung up. What the hell? Mack pulled the phone away and stared at the blank screen. His mother had just hung up on him. And had gotten flowers from someone.

There was a quick knock at his door, and Sonia poked her head inside.

"Chin hair?"

For fuck's sake.

Nearly every table at the university coffee shop was occupied when Liv and Mack walked in shortly before four. Professors chatted with students. College kids huddled around laptops and textbooks. A handful of bleary-eyed students clutched steaming lattes as if praying for salvation.

"Smells like slow-roasted hangover in here," Mack said, settling his hand on her back as they walked in.

Liv jumped at his touch, but he either didn't notice or didn't care. He pointed to a table by the window. "We can watch the entire place from over there."

Liv scanned the large open space as she sat. "I don't see her yet."

"You want something to drink?"

"Yes, God. I need caffeine." She pulled her wallet from her purse, but he held up his hand.

"I got it. What do you want?"

"I can buy my own coffee."

"I'm sure you can, but this one's on me."

She jutted her jaw to the side and thought about continuing the argument. But he would just argue back, and she was too drained. "Vanilla latte. Big. Thank you."

He nodded. "Be right back."

She followed him with her eyes to the counter, where he flashed a smile that had the young barista blushing and stammering in two seconds flat. He returned to the table a few minutes later, carrying two cardboard cups—one with a phone number scribbled on the side.

Liv rolled her eyes. "She's a little young for you, isn't she?"

Mack looked at his cup as if noticing the numbers for the first time. He shrugged. "Happens all the time."

"You're shameless."

"I can't help it if I was born with natural charisma."

"You were born full of shit."

Mack shook his head. "Drink your coffee. You're cranky."

Liv took a sip and groaned. The first hit of caffeine was always the best. She opened her eyes to find Mack smirking at her.

"You need some time alone with that thing?"

"If I say yes, will you go away?"

His quiet chuckle had the same effect as the coffee—it made her heart pound a little faster.

"How'd you find out where we'd find Jessica?" she asked after a moment.

"I have a friend who's good with computers."

Liv's spine went rigid. "Wait a minute. Did you tell someone about Royce?"

"No. Just that I needed to find someone."

She hunched in her chair. "Are you lying?"

"Jesus," he breathed.

"Because I hate liars."

His eyebrow twitched. "Noted."

Liv sat back again and stared at the door. When the door opened and a stream of students filed in, Liv held her breath as she searched the small crowd. But still no Jessica.

"Did you go to college?" she asked after several awkwardly quiet moments.

Mack sipped his coffee. "Nope. You?"

"Just culinary school."

He lifted an eyebrow. "*Just*? From what I understand, it's not exactly an easy program to finish."

His words pleased her more than she wanted to admit. "How'd you learn about running a business if you didn't go to college?"

"You don't need a degree to be a successful businessman."

"Did you not want to go to college?"

He draped an ankle across the other knee. "Is this a normal conversation we're about to have?"

"Not if you're going to be like that."

He took another sip before answering. "I couldn't afford college. I probably could've gotten a loan, but that never made a lot of sense to me."

Liv nodded. Nearly all of her friends from high school who'd gone to college were now faced with massive debt. Which was fine if they ended up with great jobs that paid the bills, but that wasn't yet the case for a lot of her friends.

"You probably could've gotten a scholarship, though. You're smart."

Mack covered his heart with his hand. "That's the first honest-to-God compliment I've ever gotten from you. I'm touched."

"Telling someone they're smart is not a compliment. It's just a statement of fact."

He looked at the ceiling as if praying for patience. "Why do you argue every single thing I say?"

"Does it drive you crazy?"

"Yes."

"There's your answer."

"What about you," he asked. "Why a pastry chef?"

A pang of something she didn't like struck her in the feels. "I liked baking with my grandma."

"That wasn't so hard, now was it?"

She rolled her eyes again.

"This was the grandma you and Thea lived with for a while?"

Her head snapped up so fast, she was surprised she didn't pull a muscle. "How do you know about that?"

"Gavin mentioned it once. He said you and Thea lived with her for a while after your parents' divorce."

"Gavin talks too much."

"Why'd you live with her?"

She shook her head. "Your turn."

He spread his arms wide. "Ask me anything."

"Why'd you start reading romance novels?"

"My mom used to read them. When I discovered they had sex in them, I started sneaking them to my bed at night."

She waved a hand. "Gross. I don't want to know anymore."

"I had to throw a couple of way because, you know . . ."

Liv faked a gag. "Teenage boys are so gross."

"It ain't easy. One day you've got this interesting thing hanging between your legs that lets you piss outside and write your name in the snow, and the next it's controlling your every thought."

"Yes, poor men, can't use their brains because all the blood goes straight to their dicks."

He peered at her through narrowed eyes. "Do you really hate men?"

"Yes."

"Really?"

"No. But I should. I've never met one worth trusting."

He tilted his head. "Not even Gavin?"

"Gavin might be the only one. And maybe Hop. But that's it."

"What about your father?"

Liv smiled. "Your turn."

He lifted an eyebrow. "Subtle."

She took a sip of her coffee. "How'd you get the money to open a club so young?"

"Dang, that's personal."

"You just told me that you used to jerk off to romance novels as a teenager."

"True." He leaned back in his chair. "I got lucky, basically."

"Win the lottery or something?"

"Sort of. I was working as a bouncer for an older man. He was looking to retire, didn't have any kids of his own, decided to help me out."

"And you turned that into four major nightclubs?"

"Yes."

"That doesn't sound like luck. That sounds like hard work and smart management."

"Did you just compliment me again?"

Liv stood with an annoyed groan. "And now I regret it."

Mack made a big play of patting his pockets. "I need a pen. I need to document this moment."

The door swung open again, and Liv sucked in a breath. *Jessica.* She looked like every other college girl in the place in her yoga pants and oversize sweatshirt. The one main difference was the haunted look in her eyes. Her shoulders literally hunched under the weight of her backpack and, probably, the secret she was carrying.

Mack followed her gaze. "That's her?"

Liv nodded.

Mack's fingers tightened on his cup. "Christ, she's young."

They watched silently as Jessica approached the counter to order. She hoisted her backpack higher on one shoulder, and as she did, her eyes scanned the coffee shop, presumably for an open table. Liv tensed in anticipation of the moment Jessica spotted her, but the girl's eyes scanned over her as if she didn't notice or didn't recognize Liv.

Probably the latter. It was amazing how many people didn't recognize her when she put on her chef's hat, so it only made sense that Jessica wouldn't recognize her out of it. The barista called her name, and Jessica picked up her coffee. There was an open table toward the back by the hallway to the bathrooms.

Liv watched for another minute as Jessica got settled at the table, pulled out her laptop and a notebook, and took a sip of her coffee.

"How are we going to do this?" Mack asked.

"Let me talk to her first. I'll wave at you when you can come over."

She set her coffee down and stood. A sudden wave of nerves brought a shaky breath from her chest. Mack reached over and gripped her hand. "You okay?"

"Fine." She pulled her hand back, not so much because she disliked the feel of his fingers on hers but because she liked it too much.

She was nearly all the way to Jessica's table before the girl noticed. Up close, recognition came fast. Jessica's eyes widened. "What are you doing here?"

"Can I sit down?" Liv asked, motioning to the open chair.

Jessica's eyes darted about. "I can't talk to you."

"No one knows I'm here."

"How'd you find me?"

"I just want to talk," Liv said.

"What do you want?" Jessica's tone was frantic, not rude.

"To make sure you're all right."

Jessica's eyes sparked.

"You're right," Liv said, claiming the chair. "Stupid thing to say."

"I have to study," Jessica complained.

"I want to help you."

"There's nothing to help with. I told you there was nothing going on." The tremble in her fingers as she clutched her pen said otherwise.

"I know what I heard and what I saw. I also know that you're terrified."

"I just want you to leave me alone."

"I can't. Not until I make Royce pay for what he did. What he has probably done before."

Jessica's eyes widened, her earlier suspicion replaced by outright panic. *"How?"*

Good question. "I'm working on it."

Jessica shook her head and started packing up her things. "Just leave it alone."

"I'm going to protect you. I promise. I just want you to know that you don't have to put up with this."

Jessica's lip trembled. "My mom is so proud that I work there. I-I'm the first person in my family to go to college, and when I got this job, my mom told *everyone*. I can't tell her about this. If I quit, she'll want to know why, and—"

"Your mother would not want you to have to endure what Royce is doing to you."

Jessica bit her lip again as if to stave off tears. "Please. Just leave me alone."

She stood. Liv reached out and grasped her wrist. "Wait."

Jessica stopped but refused to look at Liv.

"What if you had another job to go to? Would you at least consider leaving?"

"I don't know."

"You see that man over there?" Liv turned and pointed at Mack. He lifted a hand in a casual, friendly wave and then stood. "He's a friend. If you're worried about money, he will give you a job."

Jessica sat back down as Mack approached. He stopped a respectful distance away and extended his hand. "Braden Mack."

Jessica's hand trembled as she placed it in his.

"Nice to meet you. Can I sit down?" He pointed at the other empty chair.

She nodded. Mack met Liv's eyes as he rounded the table and gave her a small smile. "Liv told me a little about what happened," he said quietly, sitting.

Jessica shot a betrayed glare in Liv's direction.

"No one else knows," he said reassuringly. "You can trust me."

"Mack owns a whole bunch of nightclubs and bars in the area," Liv said.

Mack dug a business card from his wallet and slid it across the table. "My main office is at Temple. It's one of my nightclubs."

Jessica nodded. "I know that one."

"I also own several other smaller clubs."

Jessica bit her lip. "What kind of jobs do you have?"

"I'll make one up for you, if necessary."

"You'd do that for me?" Her voice held the awestruck tone of a girl who'd just met a superhero. Liv sort of understood because, in that moment, she sort of felt the same.

"You can start today if you want. You never have to go back to Royce Preston."

And just like that, the spell was broken. The utterance of Royce's name seemed to break something inside her. Jessica shook her head and shoved Mack's card in her pocket. "I need this job. The pay is better than anywhere else I can find, and the connections . . ."

"I know," Liv said. "It's the same reason I started working there too. You think your career is golden if you work for the great Royce Preston. But look at what it's costing you. No job is worth that."

Jessica's lips pinched together in a tight line. "Or maybe you just want revenge. You want to use me to get back at him for firing you. He said you would try it."

"Are you defending him right now?" At that, Mack reached over and squeezed Liv's knee.

"Do you know what he could do to me?" Jessica fired back. "All I want is to be a chef, like you. He'll ruin me."

"Not if we ruin him first."

"See? You just want to hurt him. I used to hear you talking in the kitchen. You hate Royce. You always have."

"Trust me, Jessica. The easiest thing I could've done that night is walk away. I got absolutely nothing out of defending you." Mack's fingers dug into her knee. She glared at him, and he responded with a tiny shake of his head.

Jessica snapped her laptop shut. "I wish you *had* just walked away." She hauled her backpack onto her lap and started shoving things inside.

Liv leaned toward her. "Jessica, he can't be allowed to get away with this. Who knows how many other women he has done this to? Doesn't that matter at all to you?"

"That's not my problem." She rose from her chair.

"Let us help you," Mack said calmly.

"You want to help me?" Jessica slung her backpack over one shoulder. "Leave me the hell alone."

"Jessica—" Liv said.

Mack squeezed her knee again. "Let her go. We can't force her."

Liv rubbed her eyes. "Now what?"

Mack stood. "Now I get you some barbecue."

CHAPTER NINE

An hour later, Liv took out her frustrations on an unsuspecting pulled pork sandwich while sitting in Mack's office. The thud-thud-thud of the base from the live band made her insides shake and her glass of lemonade ripple.

"I don't get it," she said, mouth full. "Why won't she leave? What possible reason would someone have to want to let him get away with it?"

Mack dipped a fry in ketchup. "Fear is a powerful motivator."

"But we're giving her a way out. What's there to be afraid of?"

"Until you've been in that position, you can't possibly know."

It was basically the same thing Rosie had told her, but Liv still didn't buy it. "No," she said, reaching for her lemonade. "Bullshit. You can't tell me a woman would willingly stay in a situation like this for any reason."

"Kind of judgmental, don't you think?"

Liv reeled back. "Excuse me, but whose side are you on?"

"Yours. Which is why I'm going to be honest with you." Mack

wiped his mouth with a balled-up napkin. "You were a jerk back there."

"I was not!"

"You basically blamed the victim."

"Screw you. I did not." But her brain betrayed her ego and started replaying her own words back to her. *Who knows how many other women he has done this to? Doesn't that matter at all to you?* She sank into her seat. "I just don't understand."

"Not everyone is like you, Liv."

She scrunched her eyebrows. "What does that mean?"

"Not everyone is willing or able to take on the world in a great big fight. It doesn't make them weak or wrong." A spark fired in his eyes, and he suddenly leaned forward on his elbows. "Did you know a woman will go back to an abusive relationship seven times on average before leaving for good?"

"Okay, first of all, I don't know why you just happen to have that statistic in your back pocket. Second of all, we're talking about sexual harassment, not domestic violence."

"We're talking about men in positions of power using their authority, whether it's professional or personal, to manipulate through fear and intimidation. It's the same damn thing. It's all one big cultural continuum." Mack threw his napkin onto his plate.

He was right. And she hated him for it. Maybe even more than she hated herself for being so ignorant. "Wow," she snarked, because she was cranky at herself. "Did you learn all that in a romance novel?"

"Believe it or not," he said, wadding up his trash, "I did. You should give them a try. I can recommend some books to get you started."

"I'll pass."

He winked. "I'm a lot less messy than when I was sixteen."

She fake gagged. "And to think I was actually starting to like you."

"No reason to fight it, Liv. Everyone eventually gives in to the Mack charm."

And now she was cranky because she was afraid he might be right.

He leaned back in his chair. "There is one silver lining in all this."

"Which is?"

He flashed the magic Mack grin. "The longer this takes, the longer you get to partner up with me."

Liv wrapped her hands loosely around her throat. "Kill me now."

"You'll see," he said, standing. "By the time we're through, you're going to love me."

Sonia poked her head in the office. "You're wanted at the bar."

Mack dropped his trash in the wastebasket. "What's up?"

Sonia put her hand to her forehead and adopted a breezy tone. "Another lonely wife."

Liv stood up. "Do I even want to know what this is about?"

"Mack has a superpower," Sonia said, rolling her eyes.

"Convincing women to embrace celibacy?"

Sonia grinned at Mack. "I like her."

Mack snorted. "Give it time."

Liv flipped him off, and Sonia clutched her heart. "Dear God, we're soul mates."

Liv stretched a fist out, and Sonia bumped it with one of hers. Mack shook his head and muttered something that sounded like *for fuck's sake* under his breath.

"Make any progress today?" Sonia asked.

Mack shook his head rapidly, and Liv's mouth dropped open. "Did he tell you?"

"Yep."

Mack groaned. "Dammit, Sonia."

She shrugged. "I can't lie. It breaks the girl code."

"Are you kidding me?" Mack said. "She's here all of ten minutes, and you already have a girl code?" He looked at Liv. "I didn't tell her *everything*."

"Your secret is safe with me," Sonia told Liv.

Mack snorted. "I wouldn't believe that if I were you."

Liv laughed and then stopped herself.

Mack pointed. "I heard that."

"You heard nothing."

"You laughed at me."

"Nope."

"I told you. You're going to end up loving me. Everyone does."

Liv rolled her eyes. "It's really sad how you need that kind of adoration."

"It's really sad how you pretend you don't."

Liv shrugged. "I'm not pretending. I hate people, and they hate me. It's a perfectly healthy relationship."

"That's not a relationship. That's an excuse. You're just afraid people won't like you, so you put on this act."

"I'm sorry, is this coming from the guy who bought a thousand-dollar cupcake to impress a woman?"

"Yeah, until *another* woman walked in and screwed that up for me."

"I had help dropping that cupcake, douchebag."

"How long do I have to keep apologizing for that?"

"Keep going. I'll tell you when it's enough."

Mack felt the weight of someone staring. He glanced up to find Sonia leaning in the doorway, watching them with way too much interest. "What?" he asked, irritated for no apparent reason.

She shrugged. "Are you coming to the bar or not?" Sonia prodded.

Against her better judgement, Liv followed.

Mack could spot an unhappy wife from a mile away.

Tight smile. Annoyed yet wistful gaze. Mournful stare at hands twisted in her lap. All while an oblivious husband stood just a few feet away, having the time of his life with his buddies, no idea that the woman he'd promised to love and cherish was one glass of wine away from walking away forever.

Christ, men were stupid.

She sat at the far end of the bar, alone, looking over her shoulder every couple of minutes to a group of men at a nearby table who were working on their fourth pitcher of beer.

Mack caught the bartender's eye and nodded toward the woman. His bartender laughed at him and nodded. Yep, this one was all his.

Mack glanced back at Liv and smiled. "Watch and learn," he said.

She flipped him off.

Mack wandered to where the woman stood, leaned on the bar in front of her, and graced her with one of the smiles his mother used to warn would get him into trouble. "Don't tell me you came out tonight looking like that just to stand here all alone."

The woman's head swiveled toward him in surprise. Her cheeks grew pink. "What?"

Mack winked. "Ah, there she is. What're you drinking?"

She looked at her empty glass. "Just water. I-I'm here with my husband," she blurted.

"Well, where is he? And why isn't he up here getting you a new water?"

She looked over her shoulder. "He's with his coworkers."

"He do this a lot?"

"Do what?"

"Take you out and then abandon you to hang out with his friends?"

She shrugged. That was a *yes*. What a fucking idiot. Men didn't deserve the gift of women.

Mack picked up her glass. "It's on the house. What can I get you?"

She shook her head. "I'm the designated driver."

So not only did Mr. Asshole ignore his wife, he'd only dragged her along so he could drink to the point of unsafe driving. Nice. "Fair enough," Mack said, filling a glass of water for her. "But I bet I can guess your favorite drink."

A perfectly groomed eyebrow arched over suddenly interested eyes. "I doubt that."

Mack studied her from the tips of her hair—balayage highlights, expensive—to her earrings—diamond studs. Then to the clutch purse next to her hands. Kate Spade. Top shelf, classy. *Classic.*

"Manhattan?"

Her mouth fell open again with a startled laugh. "How did you know that?"

Mack shrugged. "It's a gift."

"That's a weird gift to have."

"Not in my job." He looked at the table of men. "So point out which one is your husband."

The woman's face fell. "He's the one standing up."

Mack studied him. Closely cropped hair. Short-trimmed beard. Professional type. College educated and arrogant. "Let me guess," Mack said, crossing his arms. "Works in finance?"

The woman laughed again. "Impressive."

"What're they drinking?"

She rolled her eyes. "He used to just like Budweiser, but now he's into that IPA stuff. I can't stand it."

He winked. "Budweiser it is."

Mack filled a pitcher, flagged down one of the waiters, and scribbled a note on a napkin for the tray.

Compliments of Braden Mack. Pay attention to your wife, asshole, or get the fuck out of my club.

His task accomplished, Mack returned to the other end of the bar, where Liv stood next to Sonia.

"And that," he said, arms spread wide. "Is how it's done."

Liv sighed heavily and looked at Sonia. "How long have you worked with him?"

"Ten years."

"And you haven't killed him yet?"

Sonia rested her chin in her hands and grinned. "This is going to be so fucking fun."

Mack might have agreed if Liv's face hadn't suddenly turned ashen. He stepped closer. "What's wrong?"

"He's here."

Mack spun on his heel and followed the direction of her stare.

Royce. Mack reached behind him on instinct and wrapped his hand around Liv's wrist.

"He knows we talked to Jessica," she said.

"How the hell would he know that?"

"Maybe she told him. You heard what she said when she left." Mack's fingers tightened on her wrist. "Go back to my office."

She yanked out of his hold. "What? No fucking way."

"Liv, please. Let me handle this. He hasn't seen you yet."

He wasn't sure what convinced her, but Liv did what he asked. Rage turned his vision red as he watched Royce weave through the crowd, greeting fans with peace signs and high fives. He paused to snap a selfie with two women and then let each woman kiss his cheeks.

Mack tapped into his deepest willpower reserves to keep from launching into a full-fledged sprint and knocking the bastard's ass to the ground. Instead, he slowly walked to the center of the bar, hands flexed into tight fists at his sides.

Royce approached with his TV-show smile. "Mack. Just the man I came to see." He turned back to apologize to a couple of women who wanted a photo. "Sorry, ladies. Business calls."

Right. Business. This unexpected visit had all the hallmarks of old-fashioned mob intimidation.

Royce reached across the bar. Their handshake was about as friendly as a pair of boxers squaring off before a fight.

Mack met Royce's unnecessarily tight squeeze with equal pressure. "What brings you by?"

Royce dodged the question and leaned an elbow on the bar. He cast his gaze in a wide, judgmental circle. "Quite a place you've got here."

"First time in?"

"Never had the pleasure before." He dragged out the word *pleasure* just enough to convey the opposite. His gaze lingered on the dance floor, where a sea of cowboy hats bobbed and swayed in unison to a classic Brad Paisley song. His lips curled as if he'd just wandered into the unwashed masses.

Mack had never wanted to hit another human being so much in his entire life.

Actually, that wasn't true. He'd wanted to hit someone else a lot harder before, but Royce was quickly rising to a close second, and for many of the same reasons. Men who hurt women were the lowest creatures on Earth.

Mack forced his jaw to release its viselike clench. "Can I get you a drink?"

Royce swiveled again, turning that fake-ass smile back to Mack. "Sure."

Mack gestured tightly to the wall of liquor bottles on the wall behind him. "What's your poison?"

"Give me your house specialty."

"That'd be a Snot Rocket."

Royce's lips thinned in revulsion. "A Snot Rocket?"

"Shot of Jim Beam with a raw egg chaser."

"Classy."

"I can dig out a wine cooler if you prefer."

Royce lifted his hands. "Hey, I'm adventurous. Snot Rocket it is."

The bartender, who'd been hovering nearby, grabbed the bottle of whiskey, but Mack waved him off. "I've got this one."

"Making it extra special for the VIP?" Royce asked, not even a hint of self-deprecation in his tone. He really thought of himself as the VIP.

"You know it," Mack said. He poured a hefty shot, set the glass in front of Royce, and then cracked an egg into the brown liquid. "I'm supposed to warn you that consuming raw egg products can be dangerous to your health."

Royce turned a soft shade of green, but this was a battle of manhood. He swallowed once, lifted the glass, and shot it back.

"So," Mack said, bracing his hands on the edge of the bar. "What brings you by?"

"Heard you—" Royce stopped and swallowed hard as he set down the glass. The egg must've been sliding back up. "Heard you're hiring."

"I am. You need an application?"

Royce adopted the TV-show smile. "Good one. You ever wonder how I got so successful?"

"Not really."

A nerve twitched along Royce's jaw. "I like you, Mack, which is why I'm going to give you a pass on a small breech of professional etiquette."

Mack snorted. "*You're* going to lecture me about professional etiquette?"

"It's bad form to recruit someone else's employees."

Warning bells clanged in Mack's brain, but his mouth didn't care. "So is sexually harassing your employees."

Red splotches darkened Royce's cheeks. Mack realized with a start that this was the face that the public never got to see. The face that had scared Jessica to the point of tears. The face that was going to feel the brunt end of Mack's fist soon.

"Why don't you and I stop dancing around this thing? Say what you came to say and get the fuck out of my club."

"Olivia is dangerous, man. She's unstable."

"Is that right?"

"I should've fired her a long time ago."

Mack nearly cracked a tooth from the tight clench of his jaw.

"I don't know what she told you, but you listen to her at your own peril. She makes shit up." Royce shrugged. "It's sad, really, because she's talented in the kitchen, and"—his mouth curled into a lecherous sneer—"in other ways."

A blur of curly hair passed in Mack's peripheral vision before he realized what was happening.

Oh shit. Liv. "You disgusting, lying sack of shit."

Royce laughed. "Olivia. What a surprise."

Mack grabbed her arm, but she yanked free. "I have *never* slept with you. Jesus, I'd rather gouge out my own eyeballs first."

Royce shrugged again in the kind of way that said he was getting exactly the response he'd hoped for. "Told you, Mack. Unstable."

"Shut the fuck up, Royce."

"I should've kicked you in that shriveled-blob fish dick of yours when I had the chance," Liv sneered.

Royce's face exploded in red splotches.

Mack wrapped an arm around her waist and hauled her against his body. "Stop," he hissed into her ear. "This is what he wants. We get riled up and make a scene, and suddenly neither one of us has any credibility."

Liv pulled from his grasp. "You are not going to get away with this," she said, pointing.

"Hey, Olivia?" He winked. "I already have."

"Get the fuck out of my bar," Mack growled.

Liv let Mack pull her away from the bar. "Come on. Let's go." He slid his hand down the back of her arm and clasped her hand so he could tug her along behind him to his office. Curious whispers and stares cataloged the entire thing. It would be a miracle if no one had caught some of it on video.

Liv stomped into the office, hands shaking. "I have never slept with him."

"Christ, Liv. I know."

She turned around to face him. "He's going to spread that rumor about me, isn't he?"

"I won't let him."

Sonia suddenly ran in. "Shriveled-blob fish dick?"

Liv shuddered. "It's the most disgusting thing I've ever seen."

Her snark was short-lived. Her knees wobbled, and she sank against the edge of the desk. "He really is going to ruin me. The entire culinary world is going to think I had an affair with him."

Mack closed the distance between them and gripped her chin with his thumb and forefinger. "Look at me."

He tilted her face upward.

"We will stop him."

She held his eyes, and something caught in his chest. Her eyes were like mirrors, reflecting every emotion. He watched, transfixed, as anxiety hardened into determination, turning hazel into fiery green.

"You're goddamned right we will," she breathed. "Whatever it takes."

He made a fist and held it out. "Partners?"

Liv bumped her fist against his. "Partners."

CHAPTER TEN

The next morning, Mack dropped into his normal seat at the diner where he and the guys ate breakfast every other week. He was the last to arrive, which was unusual. But so were the circumstances. This wasn't their normal week.

A mug of coffee was waiting for him. He pushed it aside and leaned on his forearms.

"What's the big emergency?" Malcolm asked, tone tinged with uncharacteristic annoyance. "My wife and I have plans today."

A waitress made her way to the table and asked Mack if he was ready to order. He spared her a quick glance. "Just the coffee, thanks."

There was a moment of silence after she walked away. "What?" Mack asked.

"Wow," Del said quietly. "You didn't even smile at her."

"Who?"

Malcolm pointed. "The waitress. You didn't flirt with her."

Mack shook his head. "I don't have time for flirting. I need to talk to you guys."

"Obviously," Del deadpanned. "You dragged us out of bed."

"This is serious!"

"You get dumped again already?" Gavin asked.

Mack flipped him off. Gavin returned the gesture. Malcolm started to stand. "I don't have time for this."

Mack grabbed his arm. "Sit down. You need to hear this."

Malcolm returned to his seat with a stern glare. "This better be good."

Mack sucked in a breath and dragged a hand over his hair. When he exhaled, he settled his eyes on his friends. He knew he should feel guilty about doing this without talking to Liv first, but this was an emergency. "This needs to stay between us."

"This really is serious, isn't it?" Gavin said, growing somber.

"It is. And it's about Liv."

Gavin's whole body went rigid. "What about Liv?"

"She didn't tell you the whole story about why she got fired."

Five minutes later, the guys reacted to the story exactly as Mack knew they would because they all lived by the same code he did.

The Russian banged his meaty fist into his tree trunk of a thigh. "I will break his balls."

"What are you proposing we do?" Del asked.

"I'm not sure yet. But if he's one of those guys, we have to stop him."

Malcolm nodded. "I'm in."

Derek agreed. "Me too."

One after another, the guys nodded around the table. Only Gavin held back. He shook his head, removed his baseball cap, and ran his hands over his flattened hair. "I don't like this. I don't want Liv to get hurt."

"I won't let her get hurt. I'll protect her."

Gavin snorted. "I'd love to see her reaction if you said that to her. She has a way of doing things on her own."

Yeah. He knew. And it was sort of growing on him.

Liv raced through a shower, doing the hair and makeup thing, and got dressed before heading out to do her morning chores. A cold, misty rain dampened the grass and immediately undid the small amount of effort she'd put into her hair. Her boots sank into the soggy grass as she crossed the yard to the chicken coops. Goats bleated from inside the barn, but they'd have to wait their turn. Randy had already flown over the fence and was now perched on his favorite branch, waiting for the hens to be let out so he could reach his daily sex quota. He greeted Liv with a threatening flap of his wings.

"I'm in no mood for you today."

Randy let out an angry crow. She lunged at him but then felt guilty. It wasn't his fault that Royce was a disgusting asshole who was apparently telling everyone that she'd slept with him. A cold chill stole over her skin that had nothing to do with the weather. Just the thought of being anywhere near that man . . . she gagged.

Randy threatened her again, and this time she swung her arm out to warn him back. "I mean it, Randy. I have had it with cock-swinging fuckboys."

"Good to know."

Liv jumped and looked over her shoulder. Mack was twenty feet away and drawing closer, all smooth swagger and confidence in a pair of golf shorts and a thin athletic pullover. The misty rain that had turned her hair into a stringy mess against her neck made his own hair dance with little dots of dew. He was a goddamned Nike ad.

"What are you doing here?"

Randy flew from his perch and ran straight for Mack, feathers fluffed and wings flapping. Mack hopped on one foot and then the other to avoid the attack. "What is wrong with this thing?"

"Roosters are assholes."

Mack kicked his leg out. Randy leaped into the air and kicked with both feet. Mack stumbled back with a curse. Liv grabbed a wire basket hanging from a hook by the door of the pen and swung it. Randy finally got the message and ran off in search of a hen to molest.

Liv handed the basket to Mack. "Make yourself useful."

"What're we doing?"

"*You* are going to collect the eggs while I throw down some chicken feed."

"Collect eggs from where?"

Liv pointed to the nesting box. "Lift the lid. Look in each box to see if there are any eggs. If there are, put them in the basket. Carefully."

Mack looked at the box like death itself waited inside. "Are there chickens in there?"

"There might be. They'll move for you. Just reach under them and be gentle."

"You want me to reach *under* a chicken?"

"They'll move."

"But *under* the chicken? Like where the vagina is?"

"First of all, chickens don't have vaginas. Second of all, if they did, it's a chicken. She won't mind."

"But—"

"For God's sake, Mack, be a man."

"Hey," he said, pointing at her. "Just because I'm a man doesn't mean I should have no fears or— Wait. Chickens don't have vaginas?"

"Oh my God. Just get the stupid eggs."

Liv opened the door to the pen as Mack gingerly lifted the wooden hatch to the nesting box. He all but deflated in relief to see just one hen waiting inside. The rest had run out in search of freedom and wet dirt when Liv opened the pen.

Hazel didn't get very far, though. Randy leaped on her back and did his business. It was over in three seconds.

"Christ, Randy," Mack said, voice dripping with disgust. "Pace yourself."

Liv tossed some feed on the ground to cover her smile.

Mack lowered three eggs into the basket. "Hey, does a chicken know when it's about to squeeze out an egg, or does it just plop out?"

"I have no idea."

"How about the first time they lay an egg? They must be like, *What the fuck is happening right now? What the hell just came out of me? Maybe I'll sit on it and see what happens.*"

A puff of laugher escaped before she could reel it in. His satisfied grin said he'd heard it. Damn him.

He moved on to the next empty nest. "But seriously, what do chickens have if they don't have vaginas?"

Liv replaced the scoop in the bucket of feed. "I don't want to talk about chicken vaginas with you anymore. Like, ever."

"I'll just google it if you don't tell me, and then imagine what my pop-up ads will be like."

She sighed. "They have a vent called a cloaca. It's, like, a universal hole for everything."

"*Everything?*" He shuddered. "Why do you know so much about chicken vaginas?"

"One of the chickens had an egg stuck a few months ago. We had to help her pass it."

"This is quite an interesting life you have. Tell me again why you live here?"

Liv walked away instead of answering. She got that question a lot from different people. She didn't owe anyone an answer. Especially not Mack.

Mack followed her into the house, where she kicked off her muck boots and took the basket from him. "Wash your hands," she said, with a nod to the bathroom.

Rosie was sitting at the island with a cup of coffee and the morning paper. It was one of the things Liv loved about her. Rosie still had a newspaper delivered every morning, just like her grandmother used to. The only times Liv ever truly felt secure as a child were the mornings she spent curled up on the couch next to her grandma as she read the morning paper.

Liv swiped her wet hair back and set the eggs on the counter. "Randy is already going after Hazel. She's getting a bald spot on her neck. Maybe we should bring her in for a while."

"Poor thing. I'll go out and get her in a minute."

The water turned off in the bathroom, and Mack strode in. Rosie let out a little sigh. "Look who's back."

Mack milked it. "Rosie, you're looking beautiful this morning."

"Oh God." Liv gagged.

"Are you hungry?" Rosie asked. "I have muffins, and there's a quiche in the oven."

"I'd love one of your muffins." He winked.

Liv looked at him and rolled her eyes. "Is there anyone you don't flirt with?"

Rosie set a muffin on a plate and handed it to Mack. "So what do you two have planned for today?"

Mack took a quick bite before answering. "Cloak-and-dagger stuff."

"You never did tell me why you're here," Liv said.

"I have some things to discuss with you."

Before he could say more, though, the back door suddenly banged open and shut. The sound of twin voices filled the house. "Aunt Livvie!"

Amelia ran in, followed quickly by Ava, followed immediately by Thea.

The girls seemed happy to see Mack.

Thea did not.

"Interesting that you're here, Mack," Thea said.

Mack turned a paler shade of *oh shit*. "Hey, Thea—"

"I need to talk to my sister alone."

Mack set down the muffin. "I'll, um, I'll take the girls outside to play."

Rosie hovered nervously for a moment before deciding the safest bet was to go with them.

Liv faced her sister. "God, Thea, what the hell is wrong?"

Thea planted her hands on her hips. "When were you going to tell me the truth about why you got fired?"

Oh. Shit.

Ten minutes later, Thea paced the length of Rosie's living room. "I can't believe you lied to me."

"Technically, I just left out some information," Liv said.

Thea didn't appreciate the distinction, judging by the red splotches on her cheeks and the wild anger in her eyes. Liv swallowed and shut up.

"I swear to God, I don't understand you, Liv. Why do you keep things like this from me?"

"I didn't want to drag you into this."

"You're my sister. Your problems are my problems."

"Correction. Your problems are usually *because* of my problems."

Thea threw her arms in the air with a frustrated noise. "Where the hell does that come from, Liv? I don't understand you!"

"I have been a burden on people my entire life. Mom. Dad. Gran Gran. You."

"That is not true. Why the hell do you believe that?"

Liv stood up and waved her hands to ward off further argument and before she revealed something she really didn't want to. "It is what it is. You know the whole story now. And now you're going to go home and worry and fret, as if you need one more thing on your plate."

Thea gave her another one of those looks. "I'm your sister. It's my job to worry about you."

Liv pushed her hair off her face. "The fact that you think that is exactly why I didn't tell you."

"But did you honestly think I wouldn't find out?"

"Eventually, I guess! I didn't think that far out. I was trying to deal with it my way. Wait—how *did* you find out?"

"How do you think? Mack told Gavin and the rest of the guys this morning."

Liv's muscles spasmed. "He did *what*?"

* * *

The tension inside the house had followed Mack and Rosie outside. Even the hens were pissed. When Randy went after Hazel, she squawked and pecked at him until he backed off.

"Should we go back in?" Mack asked Rosie, who was helping the girls feed the goats.

"I think they'll come out when they're ready."

Hop ambled over. "Rosie, I need to drive over to the feed store. You want to ride with me?"

Rosie stiffened. "Come on, girls," she said. "Let's go check on some of my seeds."

"That was obvious," Mack said when Rosie was out of earshot. "What'd you do?"

Hop sucked his teeth. "She's been like that with me since I made that crack about the Equal Rights Amendment. She can't take a joke."

"Maybe it wasn't funny."

"See, that's the problem these days. No one has a sense of humor anymore. Offended at every damn thing."

Mack shook his head. "Dude, some shit was *always* offensive."

"No one minded in my day."

"Women did. You just decided their opinions didn't count."

Hop rolled his eyes, but there was a notable chink in his armor.

"So how long does that have to go on before you realize that the problem isn't her lack of a sense of humor but the fact that you need to find some better fucking material?"

Hop pointed with a gnarled knuckle. "Watch your mouth."

Mack shrugged. "I'm just saying I can help you."

Hop scoffed. "With what?"

Mack nodded toward the root cellar, where Rosie had disappeared with the girls. "How long have you been in love with her?"

"Don't know what you're talking about," Hop grumbled.

"You can play dumb all you want, but I know what I know."

"That ain't saying much."

"You can win her over. I can help you."

Hop curled his lips in like he'd just gotten his first taste of quinoa. "You think I'm going to take romantic advice from a man who can't admit when he's lusting after a woman?"

"I'm not lusting after Liv. I barely know her."

"But you knew exactly who I was talking about."

Mack sidestepped that one. "We're talking about you, old man."

"You're talking nonsense."

"You need to learn how to talk to Rosie in a language she'll understand."

"I know her language. Cranky."

Mack knew someone like that too.

Hop wiped his bandana across his forehead. "Maybe the men of your generation talk about this shit, but mine don't."

"And how's that working out for you?"

"How's it working out for you?"

Mack grinned. "Great so far."

Hop snorted. "Really? Because that doesn't look like a woman who's happy to see you."

Mack turned around in time to see Liv storming across the grass. She should have looked ridiculous in her rubber farm boots and a frayed oversize sweatshirt that looked like it had done hard time in a lost-and-found bin.

But she didn't look ridiculous. She looked beautiful.

Like a beautiful storm.

Thundering right toward him.

She stopped with a hard glare. "You told the book club?"

He winced. "That's sort of what I came to tell you."

"You should have asked me first."

Mack held out his hands. "We agreed last night that we're going to bring Royce down, whatever it takes."

"That didn't mean you could run out and tell even more people without my permission. We're supposed to be partners."

"The guys can help us, Liv."

She smacked her palm. "It's a *book club*."

"A book club made up of the most connected, powerful men in Nashville. They can help us."

A breeze picked up a single curl and draped it across her cheek. He had an insane urge to wrap it around his finger and loop it behind her ear.

"From now on, you don't do anything without talking to me first," Liv finally said. "I'm in charge."

Mack nodded. "You're in charge."

Liv nodded, satisfied.

"On one condition," Mack added.

Liv crossed her arms. "What condition?"

"That you stop doing reckless stuff."

The look of offense on her face was so genuine it was almost comical. "What have I done that's reckless?"

"Last night with Royce? We have to be smart about this. If you want to be in charge, fine. But I get veto power over stupid ideas."

Behind them, Hop snorted again.

"Look, we'll get everyone together tomorrow, and we can come up with a plan," Mack offered.

"Fine." Liv spun around and stormed back to the house. Rosie and the girls emerged from the root cellar, and before going into the house Rosie gave Hop the same look Liv had given Mack.

Mack spoke over his shoulder. "Next Friday. Eight o'clock. The Six Strings Diner."

"I ain't going to no self-help bullshit touchy-feely meeting."

"New guy buys breakfast."

"Fuck off."

CHAPTER ELEVEN

"I've made a terrible mistake."

Liv uttered the realization to herself shortly before three o'clock the next day as she surveyed Rosie's living room.

"It's going to be fine," Mack said. "I promise."

She wasn't so sure. Malcolm she totally trusted. He was smart. She'd never met a couple of the other guys but recognized both of them. Derek Wilson owned a construction company or something in the city, and she'd heard both Gavin and Mack talk about him before, so she knew he was cool.

But the Russian? She turned and looked up at Mack, voice low. "I can't believe you invited him. This house has old pipes."

Rosie walked in with a tray of cookies and a man Liv didn't recognize. He wore black-rimmed glasses, a slouchy hipster-style beanie, and a Pokémon T-shirt.

"I found a straggler outside," Rosie said.

"Who's that?" Liv whispered.

"Noah."

"Who's Noah?"

"Computer expert."

"The one who found Jessica? You said he didn't know anything about this!"

Mack held up his hands truce-like. "Okay, I might have lied about that."

Liv slugged his arm. "That's for lying to me."

She slugged him again. He covered his arm and whined. "What was that one for?"

"Just because. Are you sure we can trust him?"

"Don't judge a book by its cover. I'm pretty sure the IT thing is just a ruse and he's actually an assassin for the government."

Liv squinted. "I can't tell if you're serious."

Mack strode forward, hand outstretched. He and Noah did a manly handshake-chest-bump thing. "Thanks for coming, man," Mack said.

He did a quick round of introductions for Noah's sake, listing each man's name and what special skill he apparently brought to the table. The Russian was last.

"He's here for muscle," Mack said.

The Russian pounded his fist. "I beat him up."

Liv waved her hands. "Nope. No beating anyone up."

The Russian stuck out his lower lip. Rosie rushed over with the cookies to soothe him.

"Don't feed him any cheese," Mack said quickly.

Liv looked over. "Like, after midnight, or . . . ?"

"Just whenever."

Rosie shrugged and moved on to Malcolm. "Can you eat cheese?"

"Yeah, pretty much everyone else here can eat cheese," Mack answered.

Noah finally greeted Liv. She shook his hand and narrowed her eyes. "Do you kill people?"

He tilted his head. "Not intentionally."

Mack clapped his hands. "Let's get started."

Everyone who didn't yet have a place to sit jostled for room on one of the two couches. The Russian had already claimed Hop's recliner, which was going to be a problem if Hop decided to join them. Malcolm ended up sitting on the floor, which was going to be a problem if one of the hens decided to join them.

"Gavin and Del have a home game today, so we'll have to fill them in later on what we decide."

"What do you want us to do?" Derek asked, reaching for another cookie. "These are fucking awesome."

Rosie beamed. Hop strode in then, noticed Rosie smiling at another man, and scowled. Then he noticed the Russian in his chair, and his expression turned murderous. He jerked his thumb in a *get the fuck out* fashion. The Russian quickly joined Malcolm on the floor.

"You're late," Rosie scolded Hop. She gave him a cookie anyway.

"One of the most important things we need to do is find out how many women Royce has done this to," Liv said. "And we need to figure out how to expose him."

"Why not just go to the media and tell them what you saw?" Derek asked.

"That would violate my NDA, and I don't want to give him that ammunition to shut us down," Liv said. "Besides, reporters need to do their own research, and that could take a long time. I want to go bigger."

Mack glanced down at her, eyebrows furrowed. "Bigger?"

"I want to confront him with it at his big cookbook launch party."

"That's just three weeks away," Mack said.

"I know."

"That's impossible," he grumbled.

"Why don't we just kidnap him and make him talk?" Everyone looked at the Russian as soon as he said it. He shrugged. "Happens all the time in Russia."

Liv shook her head. "No. No kidnapping. Nothing violent."

"But maybe we could try to get him on tape admitting it," Derek offered.

Liv looked at Mack. "That could work," she said.

"But how?"

"What about at the Chamber of Commerce gala?" Derek said. "He'll be there. Maybe someone could record him on their phone or something."

"He's not going to just admit at a chamber fundraiser that he's been harassing women," Mack said.

"Maybe he'd admit it to someone who already knows," Liv said. "Like me."

It was strange how Mack's face could go from totally neutral to completely stony in a split second. "No. I don't like that. We need to come up with a different plan. That will never work."

"I might be able to help with part of that," Noah said. He leaned forward on the couch and withdrew a rolled-up wad of papers from his back pocket.

He held them out to no one in particular, and Liv grabbed them before Mack could. "What are these?"

Mack peered over her shoulder.

"I did some snooping in Royce's bank records," Noah said.

Liv choked. "You did what?"

Mack patted her on the back. "Deep breaths."

"How is that legal?"

"Technically, most of what I looked at is public record," Noah said.

"Most?" Liv squeaked.

Noah lifted one shoulder in a half-hearted apology. "Some of it may have been acquired through means of questionable legality."

"Just tell us what they say," Mack said.

Noah bit into his cookie. "I found a series of weird transactions, so I pulled them together into a spreadsheet to look for patterns and found something interesting."

Mack stood so close that he was pressed against Liv's back. "I don't get it," Mack finally said, glancing up. "What are we looking at?"

Noah nodded. "Royce's company has sent a series of wire transfers of varying amounts to a vague, nondescript charity with an offshore address. Each of those transfers was then immediately redistributed to unknown parties."

"You think these are hush-money payments," Hop said.

Noah shrugged. "If I were trying to pay people off in a way that ensured no one would ever know, this is how I'd do it."

"Can I see them?" Malcolm asked.

Mack handed him the papers. The Russian and Hop looked over his shoulder as he shuffled through them.

"Doesn't tell you anything," Hop said, sitting back. "Just a bunch of numbers that you obtained illegally, which means you'll be in as much trouble as Royce if you use them."

"Then maybe we just use them to get more information," Derek said.

"What are the rest of these pages?" Malcolm asked.

"Tax court shit." Noah took another bite of cookie. "Royce registered a—"

Noah stopped at the sound of a soft cooing. Hazel had wandered into the room, head bobbing, searching for cookie crumbs. Noah blinked. "Does anyone else see the chicken?"

The Russian's eyes lit up and he held out his arms. "Chicken."

"What were you saying?" Mack asked, agitation evident not only in his voice but in the clench of his fists.

"Royce registered a nonprofit several years ago but didn't report the taxes properly," Noah explained. "He got hit with some big fines, didn't pay them, and had to get it worked out with the tax court."

"So?"

"So it was the very next year that this new charity was created in Panama."

Malcolm's eyes bugged out. "That was seven years ago."

Noah nodded. "He's been doing this shit a long time."

Liv felt sick. Seven years? And that was just since he'd moved the fake charity overseas. But then nausea became rage, because how many fucking women had he done this to? He'd gotten away with it for *years*. And all along, there had to have been countless people who knew, who enabled him, who covered it up.

"So where does this leave us?" Derek asked.

"We obviously need to prove this money went to women he harassed," Malcolm said.

"Yeah, no shit," Mack said. "How do we do that?"

"I mean, I could keep hacking into shit," Noah said with a shrug.

"You're all high." Hop stood up from his recliner, shook his head, and started to walk away. He made it as far as the door before turning around. "You should be calling the police, not messing around with this shit yourself."

"What are we supposed to tell them?" Mack said. "Jessica has made it clear that she doesn't want to report it, so it's Liv's word against her *and* Royce."

"Well I can't be party to anything illegal. I'm a cop, dammit."

"Retired cop," Rosie said. "And no one invited you to be part of it."

"Then you're fools too," Hop scoffed. "Because I'm the only one in here with any investigative experience, and what you're talking about is an *investigation*."

The Russian began to rock, singing softly to Hazel the chicken in his lap.

"And that guy is flat-out nuts," Hop said, pointing at the Russian.

"He's a hockey player," Mack said.

"Jesus Christ," Hop muttered from the door, but he walked back to his chair.

"Right now my biggest concern is Jessica," Liv said. "She was apparently scared enough to tell Royce that we talked to her, and he was apparently scared enough about that to confront us. Things are going to get worse. I have to get her out of there."

Noah popped the rest of his cookie into his mouth. "Luckily, I can help with that too."

CHAPTER TWELVE

"You're sure this is where Noah said she'd be?"

The following Thursday, Liv eyeballed the door to the dive bar with a look that said she wasn't only skeptical but maybe a little scared too. Mack didn't blame her. The place was the ambient equivalent of a middle finger—dirty and offensive with an *enter at your own risk* vibe.

Mack shrugged. "Noah said she posted on Facebook that she'd be here tonight."

"Her page is set to private. How does he see that stuff?"

"He hacked into an overseas bank. You think he can't get into Facebook?"

She looked at him sideways. "Good point."

Mack settled his hand on her back, smiled to himself at the way her muscles twitched beneath his touch, and nodded to the door. "Let's go. Hopefully we beat her here."

The handle of the heavy wooden door had been worn smooth

over its thirty years as a student favorite, but the door itself bore the rough scars and dents of what appeared to be countless boot kicks and bouncer throws. That didn't bode well for what they'd find inside. Mack kept his hand on Liv's back as they walked in.

They both stopped briefly to let their eyes adjust to the low lighting. It was only nine o' clock, still apparently early for the college set, because fewer than twenty people were there. And those who were barely looked old enough to drink.

"I suddenly feel a million years old," he said.

"You're over thirty. To them, you are."

"Is Jessica even old enough to drink?"

"No, but I don't think they pay much attention here."

Too few places did. Mack had zero tolerance for underage drinking in his bars. His bouncers were trained regularly on the latest in fake ID techniques, and at least a dozen people a day were turned away from his clubs. Bachelor and bachelorette parties were the worst offenders. Not a day went by that someone didn't try to sneak in their younger cousin with a pretty-please bat of the eyes or a none-too-subtle slip of a twenty-dollar bill. Neither worked on his guys. Mack made sure of it.

"Let's get a table by the back so we can watch for her," Liv suggested, pulling away from his hand.

She stopped at a curved booth beneath a broken MILLER LITE sign in the far-back corner. Someone had carved a penis into the tabletop, and the vinyl cushion was more broken than not. "I shudder to think what a black light would reveal on this seat," Liv said, but she scooted in anyway.

"Stay put," he said. "I'll get us a drink so we blend in a little more."

"I'll blend in. You have some gray at the temples."

Mack's hand flew to his hair before he saw her grin. She was lying. He pointed. "Not funny."

"You're so vain."

He nodded toward the bar. "What do you want?"

"I'd ask for a Dos Maderas and Coke, but I'm guessing this is more of a Captain Morgan joint, so . . ." She shrugged.

"Lady knows her liquors," he mused, absurdly aroused by the notion. "Be right back."

The two women tending bar barely looked older than the clientele. They wore matching black tank tops with the name of the bar emblazoned across their breasts, and judging by the way the younger one kept tugging at the straps, she wasn't happy about the uniform.

"What can I get you?" she asked, flashing a smile.

"Do you have Dos Maderas?"

She blinked. He shook his head. "One rum and Coke and a Sam Adams bottle."

He carried the drinks back to the booth and slid in next to Liv. She tried to scoot over, but he slung his arm over her shoulders and tugged her back.

The side-eye she gave him carried enough attitude to fuel a sitcom. "What are you doing?"

"Blending in. We're just a romantic couple enjoying a night out."

"You wish."

He did wish. Like, all of a sudden, he was wishing it a lot. He took a long pull on his beer. This might have been a strategic mistake, sitting so close to her. She smelled good. Not like the flowery good he'd read about so many times in romance novels, but, like, just *good*. Her skin had a scent like vanilla or something. Sweet.

He rubbed his hand under his nose.

"What's wrong?" she asked.

"Nothing."

"You look uncomfortable."

"I'm not."

She shrugged, sending her shoulder into his armpit. He swallowed hard. The door opened, and they both sat up straighter. And immediately slumped again. It wasn't Jessica. A group of five women stumbled in looking like they'd gotten the party started elsewhere before showing up here.

"I'd never let that happen in my bar," Mack said.

"Let what happen?"

He pointed with this beer. "They're clearly drunk already. It's just asking for trouble."

He felt the weight of her stare. He looked down. "What?"

"You're very ethical."

"Does that surprise you?"

"Wealth and morality rarely go together in my experience."

He shifted to get a better look at her. "What is it with you and rich people?"

"I just don't trust them."

"Why? I mean, yeah, there are a lot of bad people out there making tons of money in shady ways—"

"And rigging the system to make sure no one else gets ahead."

"—but not all wealth is a sign of bad character."

"But often it is."

He raised an eyebrow, his desire to get to the bottom of things overruling the voice of common sense telling him to drop it. "This is about your father, isn't it?"

She smiled. "I didn't want to talk about him before, and I don't want to talk about him now. Nice try."

"Come on. You gotta give me something."

She shook her head and looked back at the door.

"We gotta talk about something. What else are we going to do until Jessica gets here?"

Her eyes went as round as a Disney princess's. "Kiss me."

His bottle paused halfway to his mouth. "Excuse me?"

"I said kiss me, you idiot."

Her hands grabbed the front of his shirt and yanked him closer. He nearly fell over but caught himself with a hand against the wall. "Geez, honey. You could at least buy me dinner first."

She smashed her lips against his.

Holy shit, this woman could kiss. He'd kissed enough women to know when someone knew what she was doing, and she did. He was a sucker for a good kisser. Some men liked women who could pretzel it in bed, but give him a woman who knew how to make love with her lips alone, and he was a goner.

But Jesus, this was crazy. What the hell was she doing? He pulled back, panting. "You *really* don't want to talk about your father, do you?"

Her eyes darted to look over his shoulder. "Royce's goons are here."

"What?" He tried to twist around to look, but she grabbed his face in her hand and turned him back. His cheeks were smooshed between her fingers. Surprisingly strong fingers. Kneading dough must be an actual workout or something.

"Royce has goons? What are you talking about?" It came out muffled, because his lips were smashed together.

"His security guards," she explained, not even slightly out of breath. How was that possible? He felt like he'd just run ten miles.

He tried to turn again, and this time she let him. He spotted them instantly. "Those two big dudes by the door?"

"Yep."

"They look . . ." Mack paused. "Hungry."

"I don't know how much Royce feeds them."

"What the hell are they doing here?"

"I'll give you one guess."

The two men started to scan the room. "Shit," Liv hissed, and then she did it again. She kissed him.

Only this time he was prepared. And if they were going to kiss, they were going to *kiss*. Mack palmed the back of her head and went deep, angling her face so he could slant his mouth over hers properly. She tensed against him but only for a moment. Then she sank into him. Melted. Her mouth opened wider, letting him in. Her hands opened flat against his chest.

And shoved him back. "They're not looking," she said. "We need to get out while we can."

Mack blinked. What? Right. The goons. Right. He looked over his shoulder. The two men had their backs to the room, watching the door instead. Mack grabbed Liv's hand and tugged her out of the booth.

"Maybe there's a back door," she said.

They moved quickly down the dingy hallway next to the booth and swore when it only led to a single bathroom. A sign above the door read PEE AND POOP HERE.

"Dammit," Mack said, running his hand over his hair.

"Can you see them?" Liv asked.

Mack crept to the end of the hallway and ducked his head around the corner. They were turning around again and—FUCK. "Get in the bathroom," he barked.

Liv didn't wait to be told twice. She yanked open the creaky door and ducked inside. Mack followed, turned the lock on the door, and sagged against it.

Liv looked up at him, hand over her nose. "Oh my God. We're going to need tetanus shots."

Someone banged on the door outside.

They each went breathless. Mack reached over and shut off the light. Darkness seemed to make the smell worse.

The person knocked again. "Are you done in there yet?" a young woman asked. "I have to pee."

Mack turned the light back on and turned around. He clicked the lock. Liv's hands covered his. "What are you doing?"

"The girl's gotta pee."

"It could be a trap! What if they asked her to do it?"

Mack shrugged her off and opened the door just enough to poke his head out. The girl was bouncing up and down. She saw him and let out a "Thank God."

He held up his hand. "Do you see two big guys wearing black T-shirts out there?"

"I'm gonna pee my pants," she whined.

"Just tell me where they are, and then we'll let you in."

The girl stomped her foot, walked away, and then came back. "They're standing by the door."

Mack opened the door and let her in. She stumbled, and he caught her around the waist. When she saw Liv, her eyes widened. "I'm not into threesomes."

Liv rolled her eyes. "We're hiding from those guys out there."

The girl groaned and doubled over. "I gotta go bad."

Liv pushed her toward the single stall that hid the offensive toilet. "We won't watch."

"I can't pee with you in here!"

"You're wearing a sorority sweatshirt. You expect me to believe you've never pissed in front of strangers before?"

Her eyebrows pinched together in a well-groomed pout. "Not sober."

"You expect me to believe you're sober?"

The girl giggled and swayed. "Don't listen."

Mack covered his ears, squeezed his eyes shut, and faced the corner as the girl shut herself in the stall. This would go down as one of the ten weirdest moments of his life. When he heard the toilet flush, he let out the breath he didn't know he'd been holding. A moment later, the girl walked to the door. "You won't tell anyone, will you?"

Mack winked. "I don't piss and tell."

The girl giggled and walked out.

He turned around to find Liv glaring up at him. "Is there anyone you don't flirt with?"

"Jealous?"

"You wish."

"We gonna talk about that kiss?"

She gave him her back. "Nope."

"Coward."

"What's there to talk about? It was a fake kiss, and now it's over."

He bent until his mouth brushed her ear. "It was a good kiss, and you're a horrible liar if you expect me to believe that you were unaffected by it."

She elbowed him. "You've read too many romance novels."

"And you haven't read enough."

Someone knocked again. Liv whipped around and slapped her hand over his mouth.

But it was just the girl again. "They just left, in case you were wondering," she said.

"Let's go," Liv said, throwing open the door.

Mack stopped her at the end of the hallway. "Let me look just to be sure."

He peeked around the corner again. More people had arrived, making the small room seem a lot smaller. But there was no sign of the hulking men. Liv walked up behind him. "Well?"

"I think it's safe." He grabbed her hand and pulled her beside him. Adrenaline settled, and he finally voiced the nagging question hanging in the air. "How the hell did they know we'd be here?"

"Maybe they weren't looking for us. Maybe they can see Jessica's Facebook too."

"Why would they follow Jessica?"

"I don't know. Royce is unhinged."

Mack tried to duck around a group of drunken assholes that had *date rape* written all over them. "Excuse me," he said to one of them.

The asshole swung around, all belligerent and wasted. "Excuse *you*."

For fuck's sake. "Just trying to get around you, pal."

"Yeah, well, find another way, *pal*."

One of Asshole's friends noticed Liv. "Hey, darlin'," he slurred as he swayed into her personal space. "Want to party with ush?"

"Back it up," Mack ordered, blood pressure rising.

"Fuck off, man. I'm talking to her."

Liv stepped forward. "And now I'm telling you to back it up."

"Ignore my friend," another of the guys said. "He's just drunk."

"You don't say," Liv deadpanned.

"Come on, now," he said. "Why so mad?"

"Maybe because we're just trying to get out of here and a group of walking Tinder fuckboys decides to be assholes."

Asshole Number One sneered. "God, what a cunt."

Mack saw red. He grabbed the guy's arm, twisted it, and had him chest-to-bar in one second flat in a move he'd learned as a young bouncer. The guy let out a bellow of pain, and the crowd around them gasped and jostled to watch or get out of the way.

"Apologize. Now."

"Get the fuck off me, man."

Liv tugged on his arm. "He's not worth it, Mack. Let's go."

Mack gave him another shove and stood. Asshole swung his arm around, missed Mack, and instead hit a pitcher of beer, sending it sloshing onto the floor and all over a woman standing nearby.

She swore and smacked him.

And hell officially broke loose.

"Mack! Watch out!"

Mack looked up to find Liv crawling over the bar. She pointed, but it wasn't in time. He felt the bash of a fist against his jaw, and lights exploded behind his right eye. Mack stumbled back but righted himself quickly enough to ward off another blow from one of Asshole's friends.

The next thing he knew, Liv was standing on the bar, yelling at the cowering bartenders to call the cops.

"Get down!" he yelled at her.

Asshole Number One took another swing, and Mack hit him in the gut. He doubled over and went down on one knee. People screamed and ran. Jesus Christ, what a fucking nightmare. He'd never had a fight in one of his own clubs. Never. Two bouncers shoved people out of the way and ran into the fray. Just in time to hold back one of Asshole's friends from going after Mack again. But not fast enough to stop the two women who were still fighting off to the side from knocking over a barstool and wiping out on the floor.

Mack reached out to break them up, yelling once again at Liv to get down from the bar. She did, but not in the way he'd intended. She leaped down and grabbed the arm of one of the women.

"Knock it off," she yelled, trying to yank them apart.

"Let me handle this, Liv," Mack barked.

She ignored him, because of course she did.

The women's boyfriends got into it next, shoving and swearing and knocking shit around. Liv tried again to haul one of the women up, but the woman yanked her arm away and instead sent Liv stumbling backward into the warring boyfriends. One of them whipped around and accidentally elbowed Liv in the cheek.

Things sort of happened in slow motion after that. Liv slipped and fell onto her ass. Mack shoved one of the assholes out of the way, leaped over the two women on the ground, and grabbed Liv under the armpits. He swept her up fireman-style and ignored her protests as he carried her out of the melee.

"What the hell, Mack? Put me down!"

"Knock it off," he growled, kicking open the swinging door to the outside. He set her on her feet and immediately cupped her cheeks. "Christ, are you okay?"

She tried to push his hands away. "I'm fine—"

"Tilt your head higher."

The streetlight illuminated a swollen red splotch just below her eye. Mack swore. "What the hell were you thinking, Liv?"

"*Me?* What the hell is wrong with *you*? You started a bar brawl!"

"I was protecting you!"

"From what? Bad language?"

"He called you a cunt."

"I was a bartender for three years, Mack. I know how to handle guys like that." She threw her hands in the air. "God, I was actually starting to *like* you, and then you pull this overbearing macho bullshit!"

Even as his pulse raced and his hands shook, a detached part of his brain was just like Del and the Russian, casting bets over what it would take to strip away the veneer of perfect romance hero to reveal an out-of-control alpha male, and he'd finally found it. He opened his mouth, and out came a tone of voice he'd never, ever used with a woman before.

"I swear to fucking God, Liv, you are the single most frustrating woman I've ever known."

"And you think you're one of the good guys behaving like this?"

Her words hit their mark. Adrenaline collided with anger and lust and regret into one combustible mix that took control of his senses. No, he wasn't one of the good guys. Not right now. Not when the rise and fall of her rapid breathing made her T-shirt spread tightly across her breasts. Not when he realized she was ogling him right back. Not when the sidewalk suddenly felt too small and too big at once.

His hand reached out, and his thumb wiped a drop of liquid from her collarbone. Water? Beer? He didn't know. Her lips parted, her breaths quickened. Then his thumb traced a slow path of exploration up the column of her throat, along her jaw, until it finally came to rest on her bottom lip.

They moved in a blur, and it was only that tiny bit of recognition—that she had moved too—that allowed him to give in to the fire. His mouth covered hers, and without a moment of hesitation she dove her fingers in his hair and held him there. She smelled like rum and tasted like a mistake, and he didn't fucking care. Driven by some painful urgency he neither recognized nor understood, he let out a growl, wrapped an arm around her waist, and lifted her ass to press her against the wall of the bar. Her legs widened, welcoming him into the space between.

Liv gripped his face and pulled him in. In an instant his body went hot and tight. She gripped his arms to steady herself or maybe to stop him from going full caveman. He changed the angle, and she opened wide beneath him. His tongue swept inside her mouth.

The door suddenly swung open, and a crowd stumbled out, yelling that the cops were coming.

Liv went rigid in his arms and pulled a Heisman stiff-arm to push him off her. She dropped to the ground, her feet landing on top of his. Mack turned away, hands in his hair. Oh shit. Oh shit, what did he just do?

"We need to go," she said.

"Liv," he rasped, turning. "I'm sorry. I've never—"

She brushed past him and was headed to the parking lot. "We need to get out of here."

Mack jogged to keep up. "Wait. We need to talk about this."

"No, we don't." She picked up the pace and stomped to his car. He beeped it unlocked and held open her door for her. She slid in without a word.

He got behind the wheel and looked at her. "Liv."

"Just drive."

With a muttered curse, he pushed the ignition button and jammed it into drive. Silence reigned for ten full minutes before he finally caught his breath.

He glanced over. "We should get you checked out. You were hit pretty hard."

"So were you."

"I'm fine."

"So am I."

"Dammit, Liv. I'm trying to apologize."

She snorted. "For what?"

"For . . . what I did. Kissing you like that. Without permission."

She ran a hand over her hair. "I was an enthusiastic participant, Mack. Don't get your guilt panties in a wad."

"Liv—"

She held up her hand. "Enough. Just drive me to my car."

She'd met him at Temple, and her car was parked behind the bar in the employee lot. He pulled in and killed the engine. Neither of them moved.

"Can we please talk about this?"

Liv opened her door, got out, and then bent down to look back in. "Ask Noah if he can figure out how the goons found us."

She slammed the door shut and left. What the fuck had just happened?

And how many times was she going to leave him alone with that question?

CHAPTER THIRTEEN

This was a bad day to discover she was out of foundation.

Liv peered into the bathroom mirror the next morning and tilted her face into the light. Nope. Not a trick of shadows. She had a bona fide black eye. Concealer hid the worst of it, but anyone who looked at her directly would know she'd either been in a fight or had gotten the worst sleep ever last night.

Actually, both were true thanks to Mack. Christ, that man could kiss. Not that she was surprised. He probably had enough experience to write a how-to manual. Of course, she wasn't sure which step in the instructions would include *leap off her like you've been electrocuted* and *shudder as if you need a shower*. If she'd built a shield of armor around herself over the years, his reaction was why. She should've been used to disappointment and the sting of rejection, but she wasn't. That was a fresh wound over an old scar.

Didn't matter. Kissing Mack had been a mistake. An adrenaline-fueled clash of libido and bad decisions. It would not be happening again, and that was that.

Liv blasted her curls with a hair dryer, twisted them into a bun, and then distracted herself before breakfast by paying bills. The number left over in her bank account was enough to make her stomach clench. She needed to spend a few hours today sending out more résumés and kissing ass on LinkedIn. The only place that had responded so far was the Parkway. She had an interview next week, and she figured she only had Alexis to thank for that.

On that happy note, Liv slipped into her farm boots and did her chicken chores. She tried to hide her face when she walked into the house a few minutes later, but Rosie saw everything.

"I hope there's an interesting story there."

"Define interesting."

"Sex injury?"

"Sorry. Bar fight." Liv started washing the eggs she'd gathered. "Want help with breakfast?"

"I pay you to tend to the animals and the garden—"

"Not to cook," Liv finished, smiling.

The bang of the back door interrupted her. Moments later, Hop wandered in. He took one look at Liv and scowled. "What happened to you?"

"Cage fight. The money's good."

"Where are you going all dressed up?" Rosie asked him.

Liv looked up. He *was* dressed up, at least by Hop's standards. His jeans had no stains, and his shirt had actual buttons down the front.

"None of your business," Hop said. The door banged shut again.

Liv sighed. "Why don't you put him out of his misery?"

Rosie pulled a knife from the drawer. "Because murder is illegal."

"I meant go out with him. Life would be a lot better for everyone around here. You know you want to."

"What the hell do I need a man for? I have a hand, don't I?"

"That is way more information than I need, Rosie. Seriously. I was talking about *dinner.*"

"Who are you to lecture me anyway?" Rosie said, her words broken up by the slice of her knife through potatoes. "Have you started sleeping with Mack yet?"

"Never going to happen." Her libido made a sad face at her words.

"Why? Lord knows that if I had a man like that lusting after me, I'd be naked in five seconds flat."

"Mack is not lusting after me." Angry, tongue-tangling kissing aside, he'd made it very clear he was not interested. Which was good. Because she wasn't interested either.

"What time is Thea dropping the girls off?"

"Noon."

The ding of an incoming email sounded in her pocket. Liv pulled out her phone and clicked on the email.

Her heart sank.

"What's wrong?" Rosie asked.

"It's from the Parkway Hotel. They canceled my interview."

"What? Just like that?"

Liv slammed her phone down. "It's Royce. He's blacklisting me."

Her voice was stronger than she felt. Liv sat down on a stool tucked beneath the island and lowered her head onto her arms. "Put *me* out of my misery."

Rosie patted her back. "This will pass, honey."

The simple words were surprisingly soothing. Liv stood and leaned her head on Rosie's shoulder. "Thanks. I needed that."

Rosie rubbed a weathered knuckle down Liv's cheek. "Anytime."

Mack was fifteen minutes late for breakfast with the guys. He'd slept like shit, so he felt like shit, and judging by the silent, shocked expressions when he sat down at their regular table, he looked like shit too.

They stared at him with coffee mugs paused halfway to their mouths. "What?" he growled, turning over his own mug.

"Are you okay?" Gavin asked.

"Fine."

"You didn't shave," Del said.

Mack dragged a hand along his whiskered jaw, wincing as his fingers found the tender spot where fist had met bone. "I woke up late."

A waitress walked by and stopped to fill his mug. He remembered his sunglasses then, took them off, and set them on the table. Everyone exclaimed and sat back with a collective *oh my God*.

The Russian slapped a palm on his forehead. "Are you dying?"

Mack knocked his hand away. "What the fuck? No. I told you. I didn't sleep well."

"That is why you are ugly today?"

"What the fuck is wrong with you?" he said.

The Russian shrugged. "I'm a hockey player."

It actually did explain a lot. "I'm not ugly today. I'm tired."

"You're kind of ugly. It's the eyes. Very red. Ugly."

"Fuck off."

"We're just saying you don't normally look this bad," Malcolm said.

He flipped off the entire table.

Gavin shrugged. "I'm actually glad you look like shit. I want to be the pretty one for a change."

"You're still not the pretty one," Mack said. "It's Malcolm. He's the pretty one now."

"Knock it off," Del said. "You're both pretty."

Mack picked up his menu, even though he knew it by heart, and hid his face behind it. Fuck them. They'd look like hell, too, if they'd experienced the most amazing kiss of their entire lives and then had the woman tell them it would never happen again before walking out.

"I invited someone else to join us today," he said.

"Who?" Del asked.

As if on cue, the door opened, and in walked Hop.

Malcolm followed Mack's point. "No shit," he breathed.

"I wasn't actually sure if he'd show up."

Hop's grizzled eyes scanned the busy dining room until he came upon their table. Mack lifted his hand in a wave. Hop scowled and limped over.

"No idea what I'm doing here," he grumbled, dropping into an open chair.

"You remember everyone," Mack said.

Hop gave a general nod. "Normally, we have a sort of orientation for new members, but we don't really have time for that today," Mack said. He slid a copy of *The Protector* across the table. "This is our current book."

Hop stared at the cover without touching it. "I regret this already."

"You'll get the gist of it."

The waitress appeared again then to take their orders. Mack flashed her a grin, and she ignored him. Damn. He really was ugly today.

After she left, Del leaned forward in that *let's get this shit started* way of his. "Anyone do any more reading?"

"I did," Gavin jumped in. "This book is seriously fucked up."

"It's your first romantic suspense," Mack scowled, directing his annoyance over last night's disaster at Gavin. "You can't judge the entire book by a few chapters."

"She hates him," Gavin argued. "I may not have read as many romance novels as you guys, but that doesn't seem like a great start to a relationship."

"You have to keep reading. You can't bash it until you've read more."

"Let Gavin express his thoughts," Del warned. "Every opinion is valid in this club."

Gavin grinned. "Thank you, Del."

Mack flipped him off.

Gavin returned the gesture.

Del sighed and mumbled, "I give up."

"Anyway," Gavin said, drawing out the *way* just enough to be annoying. "What I'm saying is you're always talking about how romance novels are subversively feminist, but what's feminist about a book where the woman has no say in her own security?"

"They're doing what's best for her for now," Mack grumbled.

"Who is he to decide what's best for her?" Gavin countered.

"But that's the point of the book," Mack argued. "Their journey is about learning to trust each other and overcome the adversity that the author establishes in the beginning."

"But why write a book that puts a woman in that position to start with?"

"Maybe because shit like that happens in real life? Bad shit happens to women all the time, and it's usually because men look the other way."

"So it's a metaphor?" Malcolm prompted, stroking his beard. "Interesting. I've never thought about it that way before."

Mack shrugged. "I'm just saying that if we're going to end violence against women, it's up to us to do it. We have to get after our own."

Hop groaned.

"Something to add, Hop?" Del asked.

"Yeah. Reading this shit has made you soft." He picked up *The Protector* and turned it over.

"Or maybe your generation was too hard," Mack said.

Hop bristled, and Malcolm stepped in to stave off his response. "What Mack is trying to say is that you've been raised to believe in a certain type of masculinity—"

"My brand of masculinity was crawling through the jungles of Vietnam, getting my ass shot off before you were born."

"And we appreciate your service, but what we're saying is that your brand of masculinity is tied to the inevitable degradation of women. And no one is the better for it."

Hop rolled his eyes. "Political correctness."

"What if someone made a sexual joke about Rosie?" Mack asked.

"I'd kill him."

"You think that's the right answer, but it's not," Mack said.

"You shouldn't have to care about a woman to recognize that the sexual degradation of all women is a problem. You should recognize that it's wrong simply because they're humans."

Hop snorted.

"You don't believe in equality among men and women?" Malcolm asked.

"Sure I do."

Mack raised a skeptical eyebrow.

Hop started to tick off a laundry list. "I think women should get paid the same as men for the same jobs. I think women should have equal representation in Congress. And there better be a woman president before I die. But I also think we should be able to tell some fucking jokes."

"Did it ever occur to you that the reason women don't have equal pay or that no woman has ever been elected president is because when men get together they bond over these jokes?"

Hop shrugged.

"Can we get back to the book?" Gavin asked.

"Go ahead," Malcolm said.

"It's like she just, like, up and forgives him," Gavin said. "I had to beg on my knees for a month just to get Thea to let me back in our bedroom."

"I don't think she forgave him," Mack said. "I think she realized the reality of the situation and dealt with it. You're missing the subtext."

"Bullshit," Gavin said.

Mack felt a vein pop near his temple. "This is different."

"How?"

"You two going to let the rest of us get in on this?" Del asked.

Mack bit his tongue.

"I think her anger is justified," Malcolm said. "But I don't think she's only mad about his actions. She feels like she has no control. She's been at the mercy of men all her life. First her father. Then her Secret Service agents. Now this stalker and Chase's lie. It's a metaphor."

"For what?" Derek asked.

Malcolm shrugged. "The suffocating ways that modern women are controlled without their consent every single day."

"Well, in this case, maybe it's for her own good!" Mack blurted.

"And I still think this book is bullshit," Gavin said. "He's obviously still lying to her. I don't know. I don't like this dude."

Mack toyed with a creamer packet. "Maybe there are strong emotions involved."

"So?"

"So strong emotions can make you do things you wouldn't normally do." And Mack totally, one hundred percent was not talking about himself.

"Yeah, but he's still lying to her." Gavin shrugged.

"Because he was trying to protect her."

"I'm just saying that I learned the hard way that even well-intentioned lies have a way of destroying things."

Mack slammed his mug down. "There is nothing wrong with wanting to protect someone you care about!"

Mack's outburst made the guys jump in their seats and even caught the attention of people two tables over. Great. He plunked his elbows on the table and pinched the bridge of his nose. He shouldn't even have come this morning.

"Dude, what's up with you?" That was Derek.

He was saved from answering when the waitress arrived with

their food. Things got dicey when she mixed up the order, though, and gave Del's cheese omelet to the Russian. They straightened it out before everyone suffered.

"You were saying?" Derek prodded, smiling over a pile of scrambled eggs.

"Nothing."

Malcolm leaned forward all serious-like. "You are not yourself today, Mack. Talk to us. Book club is about more than books. You know that."

He did know that. He'd just never been on the receiving end of their psychological machinations. He liked it better when he was dishing out smart-ass advice instead of needing it.

"Come on, man," Del said. "What's up?"

"I promise not to make fun of you for whatever it is," Gavin said.

Del smacked Gavin upside the head. "Shut up and let him talk."

No use keeping it a secret. Liv would tell likely tell Thea about the bar fight eventually—though he doubted she had already, because he'd made that mistake before—and Gavin would just be pissed that Mack hadn't said anything. Still, Mack hesitated before leaning back in his chair and blurting it out. "There was a fight at the bar we went to last night. Liv got hit in the face."

Gavin's fingers tightened on his fork. "Is she all right?"

"Fine. It was an accident. The guy didn't mean to do it, but . . ." Mack gave in to his own strong emotions and pointed across the table. "You didn't warn me what she was like."

"Who? Liv?"

"Yes, Liv. Who the fuck do you think I'm talking about?"

"I'm not sure what I needed to warn you about, except that she's cranky most of the time, and you already knew that."

"You could've told me that she's a pain in the ass."

"Everyone knows that," Gavin said with a smirk.

"Yeah, but now she's a pain in *my* ass."

Gavin shrugged again and spoke with his mouth full. "You're the one who insisted on partnering up with her."

"I don't get it," Del said cautiously. "Did Liv cause the fight or something?"

"No, but . . ." He made a frustrated noise. "Do you want to know what she did? I'll tell you. All hell is breaking loose, and she jumps up on the freaking bar, and when I tell her to get down, does she listen to me? Hell no. She takes a flying leap right into the god-damned middle of it!"

Gavin nodded. "That sounds like Liv."

"And then, then she had the . . . the . . ." Dammit, he couldn't even find words. "The *balls* to yell at me when I carried her out of there."

"Wait," Gavin said, a smile starting to tug at his lips. "You carried her?"

"As in, you picked her up and carried her away from the fight?" Hop prodded, getting back into the conversation.

"Yes. Which part of that don't you understand?" Mack slumped in his chair and crossed his arms over his chest. "And did you know she makes fun of romance novels? She hates them. Did you know that?"

Gavin, Del, and Derek all exchanged an unreadable glance. Next to him, Malcolm and the Russian both pulled out their wallets. Mack did a double take. "What is that? What're you doing?"

"Getting ready for the bill," Malcolm said. "Continue."

He couldn't continue, because he wasn't going to admit to what happened next. Gavin and Hop were taking the whole fight thing well, but they might not be so nonchalant if they knew that Mack had pressed Liv against the wall, kissed the ever-loving shit out of her, and was now going out of his fucking mind wanting to do it again.

"Is that . . . all?" Gavin finally asked after a long pause.

"Yes. No. I don't fucking know."

And then it happened again. Just like at Gavin's house, the guys traded bemused glances and then lost it. Their laughter shook the goddamned table and drew stares from every other person in the restaurant.

"Shut up," Mack grumbled, poking at his egg-white omelet.

"Shit," Gavin panted, trying to catch his breath. "I did not see this one coming."

"See what coming? What the hell is so funny?"

Malcolm clapped a beefy hand on his shoulder. "Mack, for someone who has read every manual out there, you sure are clueless about your story sometimes."

"Fuck off. What are you talking about?"

"Liv, dumbass," Del laughed. "You and Liv to be more precise."

The sense of total exposure sucked the air from his lungs. "No. Hell no. Look at me. She drives me crazy."

"Exactly," Malcolm said. "Look at you. You're a mess."

"You guys are full of shit." Mack started shoveling heavy forkfuls of tasteless eggs into his mouth.

"I don't know," Derek said. "I've sure as shit never seen you like this over a woman."

"Me either," Malcolm said. "Not even when Gretchen dumped you."

"Face it, man," Del said, leaning back all smug and shit. "She might be perfect for you."

Mack pointed at every man at the table except Hop. "Fuck you. Fuck you. Fuck you. And fuck you."

The Russian looked up. "You did not say *fuck you* to me."

"Fuck you too."

"Did it ever occur to you that the reason she drives you crazy is because you're attracted to her?" Malcolm asked. "It's classic enemies-to-lovers."

"Classic," Gavin said, nodding and chewing.

"I can't believe this," Mack said to him. "I thought you of all people would know this is nuts."

Gavin took a deep breath. "I only know of two women in the world who can drive a man as crazy as you are right now. I'm married to one, and the other is her sister. I say go for it."

"Go for it?" Mack parroted, his voice an incredulous squawk.

"Why not?" Gavin said. "But I probably should also tell you that if you hurt her, I will have to hurt you."

Mack slapped his hand over his heart. "Your faith in me is heartwarming, truly. I'm all squishy inside."

"I'm not trying to be an asshole. I'm just saying you have to be careful. Liv is . . . she's not what she seems."

Mack dragged a hand over his hair. "I know."

"She likes to pretend she's all tough and stuff, but it's bullshit."

"I know." It came out a growl this time, because that was what scared him the most about her. That her sarcasm, her *fuck off* attitude, and her complete distrust in men were just a cover for something else. Maybe that, above all else, was what they shared in common. They were both living a lie. A sudden sense of loneliness stole over him. Not for the first time, he felt on the outs. The odd man in the group. The man who could save a hundred marriages but was doomed to never find his own happy ending.

CHAPTER FOURTEEN

"Okay, I think that's everything."

Thea dropped the last of Ava and Amelia's four bags on the floor of Liv's living room. "But if we forgot something, you can just get it from the house."

"Who needs toys when there are goats and chickens?" Liv said, dropping to her knees and throwing her arms open for the girls. They launched themselves at her with squeals. Thea waited patiently as Liv did her best to get them riled up with tickles and raspberries on their necks.

Finally, when the girls had collapsed in a heap of giggles, Liv stood.

"You're sure this is okay?" Thea asked. "I mean the dog with the chickens?"

Liv was also watching Butter Ball. "It'll be fine."

Butter had reached that tipping-point age for golden retrievers when they stopped noticing squirrels and instead sought out the best sunbeam for a nap. As if on cue, the dog sank to the floor with a heavy sigh in front of the window, where a crack in the curtains had let in a ray of sunshine.

"How are things going?" Thea asked.

Liv looked up to see that her sister had wandered to the kitchen table, where Liv had been searching job postings. Liv strode over and shut the computer.

"I'll find something."

"That good, huh?"

Yeah. Great. Two more form rejections had come in just this morning. "I'll find something."

Thea set her purse on the table and fished out her wallet.

Liv gritted her teeth. "What are you doing?"

Thea didn't answer as she set a stack of twenty-dollar bills on the table. Liv picked them up and handed them back.

Thea refused to take them. "You're babysitting. People get paid for babysitting."

"They're my nieces."

"Use it to entertain the girls, then."

Liv shoved the money back in Thea's purse. "Don't insult me."

"Liv," Thea sighed, but whatever she might have wanted to say after that was cut off by the unmistakable clunk of Rosie's footsteps on the staircase outside. Rosie knocked once and then opened the door to peek her head inside. "Can I come in?"

The girls ran to her with hugs. "Rosie! We're staying wiff you and Aunt Livvie for three days."

Rosie walked in and hugged the girls against her legs. "I know, and I have so much planned for us. We are going to make cookies and feed the goats and collect the eggs, and Hop says he'll take you for a ride on the tractor."

Tractor rides were some serious shit for the twins. They reacted as if Rosie had just promised them unlimited ice cream all weekend. Which, in all likelihood, would also probably happen.

"What time are Mack and his mom coming for dinner tomorrow?" Rosie asked. "Isn't this the weekend his mom is flying in to look at houses?"

Thea's head whipped around so fast Liv could've sworn she heard a bone crack in her neck. "What was that?"

Great. "Nothing."

"He did say that his mom loves goats," Rosie said.

"Is that right?" Thea asked. "And you know this how?"

Liv shot a look at Rosie. She could've talked all day without bringing that up. The smug smile on her face said she knew it too. Rosie tore her gaze away and shifted it to Thea. Liv knew that look. She was about to be ganged up on.

"Okay, stop with that. Right now."

"I didn't say anything," Thea said. "Did you say anything, Rosie?"

Her work there apparently done, Rosie kissed the twins, promised them sugar, and left.

Thea pounced as soon as Rosie shut the door. "Talk."

"Oh my God, there's nothing to talk about." Liv dropped to the living room floor again to resume her aunt duties.

"He's bringing his mom here to meet you," Thea said.

"No, he's not. Rosie suggested that I invite them here. Big difference. And I'm not going to do it."

"Why not? Do you like him?"

Liv shrugged. "No."

"Oh, that was convincing."

Liv rolled her eyes. "It's Mack, Thea. Think about what you're saying."

"I am. And it's not crazy."

"It's entirely crazy. We can't go two minutes without fighting." Or getting all hot and bothered and wanting to inconveniently suck face.

Thea's small smile spoke a thousand words. "I know."

Liv shook her head and busied herself with moving the girls' bags away from the entry. "Come on, Thea. A guy like that?"

"Yeah a guy like that. Mack is true-blue. I'm telling you. I think you should give it a chance. Give him a chance."

"I don't even know what that means."

"It means you need to stop assuming every man is like Dad."

Liv paused, her breath catching in her chest. Then she stood and held open the door with a sweet—aka, *not* sweet—smile. "You're going to miss your plane."

Thea returned the smile, kissed the girls, gave them smooshy hugs, and told them to behave for Liv. Then she did basically the same thing to Liv. "Mack is a good guy," she said. "I think you'd be surprised."

She had already been surprised by Mack, but she wasn't about to admit that to Thea any more than she was going to own up to the fact that they'd already kissed. Thea would read too much into it because that's what Thea did. Her sister had an overzealous romantic streak that allowed her to believe in things like love at first sight—which, admittedly, had seemed to work out for her. She and Gavin had only dated a few months before getting married. But they were among the lucky few.

Liv couldn't afford to be romantic. If she and Mack ended up doing anything, it would be short-term and sexual. The end. Inviting Mack and his mom over to play with goats and eat dinner was not a step on the path to a meaningless sexual fling.

So why was she staring at her phone?

* * *

"I don't know." Mack's mom sighed and shook her head. "I'm not feeling this one."

Mack pinched the bridge of his nose. This was the fourth house they'd toured in the past two hours. "What don't you like?"

"Maybe I don't need a formal dining room."

"You vetoed the last one because it *didn't* have a formal dining room."

"I know, but I don't need this *much* formal. It's not like I'm going to have a lot of people around me to entertain."

Mack's real estate agent, Christopher, stood silently off to the side, his hands clasped politely in front of him. Mack would bet big bucks the man was yelling obscenities in his head. Mack sure as shit was. His mom had managed to find fault with every house they'd seen. Not enough yard. Too much yard. Too many bedrooms. Not enough bedrooms. Too close to the freeway, too far away from the city. Mack was tempted to slip Christopher a gratuity to apologize for the waste of time.

"We have two more we can look at," Christopher said after a moment.

"Maybe we should call it a day," his mom said. "I'm exhausted."

She absently rubbed her shoulder, and a burst of adrenaline made the hair on Mack's arms stand. He stuck his hand out to Christopher. "Thanks. Maybe save those other two houses for to-morrow?"

The man smiled. "I'll contact the sellers." He added with a nod, "Nice to meet you, Erin."

Mack helped his mom into the front seat and shut the door. As soon as he got into the driver's side, he looked over. "You good?"

"Just tired. I think I'll take a nap when we get home."

"You were rubbing your shoulder."

"Was I?" She shook her head. "It's fine. Just gets stiff sometimes."

Mack gripped the steering wheel. "Maybe you should have it looked at."

She made a *psh* noise with her lips. "I'm sixty years old. Sixty-year-old shoulders get stiff sometimes."

"But that's the shoulder that—"

She cut him off. "Braden, stop hovering."

She fell asleep in the car on the ride back to his house, her head bobbing gently with the rhythm of the road. Mack glanced over several times, unease turning his stomach to acid. She was being cagey again. *I'm sixty years old . . .* Christ, was she sick? Would she keep something like that from him? He tried to study her while driving but damn near ran off the road. She didn't look sick. Her brown hair was only half gray. Her weight hadn't changed. But there was definitely something going on.

He woke her up gently when he pulled into his driveway. "We're home."

She stretched and yawned. "I'm going to head upstairs and nap I think. Wake me if I'm not up in an hour."

He followed her inside, watched as she climbed the stairs, and waited until he heard the guest room door close before dialing his brother's number. Liam answered without a greeting. "How's the house hunting going?"

"Bad. She rejected every single one." Mack grabbed a beer

from the fridge and started down the stairs to his finished basement.

"Maybe she's getting picky in her old age."

Mack plopped down on the curved sectional that took up an entire wall and faced the sixty-inch TV screen. "Sixty isn't old."

"Chill, it was a joke."

The sound of kids running and screaming interrupted briefly, and Mack grinned despite his unsettled stomach as he listened to Liam tell the kids to slow down.

"Where are you?"

"Home. Lucy has a friend over from preschool."

A pang of loneliness once again joined the churning in his gut. Ever since Liam and his wife had moved to California for his job, he'd seen them less and less. They used to see each other at least every other month when Liam still lived in Iowa, but now it was every six months if they were lucky. God, he missed the kids.

"I think something's going on with Mom," he said.

"Like what?"

"I don't know. She's acting strange. And someone sent her flowers."

"I'm sure it's nothing to worry about." Liam snorted then. "Like you know how to not worry."

"I just wish she'd hurry up and choose a house. She's been alone in Iowa for a year."

"You're the one who moved to Nashville, dude. Was I supposed to stay in Iowa forever and give up a great promotion?"

"I'm not blaming you. I just don't understand why she's dragging her feet."

"Maybe she doesn't want to move. Did you ever think about that?"

Ridiculous. "Why wouldn't she want to move? There's nothing for her there."

"Except all her friends and the town she grew up in and—"

"And horrible fucking memories." Mack had moved to Nashville to get away from them. Why wouldn't his mom want to do the same? "You and the kids were the only reason for her to stay there. You're gone now. She needs to get out."

"Fine. Maybe I'm wrong. Why don't you just ask her what's going on?"

"I've tried. She just dodges the question and says she's entitled to privacy."

"She is." There was another squeal of laughter in the background. "Shit, I gotta go. I have no idea what's going on."

"Kiss the kids for me."

"I will."

Mack dropped the phone next to his hip. Liam was full of shit. His mom had no reason to stay in Des Moines. And if she didn't want to move, she would've just said so. This was her second trip out to look at houses for fuck's sake.

Annoyed, he turned on the TV and channel surfed until he found a basketball game. Sometime later—he wasn't sure because he'd dozed off—his phone buzzed with an incoming call. He glanced down, fully prepared to ignore whoever it was, but his heart leaped clear into his throat when he saw Liv's name on the screen.

He scrambled to sit, nerves shredding his gut. They hadn't spoken since the kiss. "Hey," he finally answered, then grimaced. *Hey?* That was the best he could do?

"Hi, um . . . Shoot. Hang on." Liv's voice grew distant as if she'd pulled the phone away. "It's okay, Ava. I'll clean it up. Just help your sister with the crayons." She returned to the phone. "Sorry. I have the girls."

"Right. Gavin mentioned something about that. Everything all right?"

He heard her suck in a breath, and he pictured her standing tall like she always did when she was about to blurt something out. "Rosie was wondering if you and your mom want to come over to the farm tomorrow to see the goats and have dinner."

The nerves settled into a different sensation. Relief maybe. Definitely anticipation. And something else too. A healthy shot of lust.

"Hello?" Liv said, annoyed as ever, and damn but he loved the sound of that cranky voice. It meant they were back on normal ground. "Are you there?"

"Rosie wants to know, huh?" Mack kicked back on the couch and crossed his legs at the ankle. "You're sure this isn't *you* inviting me because you miss me?"

"Yeah, pretty sure."

"Well, gee, I'll have to check our schedule tomorrow. What time were you thinking?"

"Rosie said she can have dinner ready whenever you are."

"Ah. Wow. That is super nice of Rosie."

"Right? I told her I didn't want to you to come, but she insisted."

He laughed low in his chest. "How can I turn down an invitation like that?"

"You probably should. It won't be any fun whatsoever."

Mack *hmm'd.* "Let's not be hasty. The girls probably want some Uncle Mack time."

"Why would they want that when they're having Aunt Livvie time?"

"Because I'm way cooler."

"Those are fighting words."

Upstairs, he heard footsteps in the kitchen. Mack stretched his arm over his head and yawned. "I'll go talk to my mom about tomorrow and let you know, okay?"

"Whatever. I don't really care."

He laughed again and hung up. He jogged up the stairs and found his mom standing at the stove, getting ready to start dinner. "You really don't have to cook, Mom."

She looked over her shoulder. "I want to."

"But if you're tired—"

"Let me do this for you, Braden."

The words hit him like a punch. Bile rose in his throat along with a memory he'd tried so hard to forget.

"What are you doing up?"

His mom looked up. "Making coffee."

"I can do that. You're supposed to stay in bed."

"Braden, I'm fine."

She wasn't fine, though. Her arm was still in a sling, and her face was still purple in places.

"Go back to bed. I'll bring you coffee."

She gave him a stern look that had zero effect. "I'm going to make your breakfast."

"I can make my own damn breakfast."

"Braden Arthur. What did you just say?"

Liam shuffled into the kitchen. His hair stood on end, and he was still in his pajamas. Braden scowled at him. "Get dressed. We're going to be late for school."

Liam went to their mother's side. She tucked him against her with her good arm and kissed the top of his head. She looked up then.

"Let me do this for you, Braden."

Mack blinked out of the memory, walked up behind her, and hugged her. His mom laughed, startled, and said, "What's this?"

"Just glad you're here." He kissed the top of her head.

"Are you okay?" she asked, looking over her shoulder.

"Fine." He coughed and forced a grin. "Just hungry. You're going to cut up the carrots really small, right?"

She smiled. "Of course. I know that's how you like it."

"Liv needs to know what time we're coming for dinner tomorrow. You still up for that?"

His mom smiled over her shoulder again. "Of course."

A few hours later, Mack went to bed, his stomach full and his heart doing weird fucking things in his chest. He hammered out a text to Liv.

We should be done looking at houses by 4. Be there by 5?

She responded with thumbs-up emoji.

He sent a gif of a man picking his nose.

She fired back with a gif of a woman twerking.

You right now? he replied.

She responded with a picture of herself sitting on the floor with a *help me* expression in her eyes. Ava and Amelia hung over her shoulders from behind, grinning devilishly with red stains above their lips. Me right now, Liv wrote beneath it.

Something squeezed his chest to the point of pain. Mack wasn't sure when he'd lost the capacity for humor or sarcasm, but it was gone.

He typed a question. We gonna talk about that kiss?

She didn't respond.

CHAPTER FIFTEEN

Liv didn't need to bother listening for tires in the driveway to know Mack and his mom had arrived the next day. Ava and Amelia announced it like they'd been waiting for Santa on Christmas Eve.

"Uncle Mack is here!"

Liv sent them outside to greet him in the driveway. Rosie dried her hands on a dish towel. "I hope his mom likes fried chicken."

"Everyone likes your fried chicken," Liv said.

"I'm just nervous for some reason," Rosie admitted with a little laugh. "It's not every day that you meet the parents for the first time."

Liv's heart did a weird thud-thud thing. "I'm not meeting the parents."

"Keep telling yourself that," Rosie said.

The back door opened, and Mack walked in with a twin bent over each shoulder. "I caught some stray cats," he said, catching Liv's eye.

The girls laughed. "We're not cats, Uncle Mack!" Ava laughed.

"What are you, then?"

"We're girls!" Amelia said.

Mack set them down but let them wrap around each of his legs. Behind him, the woman Liv recognized from the picture in his office walked in.

Rosie rushed forward. "You must be Erin."

"It's such a pleasure to meet you," Erin said, taking Rosie's hand. "Your farm is so beautiful."

"Thank you." Rosie backed up and looked at Liv. "And this is Liv."

Liv offered her hand. "Nice to meet you."

The level of awkward in the introduction rivaled the waiting room at a sperm bank. Mack was too busy entertaining the girls to notice. Hop, who'd been sitting in the living room as if afraid to wrinkle his shirt, walked through to do the introduction thing too.

"It's a pleasure," Erin said.

"Dinner is almost ready," Rosie said. "Would you like something to drink? Or maybe Liv and Mack can give you a small tour of the farm?"

Rosie wasn't even trying to hide her matchmaking. Liv met Mack's gaze, and he smiled. Not his normal kind of lady-killer smile, but a softer smile. It did weird things to her insides. "Let's go see the goats," she blurted.

The girls took off for the door, promising to teach Erin how to feed them. Outside, Erin laughed and tried to keep up. "They're delightful," she said. "You must love being able to spend so much time with them."

"I do," Liv said, relieved to be on safe conversational ground, which still didn't do much to calm her racing heart. Mack's presence was taking up more space than normal, and he'd barely spoken a word. "I try to see them as often as I can."

"Your parents don't live around here, is that right?"

"No," Liv said quickly. "They, um, my dad lives in Atlanta with his fourth wife, and my mom is currently living in the Virgin Islands. She moves around a lot."

A brush of fingers against her back made the breath lodge in her lungs. She wasn't sure if it was intentional, but either way, it made her insides turn to jelly.

"I miss my grandkids," Erin said wistfully. "My other son, Liam, he has two children, but they moved to California."

Liv nodded. "I've seen a picture."

"It was the right thing for their family," Erin said with a shrug, "but I miss those kids."

"I'm sure you can play grandma as much as you want with Ava and Amelia when you move here," Mack said.

Liv looked up quickly and then away.

Ava and Amelia called for them to hurry up. The girls had taken the top off the feed can for the goats and now cradled large handfuls of the pellets.

"We can show you how," Ava said to Erin.

Liv and Mack hung back while Erin let the girls fill her hands with treats and they taught her how to hold still for the goats. They stared silently at each other for a moment, like two awkward middle schoolers who didn't know how to ask each other to dance.

Mack is true-blue. I'm telling you. I think you should give it a chance.

"She's a good grandma," Liv said suddenly to cover her own thoughts.

"The best." The warmth in Mack's voice made her heart do the thud-thud again. He smoothed a hand over his hair. "The sooner I can get her here, the better. She's got no one in Des Moines."

A question that had plagued her since the first time he came to the farm finally got the better of her. "How old were you . . . when your dad died?"

Erin looked up and back at the question.

"I'm sorry," Liv whispered. "I shouldn't have asked that."

Erin returned to the goats, and Mack looked down at her. "He's been gone since I was fourteen."

Erin wiped her hands together to get rid of the feed crumbs. "Well, that was fun," she told the girls, but Liv caught a hitch in her voice. Great. *Way to go, Liv. Make things even more awkward at the NOT-meeting-the-parents thing.*

"I bet dinner is ready," Liv said. "Should we head back?"

"I'm starving," Mack said, adopting that cheesy grin that now seemed lonely somehow. Liv shook her head at the thought. What was wrong with her? She knew what was wrong with her. *We gonna talk about that kiss?* She'd thought all night about that simple text.

Mack let the girls drag him by the hands back into the house.

"He's so good with kids," Erin said, walking next to Liv.

"Ava and Amelia love him."

"He's going to be a great father someday."

Liv stumbled. Erin smiled.

Rosie had the table ready when they walked in. A platter of fried chicken sat in the center, flanked by large bowls of mashed potatoes and a hearty salad.

"This smells amazing," Erin sighed, taking a seat next to Mack.

"Livvie made a peach cobbler for dessert," Rosie said.

Mack lifted an eyebrow. "No cupcakes?"

Liv hid her smile behind a glass of lemonade.

Rosie helped Liv fill the girls' plates and got them settled at their own small table off to the side. When Liv returned to her seat, she found her plate ready and waiting for her. Mack winked.

Conservation was stilted at first. The kind of distant, meaningless chatter people do when they don't really know one another. But by the time the cobbler was served and more than one glass of wine consumed, tongues were looser.

Erin cradled her chardonnay. "Mack tells me you served in Vietnam," she said to Hop.

Hop glanced up at Rosie and then nodded. "Two years. Sixty-eight and sixty-nine."

"My brother was there in 1970."

"Infantry?" Hop asked.

Erin nodded. "He saw some things that . . . well, he never really talked about."

Hop took a drink of beer. "None of us do."

"It took us a while to become close again after he got back." Erin's face reflected a long-ago regret. "I protested the war."

"So did I," Rosie said.

"I was young, still in high school. I didn't really understand things the way I thought I did."

"Time and age have a way of making things make sense," Hop said.

"I haven't changed my mind about it, the war," Erin said. "But, looking back, I wish I had been more sensitive to the difference between the war itself and the soldiers who had to fight it."

Hop stared at Rosie. "Looking back, I wish I'd done more to understand why some people were so opposed."

Rosie's mouth dropped open, her wineglass paused middrink.

Hop shrugged with one shoulder, and he looked at his plate. "Nothing is as simple as we like to think."

Liv looked across the table at Mack, who was grinning at Hop like the man had just admitted to staying up all night reading Nora Roberts.

A half hour later, Liv walked Erin and Mack out to the car. Erin surprised her with a tight hug. "It was so nice to meet you."

Liv returned the embrace, averting her eyes to avoid the intense way Mack watched them. Erin then got in the front seat, leaving Liv and Mack alone behind the car.

"Thanks for dinner," Mack said. "This was fun."

"Yeah." Liv hugged her torso.

Mack shuffled an inch closer. His Adam's apple bobbed in his throat.

"So," Liv breathed.

Mack traced his finger down the side of her arm. She shivered and met his eyes.

"Let me know when you're ready," he said huskily.

"For what?"

"To talk about it."

She didn't exhale until his taillights disappeared.

CHAPTER SIXTEEN

Mack went for a run early the next morning before his mom woke up. When he returned an hour later, the smell of bacon and eggs lured him to the kitchen. His mom looked over her shoulder from the stove. She was dressed and ready to go. Her single suitcase sat by the back door.

Mack swiped his arm across his forehead. "In a hurry?"

"You know I like to get there early." She turned off the burner beneath the eggs and then nodded toward one of the chairs lining the island. "Sit down. I'll fix your plate."

"I should probably take a shower first."

She made a *psh* noise. "I used to feed you fresh from football practice, remember?"

Yeah, he did. Until he gave up football so he could get a job instead to help with the bills when his mom had to move to part-time at the library after the . . . the incident.

Erin filled two plates and carried them to the island. "I miss cooking for you," she said.

Mack dug in. "You can cook for me as much as you want when you move here. I won't complain."

She made a noncommittal noise.

Mack looked up from his plate. "What's wrong? You hoping I'll hire a personal chef for you?" He was teasing, but mostly to cover his own insecurity. His mom had that cagey look about her again.

Erin set down her fork and let out a long breath. "Braden . . ."

He swallowed hard. "What?"

"Maybe we should put this on hold for a while."

"Put *what* on hold?"

"I really do appreciate everything you're doing with the house search, but . . ."

Mack sat back in his chair. "Just spit it out, Mom."

"I'm not sure I'm ready to move yet."

Mack blinked several times, set his fork down, and wiped his mouth. Mostly to give himself time to formulate a response that didn't sound like a temper tantrum. "I don't understand," he finally ground out.

"You've spent so much time trying to take care of me that you missed the fact that I don't need to be cared for anymore."

A line of sweat that had nothing to do with his recent run formed along his brow. "You're alone there."

"I'm not," she insisted, leaning forward. "I have friends, co-workers."

"But no family."

"I'm seeing someone." She let out a quick breath after she said it, as if she'd been building up to that all along and now couldn't believe she'd finally gotten the words out.

Mack sucked in a breath like he'd been sucker punched. "Who?"

"He's a very nice man—"

"Who is he?"

"His name is Jason, and he's a professor at the university."

"Professor of what?" Not that it mattered, but . . .

"Physics."

"How'd you meet him?" His voice sounded like his throat was lined with glass.

"Mutual friends."

Mack picked up his plate and took it to the sink. He scraped his uneaten food into the disposal. "Why didn't you tell me? Is he the one who sent you flowers?"

"He was, and I didn't tell you because of the way you're reacting."

"How am I reacting?"

"Wounded."

Mack ignored that. "How long have you been seeing him?"

"Several months."

"Does Liam know?"

Her pause was all the answer he needed. His brother had fucking lied to him yesterday. Mack whipped around. "I'm going to take a shower."

He made it ten steps before she stopped him. "Braden, how long are you going to lie about what happened with your father?"

His hands clenched into fists. "I don't want to talk about that."

"Avoiding it doesn't make it go away."

"It has worked just fine for me until now."

"Has it, though?" She walked around to face him. "I want to see you happy and settled."

"I'd be happy and settled if you'd move here."

"No you wouldn't."

Mack uncurled his fingers. "What does any of this have to do with him?"

She placed her palm in the center of his chest. "Everything."

Mack shook his head and wiped his hand across his nose.

"You deserve to let this go," she said, patting his chest. "To be happy."

Mack sidestepped her and left her standing in the kitchen. He was happy. He was Braden-Fucking-Mack. King of Nashville's nightlife and everyone's best friend.

The ride to the airport was tense in a way that it hadn't been between them in a long time.

"You can just drop me at the curb, honey."

Mack rolled his eyes. "I can walk you into the airport, Mom."

"You're mad at me and in a bad mood, and this will be better for both of us."

"Wow, that eager to get rid of me?" He whipped into an open spot in front of the terminal and shoved the car into park.

"Look at me."

He obeyed. Briefly.

"I know you're angry and also a little hurt. I'm sorry for that."

He gave a one-shouldered shrug and immediately felt like a petulant child for it, but whatever. He *was* angry. He *was* hurt.

"I'm doing this for your own good, Braden. It's time to focus on your life for a while, finally stop worrying about mine."

Mack jumped out of the car and unloaded her suitcase from the trunk. He met her on the sidewalk on the other side of the car.

"Hey." She reached up with both hands and cupped his cheeks. "I like her."

He didn't bother asking who she meant. Mack liked her too. More than he should.

"She's good for you," Erin said, pulling away. "Tell her the truth."

Right. The truth. That would just solve everything, wouldn't it? Liv hated liars. She'd made that abundantly clear, and that was without knowing the extent of the lie he lived every single day. He was a fucking idiot if he actually believed she would just shrug and say *no big deal*. There was a reason he'd been lying for so long. And after a certain amount of time, the lie was even bigger.

Because when people learned the truth about him, about his father . . . No. He wouldn't let that get out.

Mack drove aimlessly after he dropped his mom off. He didn't want to go home. He didn't want to go to work. There was only one place he wanted to be, but it took an hour of trying to talk himself out of it before finally banging his hand on the steering wheel and turning the car around. He didn't even know if she was home. She might've taken the girls out to do something or—fuck. He just knew where he wanted to be.

He hit the button for hands-free calling and dialed Liv's number.

"Hey," she answered breathlessly.

"Hi," he responded stupidly, because he'd lost all brain cells at the sound of her voice and morphed into a walking Dick and Jane book. *Hear Mack stammer.*

"Um, what's up?"

He wiped a sweaty palm on his jeans. "What, um, what are you and the girls doing this afternoon?"

There was a pause. Long enough to cause a small heart attack.

"Um, actually, nothing. I have to . . ." she let out a nervous laugh and a restoring breath. "Alexis called and asked if I could help out at the café tonight. Her cat got bit or something, and she has to take him to the emergency vet clinic, and so I'm going to leave the girls with Rosie in about a half hour."

His heart picked up. "I can watch them for you."

Another pause. Another tiny heart attack.

"You want to watch them?"

"I could take them for ice cream or something." He cringed. Jesus, could he maybe sound a little more creepy and desperate? *See Mack wince.*

"I think they would love that," she finally said.

"I can be there in twenty minutes."

"You're sure?"

"Do I need to stop and get anything? Food or milk or whatever?"

"No." She laughed.

"I'm on my way."

"Mack, *thank you.*"

He made it in fifteen, and after pulling into the long driveway, he let out what felt like the first real breath all day. Liv must've heard his car, because she appeared on the stairs as soon as he shut off the engine. She wore a pair of jeans that made his mouth water and a plain white T-shirt. Her hair was piled high on her head.

Two pigtailed sprouts of joy raced ahead of her as he got out of the car. "Uncle Mack!"

Mack grabbed a girl in each arm and tossed them over his shoulders. They squealed and shrieked, and when he finally set them down, he found Liv staring with an affectionate smile. Whether it was for him or the girls, he wasn't sure. He just wanted to see it again.

"Thank you for doing this," she said, striding closer. She looked conflicted. "I thought about telling Alexis that I couldn't help, but she's been really weird lately because of the Royce thing, and—"

"Liv." He slid his hand around the back of her neck and squeezed gently. "I got this."

Three things happened at once.

She looked at his lips.

He looked in her eyes.

And an unspoken understanding passed between them.

They were going to talk about that kiss later.

CHAPTER SEVENTEEN

Five hours later, Alexis walked into the café just as Liv was locking the front door.

"How'd it go?" Alexis asked, slightly out of breath. She lugged a plastic cat carrier in her left hand.

Liv untied her apron. "Fine. How's Beefcake?"

"They stitched him up and gave him some antibiotics. He's going to be okay." Alexis set the carrier on the floor and shrugged out of her raincoat. "Thank you so much for doing this."

"Of course. Anytime." Liv inwardly winced. The conversation was stilted, uncomfortable. Alexis must have sensed it too, because they spoke at the same time.

"Can you stay for a little while?"

"Are we okay?"

They both stopped and laughed. "You go first," Liv said.

"I was wondering if you could stay for a little while."

Liv nodded. "For a few minutes. I left Ava and Amelia with Mack, so—"

Alexis's mouth dropped open. "You left them with *Braden Mack*?"

"He's surprisingly good with children. The girls love him."

"Oh." The way she said it was a lot like the way Thea had said *I know.*

"Don't read anything into it," Liv laughed. "He's just helping me out. That's it."

"If you say so." Alexis smiled. "What were you going to say before?"

"When—oh. Right. I just . . ." Liv bit her lip. "I just want to make sure you and I are good. We haven't really talked since the last time I was here, and we left things weird."

Alexis let out a relieved breath. "That was my fault. I overreacted."

"So did I."

Alexis picked up the cat carrier and nodded for Liv to follow her into the back. "Were you busy tonight?"

"Not too bad. Steady but manageable."

Alexis set Beefcake on the floor again. "Any progress on the job front?"

"None."

"Not even with the Parkway? I called the head chef myself."

"And they responded. I had an interview set up for next week—"

"That's great!"

"—but they canceled it for no reason."

Alexis deflated. "You think Royce had something to do with it?"

Liv shrugged. "It's the only thing that makes sense. He threatened to ruin me, and he's doing it." She sat down on a stool along the wall with a frustrated sigh. "I don't know what to do. Jessica refuses to leave. Mack even offered her a job. Any job. She won't take it."

Alexis put a bowl of water in front of Beefcake. "Maybe you should just stop."

"I can't. There has to be a way to stop him. We're trying to get a list of women who worked there before me and might have left under weird circumstances."

Alexis's hands paused. "Why?"

"So I can go talk to them. See if they know anything or if they want to come forward." Liv bit her lip as the warring voices in her head battled over whether she should shut up or plow forward. *Plow forward* won. "Do you—do you know anyone?"

Alexis stood slowly. Shook her head.

"I just need names, Alexis. That's it."

"I'm sorry, but I can't."

God, were they really back to this? "Why? I don't understand—"

"If someone hasn't come forward by now, I'm sure they have a valid reason."

"Do you know someone?"

Alexis winced. "I can't give you her name."

Liv shot to her feet. "You *do* know someone!"

Alexis's face turned stony. "You need to leave well enough alone, Liv. Didn't you learn anything from what happened with your sister's marriage?"

Liv felt the burn of her words like a giant splash of hot oil against her cheek. Wow. Liv hadn't known Alexis had it in her to go for the jugular like that. It was always the sweet and quiet ones that could surprise you the most.

Alexis sighed and apologized. "I'm sorry. That was unkind of me."

"No, you're right. I didn't help matters when Thea and Gavin were split up. I convinced Thea that Gavin couldn't be trusted because

I don't believe any man can be, and it nearly ruined their chances to get back together. That was a mistake I will have to live with."

Alexis walked over and hugged her. "I still shouldn't have said it."

Liv squeezed her friend and backed away. "I should go."

Alexis gripped her hands. "Please don't go away mad."

"I'm not." Liv looked at her feet and opted for honest. "I'm disappointed and confused. I'm trying to stop a predator. I don't know why you would try to stop me from doing that."

"Because some fights can't be won."

Disappointment burned hot and angry down her throat as Liv walked out to her car. Alexis's words bounced around her brain the entire drive back to the farm. *Some fights can't be won.* Liv refused to believe that.

A half hour later, her headlights illuminated the back of Mack's car when she pulled into the driveway, and disappointment faded into anticipation. The window facing the driveway glowed in alternating shades of blue and white as if the only light inside her apartment was from the TV. Liv climbed the stairs, found the door unlocked, and pushed it open softly. She didn't want to wake the girls. It took a moment for her eyes to adjust, but what she saw when she walked in sent her heart into overdrive.

Mack was on the couch, the girls curled up on either side of him, their feet in his lap. His head rested against the back of the couch, one arm stretched wide across the back of the cushions and the other resting on his chest, his fingers splayed wide. He was sound asleep.

Her apartment was clean too. The dirty coffee mug and oatmeal dishes that she'd left in the sink were gone. The girls' toys had been picked up and lined against the table that held the TV.

He'd even straightened up the pile of shoes by the front door. They stood in a perfect line on the mud tray.

Liv shut the door as quietly as she could, but the creak of the hinges brought a sharp breath behind her. She turned around. Mack lifted his head with a sleepy smile and raised the hand from his chest in a silent greeting. She crept closer to the couch, and he sat up straighter with a careful glance at each slumbering twin. With a wide yawn, he stretched his arms high over his head, and that was the thing that did her in. The yawn and stretch. Manly and vulnerable at the same time.

"How were they?" she whispered.

"Total devils." He smiled when he said it, so she knew he was lying. "They were great. They ran around, got dirty, all the good stuff."

"Thank you so much for doing this."

"Stop thanking me." He stood and stretched again, and this time his T-shirt lifted just enough to give her a glimpse of taut skin beneath a dusting of dark hair. "You hungry?"

"What?" She tore her eyes from his abs.

"Rosie brought food over. Want me to heat it up for you?"

"I can do it."

"I got it. Let's carry the girls in, and then I'll feed you."

They each picked up a sleeping twin, and Mack followed her down the short hallway to her bedroom. Liv avoided making eye contact with him as they laid the girls down and pulled the comforter over them. It was way too easy to imagine the two of *them* in there instead, and for all her sexed-up emotions right now, she wasn't ready for that yet.

"I'm, um, I'm going to change my clothes."

He nodded. "Food will be waiting."

He shut the door partway when he left, and Liv fanned herself. Mack in her bedroom was not something her senses were prepared for yet. She changed into a pair of sleep shorts and a T-shirt.

"Wow, I could get used to this," she said when she went back out.

He looked up from the kitchen counter. "What? Coming home to a warm meal or to an exquisite male specimen like this?"

"You had to make it weird, didn't you?" Her annoyance was fake, though. She was grateful for the teasing and the sarcasm. It was as if he'd known she needed some lightness to rise above the heavy sexual tension blanketing the room.

Mack set a plate of tuna-noodle casserole—Liv's favorite—and a glass of water in front of her. Then he claimed the chair next to her.

"So," he said, way too casually, "since you're obviously too much of a coward to talk about that kiss—"

"Um, excuse me?"

He leaned forward. "Maybe we should just talk about how you almost kissed me when I got here."

Heat raced up her neck. Busted. "Um, you mean when *you* almost kissed *me*."

"Darlin', I know when I'm about to be kissed, and that was some serious kiss foreplay."

"That's not even a thing."

He licked his bottom lip. "Oh, it's a thing. And you were doing it."

Liv crossed her arms, but her breasts were suddenly super tingly, so she tried to set her hands on her hips, but that was awkward because she was sitting down.

"You comfortable yet?" Mack teased.

She plunked her elbows on the table.

He nodded. "I happen to be an expert on these things."

Liv snorted. "I'm sure you think so."

"Aren't you even the least bit curious how I knew what you were thinking?"

"No." *Yes.*

"You probably think it's because you looked at my mouth like you wanted to drink from it."

"Wow, you *really* have read too many romance novels."

"It wasn't even the fact that your tongue darted out and licked the corner of your mouth."

Liv rolled her eyes and took a bite.

"Nope. You looked at my pulse."

Liv cocked an eyebrow.

"You stared right . . . here." Mack reached across the short space between them and pressed the pad of his thumb to the hot pulse point in her throat. "It was your biggest tell."

His thumb caressed her skin.

Her breath got stuck.

Then her food got stuck.

She started to cough. Liv glared and took a drink of her water. "I did not look there," she choked.

He leaned back, all smug and satisfied. "You're going to argue with the master?"

"Yes, because you're forgetting one very important detail." Liv inched forward until their noses nearly touched. "I don't even like you."

"I think we're beyond that, don't you?" His voice was a caress on her skin.

Liv ate several more bites before giving up. Her body was

hungry for one thing only, and it had nothing to do with Rosie's casserole.

"All done?" He reached for her plate.

"You don't have to wait on me."

"I know, but I want you to see me washing a dish."

She snorted out a laugh despite her best efforts to hold it in. "Why?"

"So you can see how sexy I am."

She tilted her head. "I admit, a man washing dishes is definitely one of my fantasies."

"Fantasies? As in plural?"

"I'm a normal woman. Of course it's plural."

"I wouldn't mind hearing about some of those."

"I don't want to scandalize you."

He turned around and dried his hands. The lazy gesture conjured dirty thoughts. "Please, by all means, scandalize me," he drawled.

Liv stood and took his hand. "You'd better come with me." She tugged him to the couch and gently pressed her palm to his chest. She gave him a soft push. "Sit."

Mack's eyebrows shot high on his forehead, but he obeyed.

"Scoot all the way back," she commanded.

"So far, I'm in total agreement with whatever you're doing."

Liv crawled onto the cushion next to him, tucked her feet up, and then lifted his left arm and ducked under it. It fell heavy across her shoulders as she snuggled into the crook of his shoulder and pressed her cheek to the spot just above his heart. She couldn't hold back the *mmmmm* that emerged from her throat.

"What are you doing?" he asked, voice husky.

"Snuggling."

"Snuggling?" He chuckled as his hand slid down her back. He stopped just above the waistband of her sleep shorts.

"Mmm-hmm."

"Snuggling is your fantasy."

"Yep."

His fingers shifted to find the bare patch of skin between her shirt and her shorts. Liv held her breath at the contact of skin on skin. Beneath her ear, his heart beat faster.

"Are you scandalized yet?" Her voice sounded like she'd just tried to gargle with straight cocoa powder.

"Completely." So did his. "Maybe you should tell me what else happens in this fantasy of yours."

"We talk."

"Dirty talk?"

"Boring talk. How our days went, movies we want to see, weird things customers ordered at the restaurant, stupid things that happened at the bar."

"I could fill up an entire day with that."

She laughed. His chin rested on the top of her head. "Why is this your fantasy?"

"I don't know."

"Must be a reason."

"I just like the idea of having someone to lean on sometimes."

She hadn't really meant to admit that, but something about the warmth of his skin and the thud of his heart had lulled her into an unguarded moment that she would surely regret later. "The night I got fired, I wished I had someone to lean on."

Beneath her ear, his heart raced. "What did you do instead?"

"Watched TV and cried."

His breath caught. "I would have held you."

"I didn't like you then, remember?"

He responded with a brush of his thumb against her waist. "What about now?"

"I'm getting there."

She felt him swallow. Hard. "What else happens in this fantasy?"

"You rub my back."

His muscles shifted, and anticipation danced along her nerves. His hand slid beneath the fabric of her shirt and began a lazy path up her spine. "Like this?"

"Yes." She closed her eyes and curled her fingers into his shirt. He was hard beneath her touch. She was weak beneath his.

"Tell me more," he murmured, voice strained beneath the rise and fall of his own labored breathing. There was no mistaking the tug of heavy desire in every exhalation.

"Maybe rub my neck."

"Now you're just milking it."

She laughed, but then she went motionless as his hand slid up farther under her shirt. His fingers began to work magic against the tight cords of her neck. She tilted her head to give him greater access. "Are you trying to get lucky?"

"I already feel lucky."

Her breath lodged in her chest. When she opened her eyes and looked up, she found the affection she'd heard in his voice also in his eyes, gazing down at her through dark pupils. Whatever they were doing—whatever was suddenly happening—it was monumental. Intimate. Hot. And so dangerous.

"Just so you know," he rasped. "I'm thinking about it again."

"About what?"

"Kissing you."

She swallowed hard. "But you're not sure?"

"I'm nervous," he said.

She could barely hear over the roar of her own blood. "Why?"

"Because I want to do it right."

"I imagine you have enough experience to make that a non-issue."

"It's not the experience that matters. It's the emotions. Mine are kind of jumbled right now."

Her chest pinched. "Wow. Sometimes I think I've got you all figured out, and then you go and say super-sweet things like that."

"Don't tell anyone. It'll blow my image."

"Maybe you could just actually get around to kissing me?"

He dipped his head toward hers and hovered there, mouth over mouth, breath to breath. She realized with a jolt that he wasn't kidding. He *was* nervous. Or maybe this was that kiss foreplay he'd mentioned. He caught her bottom lip between both of his and tugged gently and then did the same to her top lip. They stayed like that, feeling each other, adjusting to each other, to the sudden change in their relationship.

Just when she wondered whether that was going to be it, he made a growly noise and crushed his mouth to hers. His hand palmed the back of her head, his touch hot against her scalp.

If their first kiss outside the bar had been an urgent beat, a frantic dance, this one was a swaying ballad. A sweet waltz. A slow-motion union of body and mind that she never wanted to end. Insecurities would have their day, but not right now. Because right now her senses were alive with *this*. The fire between them. It sizzled and sparked and scorched.

Liv became a single-celled being. Every sense was tuned to the slow dragging of his fingers in her hair, the ragged breathing that traveled from his chest to hers, to the dip and pull of his mouth against hers.

She gave in to temptation and slid her hand up his arm, slipping her fingers inside the sleeve of his T-shirt. She felt him shudder, and suddenly his mouth wrenched from hers and began a hot descent along her jaw as his hands slid down the sides of her body. When his lips touched the tender spot where her pulse pounded, she let out a moan and squeezed the bulge of biceps beneath her fingers. He flexed just enough to make it obvious. She smiled and squeezed the muscle again and was rewarded with the flick of his tongue into the small cleft of cleavage visible above her shirt.

"You smell good," he rasped, moving his mouth to her ear.

"I smell like a bakery."

"Exactly." The tip of his tongue touched her earlobe. "You always smell like cookies or vanilla ice cream or something." His mouth kissed a path back to hers. "It drives me crazy."

This. This was what it meant to be kissed. This was what it meant to get lost in light and sound and sensation until everything disappeared but his lips, his taste, his scent, *him.* This was what she'd been missing without even knowing it.

It was also how mistakes were made. She should care, but she didn't. She should stop, but she couldn't. Her brain, her entire world could focus on one thing only—the feel of his hands on her face, his lips on hers.

By the time he finally eased his mouth away, they were both panting from heat and longing. Liv's eyes fluttered open. She found him watching her, tenderness in his expression, wonderment in the small tilt of his smile. His hand tugged hers higher so he could press a kiss to her wrist before placing it over his heart.

Oh wow. That was . . . that was the most romantic gesture

she'd ever experienced. "Mack . . ." All she could get out was his name.

"I like it when you say my name like that."

He pulled her mouth toward his again.

And then they froze at the sound of stirring in the bedroom.

Mack let out a little groan and lifted his head to listen. After a moment with no more sounds, he lowered his forehead to hers. They stayed that way for a long, quiet beat. Collecting their thoughts.

Liv's were a frantic mess. Confused and frightened. He wasn't supposed to be like this—sweet and tender. He was supposed to be Braden Mack, conqueror of women, sarcastic man-child. He was safe that way.

"Can I ask you something?" he rasped.

"Okay." Her voice barely worked.

"How do chickens have sex if they don't have vaginas?"

"Oh my God." Liv pushed him away with a laugh—a grateful laugh—and grabbed the nearest throw pillow. She whipped him in the head. "Go home."

He laughed and lunged for her, grabbing her around the waist before she could get away. He hauled her against his chest and reclined on the couch, drawing her with him. "You have to tell me," he said. "Imagine how bad those Google results would be."

She sighed. "They rub their cloacas together."

He rubbed his hands up her arms. "You should come over tomorrow night."

"I find the segue there a little disturbing."

"You can make me cupcakes."

"Really? Jeez. What an offer."

"You'd be returning my favor. I watched the girls. You can put that culinary school education to use in my amazing kitchen."

"I can't believe this, but I'm about to say yes."

He hooked both arms around his head, probably because he knew it put his biceps at their best, bulgiest advantage. "It was washing the dish that did it, right? I know I'm right."

She crawled off him. "Stop while you're ahead."

He grabbed her hand as she stood. "Hey, Liv?"

She looked down, ready for another smart-ass comment and, frankly, desperately in need of it. "What?"

He brushed his thumb over her knuckles. "My chest is yours anytime you need it."

This was the Mack that scared her most. This sweet, charming version of the man who tried so hard to pretend he didn't have a care in the world. This was the version of Mack she could fall in love with, which was the kind of foolish, naive thought she should be chasing off with a broom like she did with Randy. For all she knew, he'd shown this side of himself to a dozen Gretchens in the past year alone.

Her heart didn't seem to care, though. Not when he was smiling at her like she was the only woman in the entire world or, better, the only woman he wanted to be with.

That was a man she could convince herself to trust.

And that was the worst kind of man of all.

CHAPTER EIGHTEEN

Malcolm looked tired and annoyed when Mack sat down at their table in the diner at seven thirty the next morning. Mack hadn't called anyone else because this wasn't something he could talk about with the rest of the guys.

"What's the big emergency?" Malcolm yawned.

Mack glanced around furtively before answering. "Liv is coming over tonight."

Malcolm stroked his beard. "I see." He shook his head. "Actually, I don't see. What's the big emergency?"

"I don't want to screw this up."

"Mack, you're the one who has taught the rest of us everything we know about the manuals. You're not going to screw this up."

"I'm not talking about sex, douchebag."

Malcolm smiled. "Neither was I. So just tell me what the problem is."

Mack pursed his lips and looked away. "I'm not sure if she's . . . if she's really into me."

A puff of air burst from Malcolm's mouth. "I'm sorry. I just, I need to make sure I understand. You're worried because, for the first time ever, you have to actually work for it?"

"I'm sure that's super fucking funny to you, but I'm a goddamned wreck. Gretchen threw me off my game. I've never been dumped before, and I have no idea what I did wrong with her. And Liv is . . ." Mack scrubbed his hands over his face.

A waitress brought coffee and asked whether they wanted to order food. They waved her off.

"Liv is . . . ?" Malcolm said.

Mack had the sinking feeling that he'd never really understood how hard it was to be on this end of the book club until now. For years he'd been cajoling everyone else to spill their guts if they wanted to save their relationships without ever truly believing he'd need to take his own advice someday.

"She's skittish. Distrustful. Just when I think she's opening up to me, she closes herself off again. I don't want that to happen again after tonight."

"You really like her," Malcolm said, his voice carrying an element of *holy shit*. Mack's mood darkened.

"Look," Malcolm said, leaning on his elbows. "You know how this works. If she's scared and determined to keep her distance from you, then she's going to be vulnerable tonight because sex is a big deal. Be prepared for her to show up as her normal sarcastic self."

That made sense. It was exactly what he would've told any of the other guys. Still . . . "What do I do, then?"

Malcolm gave him an *are you serious* look. "You know the answer to that."

Sure. He knew what he'd say to anyone else. "Be what she needs in the moment."

Malcolm nodded.

But those words suddenly meant nothing to him because Liv was taking everything he thought he knew and throwing it on its head. He'd left her apartment last night feeling like the jagged edge of a knife. She'd slayed him with that snuggling fantasy and her unguarded words. *I just like the idea of having someone to lean on sometimes.* It was the loneliest thing he'd ever heard someone say, and the scary thing was, he'd known exactly what she meant. He would never admit it to his friends, but Mack had spent many nights alone in his gigantic house cursing the silence and staring at the empty space on the other side of the bed.

"It's harder than you realized, isn't it?" Malcolm said, interrupting his thoughts.

Mack drank his coffee.

"You really have no idea why Gretchen dumped you?"

"I mean, she had reasons, but they were bullshit."

"What were they?"

"It's embarrassing." Mack knew it was a stupid thing to say before he even said it.

"How many times has one of us said the exact same thing, and you've told us we had to get over it?"

Mack picked at the corner of his forgotten menu. "I know."

"You've heard every humiliating aspect of all our lives, man. It's your turn."

"I know." He puffed out his cheeks and let it fly. "She said she felt like I was wining and dining her according to an instruction manual. That it was too perfect." That still burned. "How can something be too perfect?"

"Because perfection is the opposite of authenticity, Mack."

He gulped at that because it too closely mirrored what Gretchen had said. *Eventually they want it to feel real.*

"I don't know who to be with her," he admitted quietly, shamefully.

"Just be yourself, Mack."

But what if that was the one thing he couldn't give her? If he were smart, he'd cancel tonight. She deserved better. She deserved someone who wasn't doing the one thing she hated most: lying to her.

He would just have to be what she needed. What she wanted.

Braden-Fucking-Mack.

What the hell was she doing?

Scratching an itch. That's what she was doing. And nothing more. At five past eight that night, Liv turned onto Mack's street and slowed to look for house numbers in the dim lighting of the street lamps that cast a warm, yellow glow upon the manicured lawns of the subdivision where he lived. She'd figured he lived in luxury, seeing how he was willing to pay a thousand bucks for a cupcake, but even Liv was unprepared for the overt displays of wealth that dripped from every house she passed. Massive brick and stone houses rose two stories high over elaborate landscaping, their facades illuminated by discreet floodlights designed to show off their attributes without being obvious.

She'd known enough rich people in her life to know there was rarely a noble reason for such ostentatious displays of wealth. The owners of these homes either had a point to make or had something to hide.

The latter, she knew, was always worse.

A half mile up the street, she finally found a stone mailbox with his address. She turned left into the paved driveway and drove beneath a soaring canopy of mature trees. A short distance beyond the trees, his house rose above the lawn.

The front door swung open as she slowed in front of the portico. Mack walked out wearing a pair of golf shorts and a T-shirt that hugged him in good places. He jogged down the few steps and greeted her at her car. Her heart did the thud-thud thing, but she shot it down.

Tonight was about physical release. Nothing more.

"Hey," he said, holding open her door. Before she knew what was happening, he bent and dropped his lips on hers. "Got anything to carry in?"

Speechlessness was not a natural state of being for her, but it had grabbed hold now. "Cupcakes in the back seat," she stammered.

"I got 'em."

Liv followed him inside and tried not to gape at the luxury. The entryway soared eighteen feet and was centered by a circular staircase. A marble floor was cold beneath her feet when she slipped off her shoes.

"You find it okay?" he asked conversationally, carrying the covered plate.

"Yep."

"Kitchen is this way."

This time, speechlessness was not the problem. "Holy shit," she breathed. "You have to be kidding me."

This was the kitchen of her dreams. A real chef's kitchen. A gas range with eight burners and a double oven. Oh, the things she could do in here.

"You like?" Mack's amused voice cut through her culinary fantasies as he set down the plate.

"Why do you need a kitchen like this?" she snapped, cranky for no apparent reason other than her nerves.

"Because I have to eat?" He winked.

"Do you even cook?"

He shrugged. "Sure. Frozen pizza. Sometimes I even shove a lasagna in the microwave."

Those were fighting words. Mack knew it too. His grin could've melted ice.

"You do cook," she said, realizing she'd been played.

"Of course I can cook. I'm an adult. Feeding myself is part of the deal."

She rolled her eyes.

"How about a drink?" he asked.

"Sure."

Mack pulled a chilled chardonnay from his refrigerator, uncorked it, and poured two glasses. He handed one to her and let his fingers linger against hers.

"I might need something harder than this," she said, backing away.

"I can help with that."

Laughter bubbled up from her chest with a buoyancy that broke the tension. She wanted to kiss him for that reason alone. "That was some bush-league sexual innuendo, Mack. I expect better."

He chuckled in that low, manly way of his as he shoved the cork back into the top of the wine bottle.

"You seem pretty good at that, though," she said.

"Good at what?"

She nodded at the bottle. "Sticking long things into tight holes."

He belly-laughed—an honest-to-god, open-mouthed burst of surprise that lifted his entire face and felt to Liv like winning the lottery. Unexpected, thrilling, and totally life-changing.

Mack brought his glass around from behind her but left one hand on the edge of the counter, forcing him to lean just enough that her nipples brushed against his chest. His voice and his eyes teased. "And you think *I'm* bush-league?"

She shrugged with feigned nonchalance. "I might be a little rusty at the plate."

"Haven't rounded the bases in a while, huh?"

"I could stand to practice my bat handling."

"Want a home run tip?"

"Always."

He leaned again. "It's all about how you grip the wood."

"Is this where you teach me about finding the sweet spot?"

He winked. "It happens to be my all-star specialty."

Liv fanned her face. "Damn. Is it hot in here or is it just my vagina?"

His laughter this time made her heart hop like a caffeinated rabbit. Still smiling, Mack leaned against the island behind him, one hand propped against the countertop and the other cradling the wineglass. It looked ridiculously fragile in his strong, thick fingers. The picture he presented was of unapologetic, effortless masculinity. And she had just enough swooning girly girl in her to appreciate every inch of it.

"This is an awfully big house for a single man," she said.

He looked around before returning his gaze to hers. "I won't be single forever."

"What if the future Mrs. Mack doesn't want to live here?"

His eyes registered genuine surprise. "Why wouldn't she?"

"I know it's crazy, but some women like to have a say in their own homes," she teased over the rim of her glass.

"I can adjust. I plan to treat the future Mrs. Mack like a princess, so whatever she wants, she'll have."

Liv snorted. "You really have read too many romance novels."

He lifted an eyebrow. "And you really haven't read enough." Mack sipped his wine. "You want a tour?"

No, Liv wanted to say. Because she didn't want to learn anything else about him that would suck her even more deeply into his dangerous whirlpool of stereotype-defying surprises. She didn't want to see more pictures of his family or find out which room he envisioned for the nursery one day.

"Come on," Mack said, pulling away from the counter. "I'll show you my book collection."

Liv let out an exaggerated groan. "Shoot me now."

Mack reached for her free hand and wrapped her fingers in his. "You need a little romance in your life."

He tugged her gently to follow him back down the hallway. They turned left at the staircase and walked into a den where floor-to-ceiling bookcases in dark wood boasted an entire library of not just romance novels but books on politics, history, sports, and science. Damn him. She needed him to be a mindless playboy, not a man of deep thought.

A pair of overstuffed leather chairs bracketed a brick fireplace. One looked more worn-in than the other, and an unwelcome image flashed through her mind of Mack reclining there, feet up on the ottoman, reading a book on the fall of the Roman Empire.

On the mantel above the fireplace, a line of family photos caught her attention. She let go of his hand and walked closer to them. She brushed her fingers over a gold frame containing a photo of a smiling man holding up a fish. "Is that your dad?" she asked quietly.

Behind her, he cleared his throat. "No. My uncle."

"Do you have any pictures of your father?"

"Not in here."

The catch in his voice brought her around. This was why she didn't want a tour. She couldn't afford to think of him as a grieving son who still got choked up just thinking about his father. She side-stepped him and crossed the room to the section of bookcases where he kept his romance novels.

"Which one is your favorite?" she asked, tilting her head to read the cracked spines.

"This one." His arm reached over shoulder to a shelf just above eye level. His long fingers plucked a well-loved book from the collection and held it down for her.

She took it from him and read the title aloud. "*Mistletoe Dreams.*"

"I've read it at least a dozen times."

She turned the book over to read the back cover. Her eyes skimmed over the plot. Single mom returns to her hometown and falls in love with the stranger next door. Something about a rescue dog and the true meaning of Christmas. "Why is this one your favorite?"

"You'll have to read it to find out."

She returned the book to its place. "Got anything about serial killers? I'd rather read that. Might give me some ideas about how to deal with Royce."

Mack suddenly flattened his hand against the frame of the bookcase, blocking her in from behind. His mouth brushed her earlobe. "Why did you say yes to tonight?"

Liv felt faint. "Besides wanting to see the kitchen you kept bragging about?"

"Yeah, besides that."

Her stomach pitched. *Keep it physical. Keep it meaningless.* "I've made a decision."

"Good decision or bad decision?"

"Probably bad."

"My favorite kind." He inched closer, bringing his body flush against hers. "What is it?"

She set down her glass on the shelf and turned around in the heat of his half embrace. "You and I are going to have sex."

He smacked his hand across his chest. "I'm officially scandalized. Are you suggesting we rub our cloacas together?"

"Something like that, yes, but I swear to God, if you only last three seconds, I'm going to shout it to everyone that the famous Braden Mack is a sexual fraud."

He growled something dirty and yanked her against his hard body. "If that's a challenge, I accept."

Liv backed up until she collided with the bookshelf. "You're probably curious how I came to this decision."

"Not particularly."

"I decided it made perfect sense."

"Yeah?" His mouth found the tender spot below her ear.

"We are obviously attracted to each other."

"Obviously."

"We've kissed three times, and it wasn't half bad."

He pulled back, affronted. "Half bad?"

Liv sighed dramatically. "Men and their egos."

"It's biological," he teased, nuzzling her nose-to-nose. "We like to be stroked."

"I can tell you want to have sex with me."

"What was your first clue?"

"Well, there's this." Liv reached between them and cupped the unmistakable hard bulge testing the strength of his zipper.

He gulped. "He does tend to blow my cover."

"We're spending a lot of time together anyway."

"True."

"So it makes perfect sense. Right?"

He answered by weaving his fingers in her hair and drawing her mouth to his. It was a hot, invasive, *take my breath away* kind of cinematic kiss. He lifted his head far too soon and growled against her lips. "Enough talk, Liv. Are we going to do this thing or not?"

She bit his lip. "Take me upstairs."

Mack looped his arm under her legs and swooped her up just like the night when he'd rescued her from the bar fight. Only this time, she wasn't arguing. He carried her up the stairs without speaking, his face a mask of purpose. Liv leaned into his neck and nipped at the skin below his ear.

He let out a deep growl, kicked open a bedroom door, and quickly deposited her on her feet in front of a mahogany dresser.

Keep it physical. Nothing more. Liv rose on tiptoe to kiss him, but he shook his head. "Turn around," he ordered gruffly.

She obeyed and flattened her hands on the dresser. "Am I being frisked?"

Mack's hands slid down her sides until they reached her hips. With a hard tug, he pulled her back against his erection. His mouth met her ear. "You're in charge, Liv. Boss me around like I know you want to."

Yes. This she could do. Play a role. Keep her heart out of it. Let him touch her and make her body sing like the master he supposedly was.

"Kiss my neck," she said, tilting her head.

His lips were like electricity against her skin, sending sparks down her spine. He lingered there, doing things with his tongue that left her panting in five seconds flat.

Liv covered one of his hands with hers and pulled it away from her hip. Fingers laced, she dragged it along her abdomen and stopped at the waist of her jeans.

"Tell me what you want," he rasped.

"I want you to touch me." Was that her voice? Dear God, she sounded like she was underwater.

Mack's fingers deftly flicked open the top button and drew down her zipper inch by aching inch. She sucked in a breath of anticipation as his fingertips brushed the silky barrier between her sex and his touch.

"Do it," she moaned.

His fingers shoved aside her panties. The first touch of his fingers against her hot, wet skin made her knees buckle. He caught her around the waist. "I got ya, honey," he murmured.

It was sweet and tender. Too sweet and tender.

Keep it physical. Just physical.

She moved against his hand. Seeking. Seeking. He picked up the pace, rubbing where she needed it. "Oh God," she moaned. "You're really good at this."

"I know." He nipped her shoulder.

"Your arrogance ruins it a little."

"Would you rather I be bad at it?"

She moaned an answer. He bit her earlobe, and she whimpered. He paused. "Did I hurt you?"

Her hand dove into her pants and covered his fingers. "Don't stop."

"That's it, baby. Tell me what you need, Liv," he whispered against her ear. "Boss me around."

"Put your fingers inside me."

He slid two fingers down her wet seam and plunged them inside her. Her nails dug into his hand as she cried out. Her body was the boss now, and he kept a firm arm around her waist as he did what she wanted. She rocked against his hand, and he met the pace of her hips with his thrusts.

"You're close, aren't you?" He rasped, because talking had apparently become as difficult for him as it had for her.

"Yes," she moaned.

"Tell me how to take you there. Tell me how to make you come."

"Harder." It was all she could get out, but he knew what she wanted. He used the heel of his hand to grind against her. She cried out and convulsed around his fingers. Her body went limp against him. Inside her underwear, he laced his fingers with hers. She turned her head and kissed him over her shoulder.

Mack scooped her up in his arms again, turned her, and set her on the bed. She molded into the mattress, her body limp and lithe, a satisfied flush on her skin.

"Now what?" he asked, towering over her.

"Take off your clothes."

He did it slowly, taking his time to reveal skin and muscle to her hungry gaze. There wasn't an ounce of fat on him. He had the kind of sinewy muscles that came from jogging and genes, not hours in a gym. His chest was covered in thick, dark hair that narrowed to a thin line until it dipped enticingly into the top of his Levi's.

She gulped.

He winked. "I get that reaction a lot."

She shook her head. "I knew it. Your mouth is going to ruin this."

"You have no idea what my mouth can do."

"Promises, promises."

Mack reached for her pants and yanked them off. They shed the rest of their clothes quickly, frantically. Then he lay down next to her, let out a growl, and slanted his mouth wide over hers. Hooking one arm around her waist, he pulled her onto his lap, never breaking the kiss. Straddling him, Liv gasped as the demanding throb of her desire met the hard bulge of his. At the intense pleasure, something took hold of them both, something primal, fierce, and unrestrained.

Mack's hands slid down to palm her butt cheeks, squeezing and kneading and holding them steady as he lifted his hips in an erotic rhythm against her. Liv gripped his shoulders, dug her fingers into his skin, and rocked against the hard length of him. Their groans merged into one, so she did it again as he slid his hands up the front of her body. His thick, calloused fingers brushed the undersides of her breasts and then higher still until her pebbled nipples strained beneath his hurried exploration.

It wasn't enough. "I need your mouth," she moaned.

He leaned forward and sucked one hard nipple into his mouth. Liv let out a cry and tilted her head back, her hands threading in his hair to hold him there. He lavished each breast with attention, sucking and licking until the pressure between her thighs became unbearable.

Liv might have been able to keep it that way—just physical, just her body responding to his body—if he hadn't paused, if he hadn't suddenly raised his gaze, if he hadn't shaken his head and said with quiet wonderment, "I can't take my eyes off you."

She might have been able to convince herself this meant nothing if her heart hadn't turned in on itself at his words, the look in his eyes, and the tenderness in his kiss when he tugged her mouth toward his again.

She might have been able to tell herself to knock it off with all this romantic bullshit if he hadn't been so goddamned tender. If he hadn't touched her with a reverence that made her tremble. If he hadn't smiled at her when he lifted her just long enough to sheath himself in a condom.

Maybe more than anything else that did her in was the smile.

He smiled like he was happy to be there, to be with her.

Like he was happy.

She was useless against that smile.

Liv lowered back to move against his erection. His deep, guttural groan filled her with such erotic satisfaction that she did it again. He responded with another growl and suddenly rolled her onto her back. And then the kissing began again. Slow and sexy. Her legs wide open. His hard erection nestled against her throbbing center.

"Fuck, Liv," he groaned, grinding against her, and then he was inside her.

Filling her up.

Making her soar, soar so high that she knew in an instant that the fall back to Earth was going to hurt.

* * *

Mack passed out.

He didn't know when it happened or how it happened, but one minute he was basking in the postcarnal glow of the single most exquisite sexual experience of his life, and the next he was out.

And he only knew that had happened because he woke up cold and alone.

He rose up on his elbows and looked around his dark bedroom. "Liv?"

She emerged from his bathroom. Partially clothed.

He sat up and rubbed his eyes. "What are you doing?"

"Going home."

"Why?"

"We did what I came here to do."

His first reaction was to be offended, but then he remembered what Malcolm had said. She was going to be vulnerable after this. She was going to pull away. He'd played a role all night, and so had she, and the game continued. So he went along with it.

Mack leaned back against the headboard and pretended he wasn't pouting inside. "Don't I even get a good-night kiss?"

She obliged, lingering just long enough to make him hard again. He slid his hand around her waist and tried to draw her back, but she stood. "It's better for both of us if I go."

"I definitely need that one explained because I think it would be better if you got naked again and bossed me around some more."

"It's for your own good." She threaded her arms through her T-shirt and pulled it over her head. "I have you figured out, and I can tell that you're going to need some time to process this."

The observation was unnervingly accurate. "I can process just as well with us naked in bed."

She shrugged and shook her head with a pitying expression. "Here's the thing. If we're not careful, you're going to fall in love with me. And I just can't have that on my conscience."

He barked out a laugh. A nervous one. Because damn. "What makes you think I'm going to fall in love with you?"

"Because that's what you do."

"No, I don't. I don't get my heart broken. I'm a wine-'em-and-dine-'em guy."

"Who reads romance novels and is so desperate for a woman, he spent a thousand bucks on a cupcake."

"Am I ever going to live that down?"

"Face it, Mack. You're a walking Hallmark hero."

That one stung. "Explain," he growled.

She gestured at his bedroom. "You live in a castle that you built for a princess who doesn't exist. You're a softy inside . . . I don't want to be the one who breaks that tender heart."

This time, the observation was so sharply on point that he felt the sting of it all the way through him. She was joking of course. But for one freakish moment, he worried that she could actually see right through him. "You're not kidding, are you? You're actually leaving?"

"I am."

She bent and kissed him again. And just like that, she walked out on him. Because that's what she did.

Mack listened to her feet on the stairs, the door as it opened and shut. He flopped down on his pillow. This woman was suddenly blowing his cover in every way. And he didn't fucking like it.

His phone rang five minutes after she left, and he answered without checking the name. "Change your mind?"

"Huh?"

Shit. Mack sat up straight. It wasn't Liv. It was Sonia. "What's up?"

"I need you and Liv to get over here. There's some girl here named Jessica."

Mack whipped the blanket off his legs, hung up, and quickly dialed Liv's number. She answered with forced flippancy. "Jeez, I just left. Miss me already?"

"Come pick me up. Jessica just showed up at the bar."

CHAPTER NINETEEN

Mack shut the door to his office as Jessica sat down with wobbly knees in one of the chairs in front of his desk. She clutched the flaps of her coat together across her chest, and her teeth gnawed at her bottom lip.

Liv took the seat next to her and spoke softly. "Are you okay?"

Mack leaned against the front of his desk and crossed his arms. Jessica glanced up at him nervously. "Do you want me to go?" he asked. Maybe something had happened that Jessica didn't want to talk about in front of a man. The thought made his stomach churn.

But Jessica shook her head with a quick swallow. "No, I . . . I'm just not sure what to do."

"Start at the beginning," Liv said quietly.

"I just can't do it anymore. He's so mean right now, and . . . it was bad tonight."

Mack's hands reflexively curled into fists. "Bad how?"

"Did he—" Liv stopped, as if trying to think of the right way to ask the question that hung in the air. "Did he try to harass you again like before?"

"No. Not like that."

Mack let out the breath he didn't realize he'd been holding.

"He yelled, though," Jessica said. "He glares at me every time he sees me. And he's . . ." She paused with another nervous glance at Mack. "He's trying to ruin you."

"Trying to ruin who? Liv?"

"Both of you."

Mack heard a knuckle crack and realized belatedly it was his own. "Ruin us how?"

"He's making sure that Liv can't get a job anywhere else. And I—I don't know about you. But he hates you because he knows you two are together. He has people keeping tabs on you."

In the one part of his brain that wasn't laser focused on hatred for Royce Preston and concern for Jessica, Mack waited for Liv to make some crack about them not being *together*, but she didn't, and that same part of his brain was irrationally happy given the circumstances.

"How do you know that?" Liv prodded.

"He told me," Jessica said. "He said people who crossed him always regretted it. I think . . . I think he wanted to intimidate me."

Mack had to clear his throat before speaking. "This was today?"

Jessica nodded. "I worked the afternoon shift, and when it was over, he made Geoff drive me home. To make sure I didn't come here, I guess. I don't know why he won't just fire me."

"You can't go back there," Mack said in a harsher voice than he intended.

Jessica's lower lip trembled. "I know. But I don't know what to do."

"Jessica, just quit," Liv said, taking the girl's hand. "Just don't go back. We *will* stop him."

They drove Jessica home. When they pulled into a parking spot in front of her student apartment building, Mack gave her both his and Liv's phone numbers. "Liv and I are going to figure this out," he said in what he hoped was a reassuring voice. "Call us if Royce or Geoff and the other one try to contact you or do anything to intimidate you, okay? When you're ready, there's a job waiting for you at my club."

Jessica nodded, her face downtrodden. "Thank you for helping me," she said quietly. "I'm sorry I was such a bitch before."

"Hey. No. You have nothing to apologize for."

She shrugged, lower lip trembling again. "But none of this would be happening if I had just—"

Liv turned around in the driver's seat. "None of this would be happening if Royce wasn't a piece of shit who preyed on women. That's it. End of story. *None* of this is your fault in any way."

Jessica's eyes fell to her lap as she bit her lip.

"Mack and I will take care of this," Liv said. "He's not going to hurt you or anyone else ever again."

This time, when Jessica nodded, she looked like she actually believed them.

Liv pulled back onto the freeway and headed toward Mack's house. He stewed silently for ten full minutes before speaking again. "Royce is becoming unhinged."

"He was always unhinged."

"But he's obviously getting worse, and if Jessica quits, he's going to lose his shit."

Liv took the exit for his subdivision. Mack studied her in the low lights of the dashboard. Even ninety minutes after leaving his bed, she still had a freshly sexed look about her that made his pants tighten and his heart beat faster.

Fuck the role-playing. Fuck her need for space. *He* needed her safe. "Maybe you should stay with me until this is over."

Liv's head whipped his way so fast he was afraid she'd crash the car. "What?"

"I'm worried about how Royce is ramping this thing up. Making Geoff drive Jessica home? Keeping tabs on me? He's dangerous, Liv."

She laughed and turned onto his street. "I think I'll be fine."

"I'd like to be sure."

She gave him a look that said he'd violated one of the central rules of the manuals. He'd gone too far. Said too much. And now her walls were officially back up.

She pulled into his driveway. "I can take care of myself, Mack."

"I know you can, but I'd feel better if—"

Her hands tightened on the steering wheel. "I'll call you."

"When?"

She shrugged. "Couple of days."

He gaped, heart thudding. "A couple of *days*?"

She sucked in a quick breath, the only sign that this was all bullshit. But what the hell was he supposed to do? Refuse to get out? Mack threw open his door. He'd barely had time to shut the door before she shoved the car in reverse. Mack stood in the driveway and watched her drive away.

He was left alone, once again, with the question that always seemed to follow in her wake.

What had just happened? But this time, a new question immediately followed. How the hell was he going to make sure it happened again?

CHAPTER TWENTY

Two nights later, Liv lay awake, clutching her phone to her chest, calling herself every name in the book for her own stubborn fear of falling, when a sound outside brought her upright.

Probably just a raccoon.

Or maybe one of the goats got loose.

Or Hop had decided to come back to work on the tractor some more.

But at the unmistakable scuff of shoes on gravel, she bolted out of bed, secure in the knowledge that someone was sneaking around outside her apartment. Probably a more well-adjusted person would worry first and foremost about their safety, but Liv's first thought was how annoying Mack was going to be when he was proven right that Royce was ramping things up.

Goddammit. She hated it when he was right.

Walking on tiptoe, she crept down the short hallway to the living room—just as a footstep thudded lightly on the staircase outside.

Maybe it was Rosie. It had to be, right? She just needed . . . something. At eleven o'clock at night.

Another footstep on the stairs made the hair on her arms stand erect. That was way too heavy of a footstep to be Rosie. Panting now, Liv looked at her phone and tried to calculate how long it would take the police to arrive if she called 911. Ten minutes? What if the intruder went to the main house and attacked Rosie?

Liv hit the emergency call button and dropped to the floor. A dispatcher answered almost immediately and asked her to state her emergency.

"I think someone is trying to break into my apartment."

"Okay, ma'am. Can you give me an address?"

She rattled it off.

"Where are you right now, ma'am?"

"On the floor of my living room."

"And you can see someone?"

"I hear him. I think he's coming up the stairs."

"Is he inside the house?"

"What? No. I—I live in an apartment above the garage. The staircase is outside."

"I am sending officers to your residence. Can you tell me your name?"

"Liv."

The dispatcher remained calm. "Liv, I'm going to stay on the phone with you until officers arrive."

"Do you know how long it will take?"

"I have one patrol car five minutes out."

"That's too long."

Liv army crawled to the window. The dispatcher asked her

what was going on. Liv drew back a corner of the curtain and peeked out. It was too dark to see anything.

"I don't see him, but he's definitely coming up the stairs."

He hadn't yet rounded the corner of the building.

"Liv, I need you to sit tight."

"I'll call back."

She hung up over the dispatcher's protests. Still crawling, she moved to the door. With slow motions, she reached up and winced as she turned the deadbolt. It made a low click. Liv froze. The man didn't stop, so either he hadn't heard the noise or he didn't care.

Liv grabbed the nearest object—a Birkenstock—and stood. Sucking in a breath, she whipped open the door. She took the first flight of stairs two at a time, hit the landing, and swung the shoe as if she were trying out for Wimbledon.

It connected with a face, and the man let out a surprised grunt. His arms helicoptered for one terrifying moment as he teetered on the edge of the landing. But it was long enough for Liv to realize she'd made a horrible mistake. Long enough for her to look over his shoulder and count how many steps he had to fall. Long enough for her to meet his eyes and realize this was no intruder.

"What the fuck, Liv?" Mack exclaimed.

And then down he went. Just like the cupcake, he lost his fight with gravity. He tipped backward and skidded down the ten steps to the dusty ground, his head bump-bumping against the creaky wood.

He landed headfirst on the gravel, his legs still on the stairs. He let out a groan and swore.

Guilt made her cranky. "Dammit, Mack. What the hell are you doing?"

He lifted his head. "Are you serious? What are *you* doing?"

"Defending myself from an intruder, like I told you I could."

"D-defending yourself?" He could barely get the word out. Disbelief dripped from his tone. "With a shoe?"

"It was all I could find at the moment."

Mack hoisted himself off the ground. Dust covered his jeans and his white shirt. An angry red splotch below his left eye bore the faint outline of her sandal.

She planted her hands on her hips. "Why the hell didn't you call first?"

"Because I knew you'd say no if I asked to come over, and dammit, it's been two fucking days! I wanted to see you."

"So you thought it would be a good idea to just show up?"

Mack wiped his hands on his jeans. "Let me get this straight," he glowered. "You hear a man outside your apartment, and instead of calling the goddamned police, you hurtle yourself at him without even checking to see if he has a weapon or if he's alone?"

Shit. The cops. Liv raced back up the stairs and through the door. She grabbed her phone off the floor and hit the emergency number again.

Maybe there was still time to cancel.

Too late.

Dispatch answered just as the outdoors began to dance with red and blue lights.

"Sorry for the misunderstanding."

Twenty minutes later, Liv apologized for the thousandth time. The four officers on the scene had separated her from Mack and had also questioned Rosie and Hop—who was actually there in the middle of the night, which was weird.

"I thought he was a bad guy."

"A bad guy?" the cop said.

"He's my—" She stopped and glanced at Mack, who lifted an amused eyebrow. "My friend."

Mack snorted.

It took several more minutes for the humiliation to end and the cops to leave.

"I can't believe you just showed up here," Liv said, stomping back up the stairs.

"Yeah, well, I can't believe you called the cops on me."

"Twenty minutes ago you were mad that I didn't call the cops! Make up your mind."

He followed her into the apartment.

"You have no idea the many ways I'm going to hurt you," she said.

"Promise?"

Liv yanked open the door to the freezer and grabbed the ice tray. She snatched a dish towel from the sink and banged the tray on top. A dozen cubes fell out, one sliding across the counter and onto the floor. She didn't care. In fact, she secretly hoped he'd step on it and wipe out.

In the living room, Mack plopped onto the couch with a dramatic groan, holding his hand to his cheek. Grumbling, she wrapped the ends of the towel around the ice and stalked into the living room. He had his feet on the coffee table and his head back, eyes closed. Even from across the room she could see the raised purplish bruise on his cheekbone.

Wow. She'd nailed him good.

He rolled his head and opened an eye as she approached. She thrust the ice pack at him. "Here. I don't know why I'm helping you, though."

"Because you care?"

"You scared the shit out of me."

He pressed the ice to his face. "I could use some aspirin."

Liv stomped to the bathroom, made a lot of noise banging around in the medicine cabinet, and then came back with a bottle of Tylenol.

"No water?" he asked.

"Choke on it."

"You're awfully hostile for someone who just beat up an innocent man."

"Innocent? You were sneaking around my house!"

"I wasn't sneaking. I was trying to be quiet so I wouldn't wake up Randy."

"What are you doing here?"

"*Two fucking days*, Liv." He tossed the towel aside and stood. "Maybe you do the wham-bam thing, but I don't."

Liv swallowed her guilt and shame. She'd been avoiding him, mostly to avoid her own feelings. "I told you it would be a couple of days. I was giving you time to process."

"You know what I think?" he said, moving closer. "I think *you're* the one who needed time to process things, so you made up some stupid story and left me hanging for two goddamned days."

Her body burned hot and cold at once. Hot because of the scorching look in his eyes. Cold because, damn him, that wasn't fair. He'd backed her into the kitchen. Boxed her in. If she let him stare into her eyes, he'd see right through her and realize he was telling the truth.

"This is what I was afraid of," she rasped. "You're already attached to me. I'm a heartbreaker."

Mack pressed his palms to the counter on either side of her and leaned in. His eyes had an exhausted, strung-out look to them, and she wondered for a moment whether that could actually be real. Had he really missed her? Had it really hurt his feelings that she had avoided him for two whole days?

Mack made a grumpy face. "Would it be so fucking bad if I cared about you?"

Her heart sputtered. "You don't, though."

"Don't I?"

"Maybe you think you do, but it's not real."

He groaned and rolled his eyes. "Oh please. Do continue."

"You have a hero complex and think I'm in danger or some shit, so your . . . hero hormone is firing at all cylinders."

"Hero hormone?"

"Yeah. And then we threw sex into the mix, and boom, you went full Disney prince on me."

He crossed his arms. "Wait. I thought you said I was going to fall madly in love with you. Now I don't care about you? Make up your mind."

She winced. Plot hole. "You *think* you care about me because you're the type to fall in love. But you don't really care about me."

"So your fear isn't that I'll actually fall in love with you, just that I will *think* I'm in love with you."

She looked sideways. "Yes."

He gazed down at her, the corner of his mouth tilting in a reluctant smile. "Damn, Liv, you're complicated."

She shrugged. "It's your issue, not mine."

"Well I hope you're right, because caring about you would be a major inconvenience."

"Then consider yourself off the hook."

"Thank you. That definitely makes my life easier."

"You're welcome."

"Liv?" he murmured, bending way too closely.

The unmistakable scent of him hit her with the force of a wrecking ball. The man never smelled bad. Sweaty, dirty, bloody, cocky piece of shit. He still smelled like pure lust to her. "What?" She said with a heavy rasp.

"I think you're full of shit."

He wasn't wrong. Which is why her heart overruled her brain and said, *fuck it*. Who needed gravity anyway? Liv grabbed the front of his shirt and yanked him forward. Their mouths collided, and she let him do his thing. And that thing went from a deep, hot tongue kiss to a hand up the shirt in about ten seconds flat. And after that, there wasn't much argument between her principles and her pink parts because both seemed to be on the same page. The one that said, *Sure, let's get naked*, because holy shit, what that man could do to a nipple with just the flick of his fingers ought to be illegal.

Liv moaned and arched into his touch.

Mack pinched her. "Who's the boss now?"

"You're going to ruin this with that mouth of yours."

"This mouth of mine is going to prove you wrong."

Mack suddenly dropped to his knees, and truly, Liv had no idea how it happened, but suddenly she was sans pants, and that mouth of his was licking her through the lace of her underwear, and she was hanging on to his head.

"Just so you know, I haven't actually agreed to sex again," she moaned.

"This isn't sex, honey," he teased. His left hand snaked up her thigh and stopped at the opening of her panties, where nothing but a thin layer of cotton separated his fingers from the pulsing ball of desire that so desperately needed his touch.

"It feels like sex," she moaned.

"Then you need to do it more."

She had just started to whimper incoherently when he shoved the fabric aside to bare her flesh. He did the licking thing again, and when he slid two fingers inside her, she was done. Just like that. Fireworks exploded. She bit her own arm to keep from belting out the national anthem.

He wasn't done, though. In her haze, she became aware of him nibbling his way up her body, fumbling with his pants, the sound of a condom wrapper—

She paused. "Where did you get that?"

"My back pocket."

"Good thinking."

"I like to be prepared for anything."

So did Liv, but she wasn't prepared for him to hoist her in his arms, press her against the apartment door, and enter her with a powerful thrust. Maybe he hadn't exactly been prepared for it either because he didn't move for a moment. His forehead dropped to her shoulder, and he made a noise that was half pleasure, half pain, and lord did she understand that. The door handle dug into the curve of her butt cheek, but the feel of him inside her was so intense that she didn't care.

And then he started to move. Hard thrusts that pounded her harder against the door, which made her intimate muscles start to pulse again like the rockets' red glare. Mack covered her mouth with his to smother the sound of her bombs bursting in air.

Mack grunted, his hands digging into her backside where he held her. She clung to him, arms around his neck, legs around his waist.

"Liv," he suddenly groaned. "Ah God."

He came with a final hard thrust and another grunt.

She had barely returned to Earth when she felt him yank up his pants with one hand and then start carrying her toward the bedroom.

"What are you doing?"

"Taking you to bed."

"No. Nu-uh. You're not staying."

"Yes, I am. I don't do this kind of thing. I don't do the sex-and-run thing, Liv."

She expected him to drop her on the bed, but he didn't. He bent and gently lowered her, shedding the tough-talking alpha thing as quickly as he'd shed her pants from her body. He gazed down at her in a way that reminded her why she'd avoided him for two days, because a girl could get attached to a look like that, and wouldn't that be the dumbest thing in the world?

"I just want to wake up next to you," he said quietly. "Is that all right with you?"

She didn't actually agree before he lifted the shirt over his head and dropped it on the floor. His jeans quickly followed. She barely had time to scoot out of the way before he pulled back the covers and slid under them. Liv clutched the comforter to her chest.

He rolled his head and let out a laugh. "You scared of me?"

Scared? Yes. He terrified her.

"Night, Liv," he yawned. And then the bastard closed his eyes. His breathing slowed to an even rhythm within minutes. How the hell could he sleep? Her entire body was on fire. One prompt, and she would climb on top of him. But he seemed completely unaffected by their proximity.

Men. They could turn their emotions on and off like faucets. It wasn't fair.

"Jerk," she whispered.

"What did I do this time?"

Liv gasped. "I thought you were asleep."

"I know. I was letting you admire me."

"I hate you." She flopped on her side to face away from him. Behind her, the bed dipped and shifted, and a heavy arm fell across her waist. He tugged her against his chest. The contours of his rock-solid body molded against her. If she scooted her hips back just an inch, she'd probably feel his you-know-what.

"I'm sorry for scaring you," he said quietly. Sincerely.

She rolled over to face him. "I'm sorry for not calling." She could at least give him that much.

Mack slid his hand up her side until it framed the outline of her jaw. She didn't need encouragement. She leaned into his kiss. Into him. Until she found herself on her back once again. He slid his hand down her side, hooked his hand behind her knee, and drew it over his hip.

"I used to think I knew what I was doing with women, Liv," he whispered. "But then I met a certain pastry chef, and my whole fucking world turned on its head."

Sometime later, she fell asleep in his arms, wondering whether he knew what he'd done to her with those simple words.

CHAPTER TWENTY-ONE

She awoke sometime later with the heavy weight of his body on her.

What the—?

"Be quiet." His hand covered her mouth, and his lips brushed against her ear as he whispered. What the hell was he doing? Was this some kind of kinky sex game? She squirmed beneath him, but he held tight.

"Is this payback for hitting you?" she hissed.

"Just listen to me," he ordered. "There's someone downstairs."

She rolled her eyes. Yeah, right.

"I want you to lock yourself in the bathroom—"

What? No way. She shook her head beneath his hand.

"Jesus, Liv. Just listen to me for once!"

And that's when she heard it. The unmistakable squawk of a pissed-off man-hating rooster.

Mack yanked on his jeans and raced down the stairs. Liv, of course, refused to stay inside.

"Help!" The cries of a desperate man were drowned out only by Randy's vicious screech. Mack leaped off the bottom step and ran into the driveway, where a shapeless form lay on his back, arms raised to ward off the talons.

"Who the hell are you?"

"Help," the man cried again, hands now over his face.

The man suddenly swung his arm wide and knocked Randy away just far enough to roll and dodge another attack. With his butt to them, he rose on all fours. "It's me," the man bellowed.

"I don't know who you are."

He stood and turned around, and by now Liv had joined Mack's side. She let out a surprised scream.

"Geoff."

"Christ," the man barked, covering his ears.

"What the hell are you doing here?" Mack boomed.

"Livvie!" Another man's voice. Hop. This time from the house.

Liv turned. Mack turned. Geoff turned. And all three let out a collective scream because—

"OH MY GOD, WHY ARE YOU NAKED?" Liv covered her eyes.

Mack understood her reaction. Jesus God, Hop was naked. Running. Naked.

And then Geoff let out another startled grunt because Hop was flying in slow motion through the air in a tackle that would've made the NFL proud. Dust rose in a cloud around them as they hit the ground, Hop on top. Bare-ass naked.

"Oh God," Liv groaned. "I'm never going to recover from this."

Hop had an arm to the guy's throat. "You have five seconds to tell me who you are and why you're here."

Geoff grunted and gasped for air. Hop lessened his hold.

"It's one of Royce's goons," Liv said.

The back door to the house banged open again. Rosie ran out wrapped in a robe, her hair flying wildly around her shoulders. She carried a pair of men's jeans and a flannel shirt in her hands. She handed them both to Hop and gave him *eyes*.

Liv's mouth dropped open. "Oh my God."

"We can talk about that later," Rosie admonished. "What the hell is going on?"

Hop quickly filled her in with the slim details they had. Rosie clutched her robe.

Hop hauled Geoff to his feet. "What the hell do you want?"

"To help," Geoff panted.

"Bullshit," Mack barked.

"I swear." Geoff wiped his face with dirty hands. "I don't want any part of Royce's bullshit anymore."

Hop was unmoved. "How do we know we can trust him? This could be some kind of trap."

"It's not a trap," Geoff said. "I swear. Just listen to me. Please."

"Talk."

Geoff pressed the ice pack Rosie had given him to his cheek and kept a wary gaze trained on Hop, who—thank fucking God—had put on his jeans.

"I want to help."

"So you said," Mack said, arms crossed. "Help with what?"

"I know you guys are trying to expose what Royce is really like."

"No idea what you're talking about," Hop said.

He'd gone into full cop mode, and Mack had to admire the act. Geoff actually blinked for a moment as if he'd been wrong maybe.

But then Geoff got wise. "Jesus, I'm not recording this or anything."

"We're supposed to just trust you?"

"Want me to fucking strip?"

Hop smacked him upside the head. "Watch your fucking mouth."

"Please don't strip," Liv said. "I've been subjected to enough unsolicited balls lately to last a lifetime."

Mack hoped his weren't among them.

"I swear to God, I'm here to help you," Geoff said. "I didn't sign up for this crap. I thought I was going to be a bodyguard! But he's lost it, I swear."

"What does that mean?"

"He's paranoid!"

"Slow down. What does he have you doing instead of being a bodyguard and intimidating my future employers?"

"You know about that?"

Liv nodded. "We know about that."

He shrugged. "At first it was just, you know, watching your Facebook accounts and shit to see if you talked about him."

"And then?"

"Then, when Jessica told him you guys came to her campus, he lost his shit. He . . ." A deep swallow revealed either shame or trepidation at whatever he planned to say next.

"He what?" Mack growled.

"He made us start following her everywhere. And you."

The last two words rang the loudest.

Mack cursed, and Hop pointed. "See. This is what I was talking about. You guys went and messed around in shit you had no business—"

Rosie rested a gentle hand on his arm, and miraculously, Hop quieted.

"He's gone crazy, though. Even worse since Jessica quit," Geoff said. "I don't want to be part of it anymore."

"So why don't you just quit?" Mack challenged. He still didn't trust this douchebag.

"Just leave and let him get away with this shit? No fucking way, man. I have little sisters. If someone pulled this shit with them, I'd beat his ass."

Mack resisted the urge to point out that a man shouldn't need little sisters to recognize how wrong Royce's behavior was, but this didn't seem like the time.

"Do you know any names of the women he's done this to besides Jessica?" Liv asked.

"No."

"Where might we find that information?"

"His office. He keeps some kind of secret record in there."

"Bullshit," Hop grumbled. "No one would be that stupid."

"Have you met him?" Liv countered. "He's an arrogant prick who thinks he can get away with anything. It would never occur to him that anyone would uncover his dirty secrets."

"Or that anyone would violate his trust," Mack added, his eyes trained on Geoff.

"I'm not loyal to that dirtbag," Geoff said. Then, with something akin to admiration in his eyes, he looked at Liv. "That's why you scare him, I think. He knows you think he's a piece of shit and have never been loyal to him. He's not used to people he can't intimidate or pay off or impress."

A swell of pride flushed Mack's chest with heat.

"Then what exactly can you do for us?" Hop asked.

"What do you want?"

"We need names," Liv said. "We need to know how many women he's done this to and how much he's paid them."

"Those would be in the files."

"Can you access them?"

"I don't—I don't know. But I know where they are."

Mack raised his eyebrows and nodded toward Liv. "What do you think?"

"I think we should trust him. This is the best information we've gotten so far."

"I agree," Hop said. "Let's get everyone together tomorrow and make a plan."

Geoff stood and handed Rosie the ice pack. "Thank you, ma'am. I should probably get going."

"Nonsense," Rosie said. "It's late. Just stay here."

Mack and Hop made matching noises of *what the fuck*, but they were overruled by a single look.

They watched Rosie escort Geoff to the downstairs bathroom. Liv stood and said she needed a glass of water.

"So . . ." Mack said when she was out of earshot. He motioned toward the bathroom. "That looked promising."

"Fuck off," Hop grumbled.

"You could just say thank you."

"I'm not thanking you for shit."

Mack grew somber. "We're in over our heads, aren't we?"

Hop nodded. "Yep."

"You think we should stop?"

Hop hit him with a stare as certain as he'd ever seen. "Not a fucking chance. I'm in."

CHAPTER TWENTY-TWO

The guys, minus Del and Gavin, who had an away game, arrived at the farm just before noon to plan the next steps. Geoff sat in the corner like a hostage, alternating between biting his nails and eating cookies.

"What good does it even do us if we get a list of names?" Malcolm asked. "They've all likely signed NDAs. And if any of them wanted to come forward, they would have done so by now."

"We don't have to release names," Liv said. "All we need to confront him with are the numbers. We can leave names out."

"It would be enough proof to leak to the reporters at his cookbook event," Derek said. "No one has to be identified. No one has to know where they came from."

"I can cover our tracks," Noah said.

Liv didn't doubt it. But it still made her stomach hurt. "Just to be clear. We're actually talking about doing this, right? Breaking into Royce's office?"

Mack stood in front of her, close enough that he could keep his voice low, close enough to be obvious. "You're in charge," he said. "If you're not comfortable with this, just say so."

She wanted to kiss him for that but held back. She wasn't sure where things stood between them after last night, but she still wasn't quite ready for the *public display of affection* thing.

"I just want to make sure we're all in agreement about what we're getting ourselves into," she said. "Royce has done enough damage. I don't want any of you to suffer from bringing him down."

"Then we'd better be sure we don't get caught." Hop said.

The plan came together quickly. Derek would arrive first and park himself at the bar to keep an eye out for Royce. Malcolm and his wife would make a reservation in the VIP section—

"Order the Sultan," Liv said. "It'll send him into fits."

That would keep Royce occupied while Geoff snuck Mack, Noah, and the Russian through the back door and up to the administrative offices.

"What about me?" Liv asked.

"You'll stay here," Mack said.

"What? No way!"

Mack faced her. "Liv, you can't go. Royce will know something is up if he sees you."

"Um, I could say the same for you."

Mack clenched his jaw. "It's not safe."

"It's no less safe for me than for you."

"He's right, Liv," Hop said.

"This is so sexist!"

Mack dragged his hands over his hair. "Liv, on this issue, please let me be in charge."

"Uh, no. I'm the one who started this. I'm not going to stay behind while you guys take all the risks."

Rosie walked in and handed a hen to the Russian. "Maybe you could stay in the van," Rosie suggested.

Liv spun and gaped at her. "I thought you of all people would take my side."

Rosie shrugged. "I'm a little biased on this one."

"So am I," Mack said quietly. "I need you safe."

The look in his eyes made her heart do a thing that she didn't like because she wasn't ready for it, wasn't ready to trust it, so she did the thing she always did. She got cranky. "I can't talk to you when you're like this. You're acting like a, like a . . ."

He lifted his eyebrows.

She planted her hands on her hips. "Like an overprotective boyfriend."

Mack threw his hands in the air. "That's because I am! Maybe you haven't noticed after last night, honey, but I'm hooked."

The sentence exploded in the room and covered everyone in its guts. Liv blinked, sucked in a breath.

The deafening silence was followed by a quiet whisper.

"I knew it," the Russian said.

Chaos erupted as the guys dug out their wallets and started throwing money at the Russian.

The Russian stood and lifted the chicken in the air to dance. "I won the bet! I won the bet!"

"There was a bet?" Liv hissed.

Mack held up his hands. "I had nothing to do with it."

Hop stood and yelled at everyone to shut up. "This is serious shit we're talking about."

His cop voice brought the room under control.

"Liv, you ride in the van with me. Malcolm, make the reservation for eight if you can. Noah, you said you have a van we can use?"

Noah nodded, grinning like a gamer who'd just gotten an upgrade. "Oh yeah."

"You have to be shitting me."

At seven o'clock, Noah pulled up in front of Mack's house in a dirty white van that couldn't have been more obvious in its nondescript creepiness if he'd spray painted "Free Puppies" on the side.

Liv, Hop, and Mack stared in silence. Noah rolled down the passenger window. "You ready?"

Mack wrenched open the door. "Are we going for child-molester chic in this thing, or what?"

"This is a good van. I got laid for the first time in this thing."

"And I'm out." Hop backed away, hands raised.

"Don't worry. I took the seats out a long time ago."

"When?" Hop grumbled. "During the Clinton impeachment? This thing is ancient."

"Yeah, I was in elementary school during the Clinton impeachment."

Hop flipped him off.

Noah gestured for everyone to get in. "This was one of my grandpa's vans for his roofing business."

"Great. Because a roofing van is definitely what we need," Mack said.

Noah got out, rounded to the passenger side, and opened the sliding door to reveal a cavernous back full of computer equipment and some kind of radio shit that lined one entire wall. Computer screens provided a 360-degree view of the outside of the van.

Everyone stilled. "This really is a surveillance van," Mack said. "You weren't lying about that."

Noah slid back behind the wheel. "Nope."

"Why exactly do you have this?"

As Liv and Hop got settled in the back, Noah eased out onto the street. "All IT professionals have one."

"You work for the CIA, don't you?" Liv said from the back.

"The CIA can't operate domestically."

"Which is a totally natural response."

"The NSA, on the other hand . . ."

"I can't tell if you're joking," Liv said.

"No one admits if they work for the NSA, Liv."

The Russian's house was just three miles away from Mack's. They found him waiting outside in the driveway wearing black tactical pants, a black T-shirt, and a mobster-style leather jacket. He carried a black workman's lunch box, the kind they used on construction sites.

After a brief silence, Noah spoke for them both. "What exactly is going on there?"

Mack sighed and dragged his hand down his jaw. "I told him to wear dark clothing."

Noah parked, got out, and went around to open the back doors. The Russian climbed in, his massive hulk taking up most of the space. He sat on the floor, knees to his chest, the lunch box resting next to him.

A few minutes after Noah started driving, a rustling in the back seat made Mack turn around. The Russian was riffling through his lunch box and handing out snacks to Hop and Liv.

"What are you doing?" Mack asked.

"I'm hungry," the Russian answered.

"You packed *food*?"

"I get very hungry."

"There'd better not be any fucking cheese in there." Mack turned back around in his seat. "This is quickly becoming the worst idea in the entire history of bad ideas."

"Here they come."

Just before eight, Mack sat up straighter in his seat and watched one of the computer monitors in the back of the van. They'd parked the van on the top floor of the parking garage overlooking Savoy. Malcolm's black SUV stopped at the valet stand in front of the restaurant. A black-attired driver opened the door for Malcolm's wife, Tracy.

"I can't believe we're really doing this," Liv breathed, scrunched next to Mack on the floor. He took her hand, and she laced her fingers with his. That's how nervous she was.

"It'll be okay," Mack reassured her. He kind of wanted to lean over and kiss her head, but that was probably pushing it.

Less than a minute passed before Geoff reported in. "They're being seated."

Then a few minutes more. "He's coming out to greet them."

"That's our cue," Mack said.

Mack turned to his left, where Liv sat biting a fingernail. "It'll be okay."

She nodded. "Be careful."

Fuck it. He dipped his head and kissed her hard and fast.

He, Noah, and the Russian jumped out of the van and jogged down the stairs. They were all winded by the time they reached the ground floor. They rounded the corner into the alley behind the restaurant. Ahead, a back door to the restaurant swung open. Silently, all three ducked inside.

Geoff guided the door closed with a silent click. He handed Mack a key card.

"Whose is this?" Mack asked.

Sweat dripped from Geoff's chin. He was nervous as shit. "No one's. It's the generic card that we use for deliveries."

"So they can't track it. Perfect."

They'd entered the delivery bay of the restaurant, which was probably bustling during the day but was thankfully deserted now. The place smelled like dirty concrete and motor oil. A door at the far end was illuminated only by a red EXIT sign.

Geoff pointed to it. "That's the staircase. Do you remember what I told you about how to get there?"

"Turn left at the top of the stairs," Mack said.

Geoff nodded and wiped his hand down his face.

"You're sure the office is unlocked?" Noah asked.

"I just unlocked it myself. You have ten minutes."

"Let's go."

"Talk to me," Hop ordered through the earpiece.

"We're in," Mack answered. "Headed up the stairs now."

Mack remembered Geoff's instructions from earlier. There were two main staircases to the upper floors. The one from the back, which they were taking, was used mainly for daytime staff, so it would be empty this time of night.

The screens of computer monitors bathed the entire administrative floor in a soft blue glow when they snuck out of the staircase. The office they wanted was at the end of the hallway and to the left, Geoff had said.

"Hurry," Mack hissed.

The three of them crept across the carpet until they spotted the office Geoff had described. Mack held his breath as Noah gripped the door handle with his gloved hands. They were really doing this. Jesus Christ.

With a quiet turn of the handle, they were in.

Mack let out a breath and followed Noah inside, the Russian on his heels.

Mack motioned to the door, and the Russian nodded. He took up a guarded position by the door to keep watch while Noah and Mack crossed the small space to the desk. The computer was on but needed a log-in.

Mack swore under his breath. "You're sure you can do this?"

Noah sat down in Royce's chair and immediately started pounding the keys. It was like watching Mozart compose a symphony the way Noah manipulated the computer. Seconds later he was in.

"Jesus, you did that fast."

"People don't give enough thought to passwords," Noah said. He dug a thumb drive from his pocket and shoved it into the port on the side of the computer.

Mack turned away to study the office. He glowered at the picture of Royce with his wife.

"Ten minutes," Hop said into their ears.

Sweat rolled down Mack's face. The Russian was at the door, ready to take out anyone who happened to come upon them.

Noah's fingers flew across the keyboard.

"How do you even know what you're looking for?" Mack asked.

"Don't talk to me," Noah snapped.

"Liv is driving me crazy for an update," came Hop's voice.

Mack smiled. "Tell her we're fine."

Except they weren't. Noah was swearing and banging on the keys.

"What's wrong?"

"I said don't talk to me!"

A car horn on the street outside nearly sent Mack jumping clear to the ceiling. "Hurry the fuck up," he griped.

"I'm in," Noah breathed.

Mack raced over to watch as Noah called up list of files. "What are we looking at?"

"I'm just going to download it all."

"How long will that take?"

Noah ignored him. Mack clasped his gloved hands into fists and banged them against his forehead.

"Almost done," Noah said. "Five more seconds."

Mack counted down in his head.

"I'm out," Noah said.

Mack let out a relieved breath. "Let's go."

Noah pulled out the thumb drive, clicked out of whatever file he'd been in, and then backed away from the computer. The Russian held up his hand before they could leave, looking back and forth down the hallway before giving them a nod.

They made it halfway down the hall before they heard footsteps.

Shit. Shitshitshit. Mack met Noah's equally alarmed gaze. The Russian spun around.

Whoever they were, they were coming right for them. Mack grabbed Noah and threw him under a desk. The Russian wrapped his fingers around Mack's wrist and yanked him behind a half wall separating one cubicle from the next.

Two male voices were coming. The night security guards Geoff had warned about. Oh fuck. Oh shit.

And then suddenly the Russian let out a soft moan.

"Oh no." Mack peered closer at his face. "Oh shit, no."

"What?" Hop hissed through the earpiece.

"I think there's something wrong with him," Noah answered into the microphone.

"Wrong with who?"

"The Russian dude. He's got a weird look on his face."

Mack grabbed the Russian's lapels and dragged him close. "Breathe. Breathe through it."

The Russian started to pant like he was in labor.

"What the fuck is going on?" Hop barked.

"I don't know!" Noah hissed.

"What did you eat?" Mack whispered.

"No cheese. Just vegan cheese."

"You can't eat vegan cheese!"

"It's nondairy. Nondairy."

"It's still fucking cheese!"

The Russian groaned again, and even in the low light of the computers, Mack could see as the color drained from his face.

Sweat ran down Mack's back. "You gotta squeeze your cheeks, man. Squeeze and breathe, because if you let that go right now, we're done for."

"Are you kidding me?" Noah hissed. "Is this about a fart?"

"You don't understand," Mack said, looking sideways. "He doesn't just fart. It's like ripping open a sewer line and—"

A soft Russian chant cut him off.

Panic set in. "This is bad. This is so fucking bad."

"Can't he just let it out silently?" Noah asked.

"It's not the sound we're worried about. It's the goddamned smell."

"This is a joke, right?" Hop said through the earpiece.

"I can't hold it," the Russian groaned.

"You have to."

"Not healthy to hold it in," the Russian grunted.

Mack shook him. "It's not going to be healthy for you if you let it out either."

The Russian groaned and wrapped his arms around his abdomen. His face twisted in pain. Outside their hiding spot, footsteps drew closer. Mack smacked his hand over the Russian's mouth. Sweat poured like a river down his face.

He couldn't believe it. He was going to get busted for breaking and entering and a hundred other offenses because of a goddamned fart.

And not even one of his own!

But as it so often happened in the manuals, a sudden epiphany broke through the haze of panic. Jail would be worth it because he was doing this for Liv. No one else. He had officially fallen for her. Enemies-to-lovers was no longer just a fictional trope for him—it was his fucking life.

"What the hell is happening in there?" Hop barked into their ears.

The light from the security guards' flashlights bobbed back and forth across the floor, closer and closer.

The Russian sucked in a breath and held it.

The guards passed by.

The Russian exhaled.

And the smell of death filled the air.

Noah fell onto all fours and crawled, gagging. Around the corner, someone shouted. "Goddamn, dude. Did you just fart?"

"That wasn't me," the other guard replied.

There was a moment of silence when the two men realized what that meant.

Mack grabbed Noah buy the arm and hauled him up. "Run," he hissed.

The last thing they heard as they hit the stairs was a disgusted cry. "Oh my God. What is that smell?"

"I think I shit myself." The Russian could barely walk much less run downstairs.

"Then you're walking home," Mack hissed. "You nearly got us caught!"

"Jesus fucking Christ," Noah gagged, gasping for air. "What the fuck? What the fuck is wrong with him?"

"He has digestive issues."

"Oh my God, it's like he slaughtered a cow in his colon."

They burst through the back door of the delivery bay and ran down the alley. A squeal of tires greeted them as the van pulled up. Liv threw open the door. "Get in!"

Mack jumped in first, followed by Noah, and lastly the Russian.

"What the hell happened in there?" Liv yelled.

Noah pointed at the Russian. "He farted."

"Forget all that," Hop growled from the driver's seat. "Did we get it?"

Mack slumped against the wall of the van. "We got it."

Noah hauled his laptop onto his legs, briefly let his head fall back against the wall so he could catch his breath, and then powered it up. He shoved the thumb drive in.

Mack looked at Liv. He wanted to put his arms around her but held off. She looked skittish again, worried. Probably it was because of what had just happened and had nothing to do with them, but he wasn't going to take any chances.

"This is going to take me a while," Noah said. "I need to go through all this shit and see what's here."

"Fine," Mack panted. "The Russian needs a shower anyway."

"False alarm," the Russian said. "It was just a fart."

The drive back to Mack's house was quiet and tense. Noah carried his laptop into the house and set it up at the island in the kitchen. Mack handed out cold beers.

"How long?" he asked Noah.

"I don't know," Noah said, ignoring the beer. "Maybe an hour. Maybe twenty minutes. Leave me alone."

Mack caught Liv's gaze. "I'm going to go change my clothes," he said, hoping she got his hint. The hint being, *I'm going to take my clothes off, and it would be cool if you did too.*

She didn't or was just back to being standoffish. "I'll wait down here," she said.

But when he came back down ten minutes later, she was gone. He found Noah, the Russian, and Hop wearing matching expressions of *oh shit* in front of the computer.

"What?" Mack growled. "Where'd she go?"

"You need to see this," Noah said.

Mack stomped over and looked down at the screen. "I don't understand. Is this a list of former employees?"

Noah gulped. "It's a list of women who've been paid off."

And there at the top was a name he knew.

Alexis Carlisle.

CHAPTER TWENTY-THREE

It was just before closing time at ToeBeans when Liv walked in.

Alexis stood at the counter in her cherry apron, waiting on a woman who was super excited to get the day's last cookies at half price. At the sound of the door, Alexis looked up and then waved with a smile. It died quickly on her lips.

Liv marched around the counter. "I need to talk to you."

Alexis glanced apologetically at the customer, who was signing her credit card slip. "Um, can it wait?"

"No."

Alexis asked the young man working the espresso machine to finish the transaction. Then she turned with an annoyed look to walk into the kitchen. The cook was cleaning the kitchen, so Alexis led Liv to her office. It was no bigger than a bathroom, with barely enough room for a desk, chairs, and filing cabinet. Liv had to wedge herself against the wall to shut the door.

Alexis crossed her arms. "Okay, that was seriously rude out there. What is going on?"

"I have the list."

Alexis swallowed hard. "What list?"

"The list of people who've been paid off by Royce."

Alexis paled and she shook her head. "We've been over this a hundred times. I am not going to tell you anything."

"Your name is on the list!" Her friend jumped at the sound of Liv's shout. Liv didn't have the time or patience to feel bad. "Why is he paying you? Why are you protecting him?"

A spark of fire lit up Alexis's eyes. "I'm not protecting him!"

"You have a chance to help me expose him. Right now. And you're not willing to do it. So I'm sorry, but that makes you no better than any of men who've covered up for him."

Alexis slammed her hands on the desk. "How dare you! How goddamn dare you walk in here and say that to me? You have no idea what you're talking about or what I've been through."

Liv took it all in at once. The shimmer of rage tears in Alexis's eyes. The tremble in her lip. The color in her cheeks.

"Oh my God," Liv breathed, knees weakening, the adrenaline crash making her nauseous. "Oh my God, Alexis. How could you not tell me?"

She instantly regretted the question, but confusion and betrayal had taken hold of her tongue. "You let me work there and never even warned me. After you left, you didn't even warn me what he was like."

Alexis shook with indignation. *"That.* That right there is why I never told you. Because it's all about you. Do you have any idea what it was like for me? Do you even care?"

"You have a responsibility to other women!"

"Do you hear yourself? You walk in here so full of judgment—"

Bile stung Liv's throat. "I'm not judging you."

"Are you serious? All you've talked about since the minute you got fired is how you'd never stay in situation like that and you can't understand a woman who'd let this happen to her."

"That's not true." Except it was. Even Mack had called her out on it.

Alexis's expression turned mournful and furious at once. "Do you honestly think I didn't want to tell you? To unburden myself just once of the secret I was hiding? But I knew that I couldn't. Because you use weakness as a weapon. You're so ashamed of your own mistakes in life, so afraid of your own fragility, that you accuse everyone else around you of being soft just for the crime of basic human frailty."

Her words were like shards of glass. They stabbed, shredded, and left Liv bloody. Somehow Liv's voice found its way through the wreckage to stammer out another weak denial. "That's not true."

"I'm not helping you, Liv. I've endured enough because of Royce Preston. I got out, and it's over for me. And you have no right to expose those women and subject them to something you can't possibly understand. If you want to be the big hero and take on Royce, be my guest. But don't drag us into it just because you have something to prove." Alexis's hand trembled as she pointed to the door. "Now get the hell out of my life and don't come back."

Two hours later, Mack was officially worried because Liv wasn't responding to any of his text messages. Noah, Hop, and the Russian left just after eleven.

Just before midnight, Mack texted again. I'm worried. Just let me know you're OK.

His doorbell rang.

He barely had time to open the door before Liv barged in. He stumbled back in relief and also a little bit of anger. "Christ, Liv, where have you been—"

Her arms went around his neck, and she silenced him with her lips. Even as he went weak-kneed, the logical part of his brain recognized that this wasn't right. Her actions were almost desperate. Something was wrong.

He snaked one arm around her middle and pulled her inside, kicking the door shut with his foot. "What happened?" he mumbled against her lips.

She claimed his mouth again, this time using the distraction to back him into the living room. He went willingly because he was powerless against the way she made him feel, against the havoc she wreaked on his senses with a single touch.

They stopped in the middle of the room, and he broke the kiss with a guttural groan. "Talk to me. What happened with Alexis?"

She burrowed her face into his chest, tangling her fingers in his shirt.

"Liv."

She backed away, letting her arms fall against her side. "She's been lying to me all along. For *years*."

Mack swallowed against the stinging taste of something sour and sinister in his throat.

"She didn't trust me," Liv said, voice flat. "She said I'm judgmental. That I use weakness as a weapon."

The instinctive need to protect her brought his hand to her face. "Then she doesn't know you."

Liv looked up at him with an expression that reminded him of the day when she'd come to his office and demanded that he hire Jessica. Just like that day, her eyes betrayed a battle inside—the need to believe his words, to trust him, but no idea how. But this time Mack was struck with the sickening realization that she had no reason to trust him, to believe him.

Because he was lying to her too.

He had fallen for her. Hard. And he was lying to her.

His voice was like gravel. "Liv—"

She interrupted him. "She's not going to help us. She won't come forward."

"Maybe she just needs time."

"We don't have time!" She shook her head and faced him with an expression that usually preceded words he didn't like. "We don't have time to wait for anyone else to do this."

Mack tilted her face up. "Meaning?"

"This is my fight. I started this. I need to be the one to finish it."

"Liv—"

She pulled from his touch. "The chamber gala is tomorrow night."

"What about it?" he asked, dread making sweat pool under his arms.

"I'm going to do it. I'm going to get him on tape."

CHAPTER TWENTY-FOUR

"It isn't a bad plan, Mack."

Liv, Noah, Hop, Derek, Malcolm, and the Russian sat at the island in Mack's kitchen the next morning. Noah winced as he said the words, as if anticipating Mack's response.

"It's a horrible plan! She can't face him alone."

"I won't be alone," Liv protested. "You guys can listen in—"

"No."

"And Derek will be in the room with me. Royce won't connect us."

Mack clenched his hands into fists. "No. There has to be another way to get a confession."

"How?" Liv countered.

"I don't know," Mack growled.

Noah coughed quietly. "I can get her wired up—"

Mack's had nearly blew off. "Wired up? Do you hear yourself right now?"

Liv tried to calm him down. "We're talking about Royce here. It's not like he's a kidnapper or a murderer."

"You never know what people are capable of when pushed, Liv." He shoved his hands through his hair. "This is a bad idea."

"Do you have a better one?" Liv fired back.

Mack threw up his hands. "Yes, how about anything that doesn't involve you directly confronting Royce? What if he finds out you're recording him?"

"He won't," Noah said.

"How do you know?"

Noah's face went blank, but, like, in a *stop asking questions* way. "Because I know how to do it."

Mack paced for several minutes.

"You have to trust me," Liv said.

"I do trust you. It's Royce I don't trust."

"Then trust that I can handle him. I worked for him for a year. I know what he's like, how to talk to him."

Mack stopped pacing. "I should be going with you."

"No. It'd be way too suspicious."

Mack felt the sour sting of desperation in the back of his throat. "There are too many things that could go wrong."

"I'll be in a public place. What could he possibly do?"

"He could drug your food," Mack said, suddenly scowling.

She laughed. "I won't eat."

"He could stab you under table with syringe full of radiation poison that kills you slowly, said the Russian."

Everyone stared at the Russian. He made a *what* gesture with his hands. "Happens all the time in Russia."

"Here's what I'm thinking," Mack said. "We send two guys ahead of you—"

"No. I have to go alone."

"Two guys he doesn't know and can't connect to you," Mack said. "They can grab a table before you get there and keep an eye on things. If anything bad goes down, they can save you."

"*Save* me?"

Across the room, Hop dragged his hands down his face and muttered something that sounded like, *here we go.*

"It's just a word, Liv."

"I can take care of myself, Mack."

"We should come up with a signal, just in case," Derek said.

"Knock over the salt shaker," Malcolm offered.

The guys all started to nod enthusiastically.

"Was that in one of your books?" Liv asked.

They nodded again.

Mack's scowl deepened.

"Everything is going to be fine," Liv said. "Royce won't do anything in public that could end up on Instagram."

"But what about after? What if he follows you out?"

The Russian cracked his knuckles. "Then I will break his balls."

The shower was running in Liv's apartment when Mack arrived just before five that afternoon. Noah would pick them all up at six. Except for Liv. She would drive herself. Mack had spent a good half hour protesting that part of the plan, but he'd lost.

They hadn't had a single moment alone to talk since last night, and he had things he needed to say before she left. Because something about tonight felt ominous, and he couldn't let her walk out without him making sure she understood a few things. There would be time later for him to tell her the full truth, and he would. But right now, he just needed to—

The shower shut off. Mack cleared his throat. "I'm here," he called out.

"Okay. I'll be out in a second."

She emerged in nothing but a towel. *See Mack drool.* "Liv," he croaked.

"Are you all right?"

"Fine."

She gave him an amused look and walked past him into her tiny kitchen. "I need coffee," she said.

Mack watched her go through the motions of filling the coffeepot. Urgency drove his feet to where she stood. He slipped an arm around her waist and tugged her firmly against him until she was molded against his chest. "Do you feel that?"

"Uh, is this where I'm supposed to say, is that a baseball bat in your pants, or . . . ?"

He ignored her sarcasm. "I'm talking about my heart, Liv."

He felt her breath catch before she exhaled quickly. "It's racing," she whispered.

He lowered his forehead to rest against the back of her head. "It's been like this since the minute you kissed me in that bar, and I can't get it to stop."

"Do—do you want it to stop?"

"Only if yours doesn't race too."

Liv slid her hands to cover his against her stomach. He reacted immediately, lifting his fingers to lace with hers and then curling them together into a tight, tangled fist. Liv rubbed her thumb against his, and he rubbed back. All the while his forehead remained pressed to her head, his breathing warm and fast against her hair, his other hand splayed across her stomach, branding her with his touch.

"Liv," he whispered, the questioning lilt making him sound young and vulnerable. "Am I the only one feeling like this?"

Liv flattened his palm over her pounding heart, his fingers brushing the tender swell of her breast above her wet towel. "I lied to you," she whispered.

Mack froze. "About what?"

"All that stuff about me giving you time to process and not wanting to break your heart?"

He smiled softly. "I remember."

"I was talking about me."

Mack nuzzled her hair, his heart in his throat. "I know."

"I was protecting myself, because . . . I was afraid of getting too close to you."

"Why?" His voice barely sounded human beneath the layer of emotions clogging his throat.

"I don't know how to do this. How to trust."

Trust. There was that word again. That fucking word.

"My father . . ." She paused to swallow. "He used to lie to us all the time. Say he'd call and then not do it. Promise we could spend a week with him during summer break and then have excuses why we couldn't. I don't know how to believe in people."

Believe in me, he silently pleaded. Mack tightened his hold on her, his body trembling with the need to tell her the truth. He could do it. Right now. All he had to do was open his mouth and say the words, tell her the truth about him and that she was the only woman in the world he trusted to know the truth, the only woman he could imagine telling the truth to, and then maybe . . .

Maybe what? She'd understand? Kiss him and make it better?

Or would she walk away in disgust?

Sweat pooled under his arms. With a long exhale, Mack dropped his face to her bare shoulder. She leaned her head back against him and held him as if she sensed that he needed . . . something.

Then she turned her face and kissed him. Sweetly. Softly. "I have to get ready," she said.

And then she slipped from his grasp.

CHAPTER TWENTY-FIVE

"Can you hear me?"

Liv spoke quietly as she stepped off the elevator on the top floor of the Parkway Hotel. Her heels sank into the carpet, and she paused just long enough to steady herself before following the sounds of the gala in the ballroom at the end of the hallway.

"Gotcha, Liv," came Noah's response. "Check in again when you get in the room."

Her stomach clenched with every step. What if she failed? What if Royce refused to talk to her, or what if he did talk to her but revealed nothing? What if he spilled his guts but it was too loud in the ballroom for Noah to pick it up on tape?

"Liv." It was Mack this time, and just the sound of his voice calmed her racing heart. "You don't have to respond, but I just wanted you to know I'm here."

I'm here. Such simple words, but they carried so much meaning. How could someone be so good at saying so much in so few words? How had she misjudged him so completely?

Am I the only one feeling like this?

No, she'd wanted to say. *No, you're not alone. I'm feeling it too.*

She regretted not saying it. She regretted not letting him come with her. She regretted her fear, her insecurities. She regretted that she couldn't be as open with her emotions as other people, that her past made her doubt and distrust. She regretted that she hadn't turned in his arms and told him her heart raced for him too and she never wanted it to stop.

A man in a tuxedo stood by the doorway to the ballroom and greeted her. "Good evening. May I check your ticket, please?"

Liv opened her clutch purse and withdrew the invitation Derek had given her. Satisfied that she wasn't a party crasher, the man smiled and opened the door for her. Liv was hit with the sudden swell of sound—laughter, conversation, clinking glasses, and music from the live oldies band. Twinkling chandeliers cast the room in a soft yellow glow, just low enough to perfectly catch the light of diamond earrings and a hundred sequined dresses. If rich people knew anything, it was how to take advantage of their surroundings.

Liv paused another moment to get her bearings. "I'm in," she said, looking down so people wouldn't notice her talking to herself. "Can you hear me?"

"Loud and clear, Liv."

Relief gave her confidence to walk, to enter the party, to paste a smile on her face. A waiter approached with a tray of champagne flutes. Liv accepted one with a quiet thanks and took a small sip. She didn't really want it, but she feared she'd look out of place if she didn't take it.

"Derek is sitting at a table for the city," Noah said into her ear.

Liv studied the room, which was set up like a wedding. Round tables dotted one half of the room, where people in various levels of formal dress sat with plates of food and drinks. Some tables were reserved, with the names of sponsoring companies on placards high above the floral arrangements. She scanned each card until she found the one for the City of Nashville. Derek and his wife glanced nonchalantly in her direction but quickly looked away.

"I found him," she responded.

"What about Royce?" Mack asked.

On the other side of the room was a long bar surrounded by tall cocktail tables for mingling. In the center was a dance floor that very few people were taking advantage of.

"I don't see him yet," she said softly.

"Look for the flash of cameras," Mack answered. "That'll be him."

Liv smothered a snort of laughter behind the rim of her glass. Once again, she wished he were standing next to her instead of sitting in a van outside. She wanted his hand on her back, his strength and his warmth. She needed him, and the most amazing thing about that was that she wasn't afraid to admit it. She needed him and didn't mind. Was that what it meant to trust someone? Was this how it felt to trust someone?

A round of boisterous laughter from the bar brought her gaze around. A large group of people stood in a circle, fawning over someone who was eating up the attention and the adoration like a dry sponge under a faucet. It could only be Royce. Liv walked closer. The man turned, and her heart stopped. Royce. He tilted his head back to laugh at something a man said, and he patted the guy on the back all buddy-buddy-style. Then a woman asked for a picture, followed quickly by another.

Those people had no idea who he really was. What he was capable of. That behind that amiable facade was a monster.

Which was why she was doing this.

"I see him," she whispered.

"Okay. We'll stay silent after this," Noah said. "But we're here."

"You can do this, Liv," Mack said next. "You're the bravest person I've ever met."

His confidence became hers. Liv squared her shoulders, downed a large gulp of champagne, and stalked forward. She set down her glass on a cocktail table as she approached the group and tucked her purse under her arm. The group was reluctant to let a newcomer into their midst, but Liv finally squeezed through just enough to be seen. She waited for him to turn, to spot her. Her heart beat so loudly that they could probably hear it in the van.

Royce finally looked her way, and there was a split second of disbelief followed by a total lack of emotion. "Olivia," he said, adopting that sickeningly fake voice of his. "What a surprise."

"Hello, Royce."

"You're looking beautiful this evening," he said smoothly.

She shrugged, *aw shucks*–like. "This old thing?"

Curious faces watched their exchange. One of the women standing next to Royce looked on with what could only be described as annoyance that an interloper had stolen his attention. Did the woman not even know Royce was married? Not that he ever let that stop him from engaging in a nighttime snack, but Jesus.

Liv extended her hand to the woman. "Liv Papandreas. I used to work at Savoy."

The woman's smile didn't quite reach her eyes. "Oh, wow! How exciting!"

"It was definitely interesting."

"You're a chef?"

"Olivia *was* a pastry chef," Royce said, interjecting himself because he couldn't help it, but also probably because he was afraid of what Liv would say. Good. She wanted him afraid and nervous.

"What's a pastry chef?" the woman asked.

"Mostly I made desserts. My specialty was the Sultan."

That earned a round of oohs and aahs because everyone had heard about the Sultan.

"I've always wanted to try that," a man said. "Not sure I can afford it, though."

The man laughed nervously then with a glance at Royce, as if afraid he'd insulted him.

Liv waved her hand. "Don't worry. It's just a cupcake. The ingredients actually only cost about two hundred dollars."

Royce's face went stony and dark. He recovered quickly with a laugh. "You're sharing state secrets, Olivia."

The group joined him in a kind of relieved laugh, as if they knew he was simmering.

She briefly pictured Mack in the truck, listening in. It gave her courage to plow forward.

"Royce, I was hoping to steal you away for a moment. May I?" She gestured toward the dance floor.

The woman at his side shot him a wounded look, as if she'd been promised a dance. But Royce was a shark after a meal, and he wasn't going to miss this chance to take a bite out of Liv's torso. Little did he know she was the one who smelled blood in the water. He was wounded and didn't even know it.

He forced another smile, this one sinister. "Of course. I'd love to."

The crowd parted to let him pass as if he were a goddamned

king. Their heavy stares weighed on her back as she led him to the dance floor. The band had just started a slow song, and other couples were quickly joining them.

Liv's skin crawled when Royce placed his hand on her lower back and drew their bodies together. She was going to need an hour-long shower to get clean after this. He smelled like champagne and cologne, a cloying combination that would forever ruin both for her.

Royce gripped her hand more tightly than was necessary, and when he spoke, his voice was a cold, menacing whisper. "What do you think you're doing?"

"Networking. I'm still looking for a job, unfortunately."

Royce's eyes darted around the room as if he was afraid just to be seen with her. She really liked him like this—scared.

"I even applied here," she continued conversationally. "The Parkway was looking for a pastry chef, and I got as far as an interview request, but then poof. They canceled on me for no reason. Don't suppose you know anything about that?"

He clenched his jaw. "It's a tough market."

"Especially when someone is spreading rumors to ruin you."

The fingers on her waist pressed into her flesh. "I warned you."

"Indeed you did."

He met her eyes—his were cold, dark, hard. "If you're looking to apologize, it's too late. You had your chance."

"I actually think of this as *your* chance." Sweat trickled down her back, and she prayed he couldn't feel the dampness through the thin material of her dress.

"Don't even think about threatening me, Olivia. You are way out of your league."

She let out a practiced sigh. "You're right about that. I can't compete with you. You have every former employee from here to the ends of the Earth terrified to say a single bad thing about you."

"You should've come to that realization a lot sooner."

"How about just a truce instead?"

A single overly groomed eyebrow arched as he gazed down at her. "A truce implies we both give up something and get something in return. We're beyond that."

"I only want two small things from you."

"I'm not giving you shit."

She kept going before her body gave in to the urge to tremble. "First, I want you to promise to give Jessica a good recommendation."

A muscle clenched along his jaw. "And second?"

"That you stop trying to ruin me in the industry. I don't need a good recommendation from you. Just stop sabotaging my job interviews."

A look of genuine surprise crossed his face before he covered it with a sarcastic sneer. "I told you. I don't give second chances."

"Are you sure you want to take that risk? I mean, I could just sue you, and then we'd get into things like disclosure, and, God, that would be so messy, and—"

He gave up all pretense of politeness for the sake of appearance. He yanked her hard against his body and glared. "Try it. I will fucking bury you. I have more money than you can dream of."

She shrugged in what she hoped was a calm, casual gesture, but inside she was shaking and on the verge of puking. He still hadn't said anything that couldn't be explained away. "Like I said," she laughed. "It's messy. Wouldn't it just be easier to come to an agreement of some kind?"

He vibrated with rage. "What kind of agreement?"

Liv swallowed hard. "You tell me. What do I have to give you to get you to back off?"

"A signed statement," he hissed.

Her heart stopped. This was . . . this was getting close. "A signed statement saying what?"

"That you didn't see a goddamned thing."

Shit. Was that enough? Did she have him yet? It didn't seem like enough, but if she were smart, she'd agree and leave and hope this did the trick. But she wasn't smart. She was enraged and scared, and when she felt like that, she did crazy things, like opening her and mouth when she should keep it shut.

"Is that how you do it? How you keep your dirty little secret? You intimidate women until they sign statements saying it never happened, they never saw anything, you never touched them?"

Royce let out a weary sigh, as if suddenly tired of having to deal with this inconvenience. "Do you really think I don't know how to do this after all this time?"

Her pulse spiked again, but this time from elation. Holy shit. They had them. She had him! He couldn't possibly explain that away. He was all but admitting it!

"Yes, I suppose you do," she breathed, trying to school her features. "I think I can agree to your terms."

He winked. It made her blood turn to ice. "Good girl. You always were smart."

"Thanks, I think." She tried to back away from him, but he held firm. Her pulse skyrocketed.

"I've always liked you, Olivia. I'm glad we've come to an agreement."

"Me too." Liv tried again to pull away, but his fingers dug into her lower back. She couldn't get away without causing a scene.

Royce smiled in a way that suggested she'd just walked into a trap. A burst of adrenaline filled her veins, and the image of a radio-active syringe came to mind. She realized with a sickening dread that she couldn't even motion to Derek for help. She was facing the wrong way and was hidden in the crowd of other dancers. She could only pray that Noah and Mack were talking to him.

"You know what?" Royce said, his tone way too casual. "In honor of our new truce, I think I'm going to give you some free advice."

"Let me go," she whispered.

"I'm concerned about your choice of companionship lately."

Liv tried to keep a neutral expression, but ice ran through her veins. "I don't know what you're talking about."

"Braden Mack, of course."

Rage made her tremble, her vision blur. "Braden Mack is a thousand times the man you are and always will be. You don't get to say his name. You don't even get to think his name."

"You know what's funny about that?" Once again, Royce's face became calm. Frighteningly so. As if she'd just given him the perfect segue. "His name is exactly the problem."

Mack could hear voices, but they were muted and murky beneath the roaring of blood in his ears. The van was suddenly too small, too hot, too fucking far away from her.

"Dude, are you listening to this?" It might have been Noah who said it, but Mack was too focused on getting through to Liv before it was too late.

"Liv," he said into the microphone. "Liv, listen to me. Get away from him. Now."

Her voice through the earpiece was suddenly timid as she spoke to Royce. "Wh-what are you talking about?"

"Liv, please." Shit. Please, God, she couldn't find out like this. She couldn't find out from *him*. "You have to listen to me."

Noah leaned into his mic. "Derek, what's going on in there? Can you see them?"

If Derek answered, Mack didn't hear. He could only hear Liv. And Royce. And the sound of his entire life crashing down.

Royce's voice filled the van. "See, that's what I was afraid of, Olivia. That he didn't tell you the truth. You should be thanking me for saving you from that . . . that murderer's son."

Hop grabbed Mack's arm. "What the hell is he talking about, Mack?"

Mack shook Hop off and once again tried to plead with Liv. "Babe, please. Listen to me."

"You're a fucking liar," Liv hissed. But the tremble in her voice betrayed her through the microphone.

"Mack is the liar, Olivia."

Mack's stomach lurched. He was going to be sick. It couldn't come out like this. *I hate liars.* Why hadn't he told her the truth when he'd had the chance?

"Or should I say McRae? That's his real name. Braden McRae."

"Liv, please." Mack dragged his hands over his hair. Noah was yelling at Derek. Hop was yelling at Mack.

Mack heard none of it as Royce continued. "Son of Josh McRae. Murderer. Wife beater. Serving a life sentence at the Iowa State Penitentiary."

Liv sounded small when she spoke. "You're lying. His father is dead."

"Liv," Mack tried again. His voice was broken.

"Let me go," Liv pleaded.

There was a rustling sound and then Royce's sinister voice. "I always win, Olivia. Always."

Another rustling sound and then panting. As if she were running.

Mack swallowed hard. "Liv, listen to me."

"Shit!" That was from Derek.

"What's going on?" Mack demanded, sweat dripping down his face.

Hop grabbed his arm again. "You sonuvabitch. What fucking lies have you been telling her?"

Mack yelled into the microphone. "Derek, what is happening?"

"She's leaving. I'm trying to follow."

Mack crawled to the back doors of the van—

Noah grabbed his arm. "Mack, what are you doing?"

Mack threw open the doors and leaped from the van.

"Mack, wait!" Noah yelled. "If he sees you, you'll blow this entire thing!"

Footsteps pounded behind him as he ran toward the back of the building. Noah grabbed him and swung him around and— what the fuck?—tossed him effortlessly against the wall. Where the hell had that strength come from?

Mack shoved at him. "Get the fuck off me. I have to find Liv."

Noah grabbed his shoulders and held him against the wall. "She's gone, man. She left."

Mack threw Noah's arms off. "What do you mean she's gone?"

"Derek said she took off. He doesn't see her. And you can't go running in there."

"I have to talk to her," Mack said, sinking against the cold brick. "I have to . . . I have to tell her. I have to tell her why."

Noah bent at the waist, panting. When he stood, he wiped his forearm across his brow. "Get back in the van. That's all we can do right now."

No. That wasn't all he could do. He had to find her. Before he lost her forever.

CHAPTER TWENTY-SIX

It was nearly eleven o'clock when the Uber pulled into Thea's driveway. The only light in the house was from the master bedroom, which probably meant Thea was still awake and reading. Or having phone sex with Gavin. Either way, Liv regretted having to interrupt.

After ditching the gala, she had driven aimlessly, phone off, heart bleeding. She'd run out of gas just outside of downtown and had called for a car to bring her here. Liv thanked the driver and got out. She glanced up at the house just in time to see the bedroom curtain peel back. At least she wouldn't have to knock. Her shoes wobbled on the uneven brick sidewalk that led to the front porch. The porch light flickered on when she reached the steps, and then the door swung open.

Thea walked out in a sweatshirt and flannel pajama pants. "Oh my God, where have you been? Everyone is going crazy—oh my God, what's wrong?"

And then, for the first time in a long while, Liv threw herself into her sister's arms and burst into tears.

* * *

Twenty minutes later, Thea rose from the couch and started to pace. "There has to be a reason he lied."

"Does it matter?"

"Of course it matters! He didn't just lie to *you*. He lied to everyone. There has to be a reason. Don't you want to give him a chance to tell you why?"

Liv shook her head. "I can't think right now. I don't know what I want." She choked on her own emotion. "I knew better than to fall for him."

"Yet you did anyway. That should tell you something."

Yeah. That she was a fucking fool.

Thea sank down next to her on the couch and took her hands. "I know you have a hard time trusting people, but—"

"This isn't about trust! It's about how I never seem to be worth the truth!"

Liv shook as the words exploded from her mouth, shocked that she'd actually said it out loud. Thea sank against the couch cushions. "What does that even mean?"

"*You're not worth all this trouble.*" Liv whispered. "That's what he said."

"*Who?*"

"Dad."

Thea shook her head. "When? When did he say that to you?"

"That day when I took the bus to see him."

Thea's shoulders slumped with the weight of the memory. The horrible memory of the day Liv ran away at thirteen, hopped on a bus, and showed up at their father's house for the summer visit he'd promised.

"All those years, he'd been lying to us, telling us that he just didn't have time or space for us, and instead . . ." She shrugged. "It was a lie. He had a massive house. He just didn't want to fight with his new wife." Who'd wanted nothing to do with them. Who'd refused to let them live there or visit.

Thea took Liv's hands again. "I don't understand. When did he say—"

"That I'm not worth the trouble? Before he put me back on a bus and sent me home."

Thea paled. "You said you came home on your own. That he wasn't even there when you showed up. That *she* was the only one there."

"I didn't want you to know." Irony brought a sad laugh from her burning chest. "I lied."

Thea's face crumpled. "Oh, Liv. I'm so sorry." And then suddenly rage replaced Thea's sorrow. "God, I am so sick of us paying the price for our parents' bullshit." Thea dropped to her knees in front of Liv. "Listen to me. I almost lost Gavin because of the baggage that they saddled us with. Don't lose Mack over it too."

"This is different."

"How?"

"I—it just is."

Thea's eyes managed to convey both pity and disappointment in a single glance. Liv hated both. She looked away. She couldn't explain something to Thea that she barely understood herself.

Thea's phone trilled softly with an incoming call. She pulled it from her pocket and looked at the screen. Her eyes immediately flew to Liv's. "It's him again."

Liv's stomach dropped. "Don't answer it."

"Liv, he's so worried. He's going crazy."

"I—"

Thea answered at the last second. She didn't bother with a greeting. "She's here."

Mack raced inside Thea's house, his face stormy and his voice thunderous. He ignored Thea, palmed the back of Liv's head, and crushed his mouth onto hers.

He pulled back just enough to rest his brow on hers. "Do you have any fucking idea how worried I've been?"

A squeak from near the stairs was his first indication of Thea's presence.

"I'm going to just, uh, go upstairs, I think, and let you guys talk," Thea said. Her feet beat a soft staccato up the stairs.

Mack ignored her as his scattered thoughts cataloged Liv's appearance like puzzle pieces he couldn't fit together. Red dress. Soul-shattering curves. Curly hair long and loose atop bare shoulders.

Eyes that had once gazed upon him with passion now stared with betrayal.

"Braden McRae," she whispered.

His hands fell to his sides. "I don't use that name anymore."

"Why did you lie to me?"

Mack looked at the floor. "Because I've been lying to everyone for so long I didn't know how to tell you the truth." He lifted his gaze, and his heart shattered at her blank expression. "My father was an abusive alcoholic who used to beat my mother. Us too. My brother and me. We weren't spared."

A tear slipped down Liv's cheek. "Oh, Mack. I'm sorry."

Mack dragged a hand over his hair. "One night he got in a fight at a bar, and he killed a man. No remorse. Just nothing but anger. And then he came home and continued to take it out on her."

His voice cracked, but he couldn't stop. He wouldn't, not until she knew everything. "The thing is, I was there when it happened. And I didn't do anything. I was too scared to protect her. I grabbed my little brother and hid in the fucking closet like a goddamned coward until it was over, and by then, it was too late. I thought she was dead when I found her."

Tears dripped from her chin. He wondered if she even knew she was crying.

"You asked me why I started reading romance."

She nodded, sniffling.

"It was when she was in the hospital. I found one in the waiting room while she was in surgery." He looked at Liv, but he didn't really see her. His brain and mouth were no longer connected. The whole world wavered like he'd been dropped into the deep end of a pool. Everything was murky, thick, confusing. "I loved those stories. Not because of the sex, although"—he managed a sad laugh—"they really did teach me everything I know. I loved them because good people always won in those books. Men were always heroic, and if they weren't, they got what was coming to them. Always."

He shook his head. "I changed my name when I was eighteen. Legally. I didn't want anything connected to him."

Liv rose and walked toward him. He wanted to grab her and hold her, but her body language screamed KEEP AWAY.

"Braden," she whispered.

His heart skipped at the sound of his real name on her lips.

"I'm so sorry you went through all that."

"I should have told you," he said, voice thick.

"Why didn't you?"

"I—"

"You had so many chances to tell me," she said, her voice getting stronger. "How many times did we talk about your father? You lied to my face."

"We barely knew each other at first, Liv. Why would I tell you something that I've been lying about to everyone for years?"

It was the wrong thing to say. Her face became a mask of calm certainty. "You're right," she said. "We barely knew each other. Maybe we still don't. Which is why this entire thing between us has been crazy. But that's all it was. A crazy little fling, and now—"

Mack shook his head. "Don't say it."

"Maybe it's best that we just end it now."

Pain sliced through him as sharply as if she'd stabbed in the chest. "Why? Nothing has changed. Nothing. My name doesn't change the fact that I have never felt like this before."

She waved a hand, sarcasm taking over like a suit of armor. "You'll get over it. Next week someone else will drop a cupcake in your lap."

"Knock it off with the bullshit. It's childish."

Her face flashed with shame.

He turned around and laced his hands on top of his head. The floor wavered before his gaze. "I'm just a man with a heart," he said, turning back around. "Whether my name is Braden Mack or Braden McRae. I'm just a man with a heart, and you're breaking it."

"I can't do this," she whispered, sinking onto the couch.

"You think this is easy for me?" He dropped to his knees in front of her. "I'm scared shitless right now because I have no idea what that look on your face means. And after what we've shared, if you kicked me out right now, I'm not sure I'd recover."

Cupping the back of her head, he forced her to look at him. "Give me a chance. Please."

Her gaze locked with his, challenging him.

His hand moved around to her cheek.

"I never planned on you," she said.

"I never planned on you either," he said, his voice low and husky. "But we can figure this out. We can make this work. I'll never lie to you again about anything. Just *trust me*."

And that's when he lost her.

Her face went slack. Her eyes went blank. She pulled away from. "I'm sorry. I can't do this."

Mack barely felt his body as he stood. "Are you sure this is what you want?"

"It doesn't matter. This will always be between us. I'll always be wondering if you're telling me the truth."

Mack went numb. "I'm not your father, Liv."

Her eyes went dark. "And I'm not the princess from your romance novels. This is one story that's not going to have a happy ending."

Mack didn't remember leaving. Didn't remember driving his car. Didn't remember anything except sitting in his driveway.

There was no happy ending for him. There never would be.

And he was a fucking fool for ever believing there could be.

CHAPTER TWENTY-SEVEN

For the first time in her life, Liv was grateful to be unemployed with zero responsibilities.

The next morning, Thea drove Liv back to the farm, where Liv immediately climbed into bed. She stayed there all day with the blankets over her head and a box of tissues at the ready. She rose three times to pee and one time to tip the crumbs from a bag of Doritos down her throat. Shortly after seven that night, Rosie knocked quietly on her bedroom door and told her she'd left tuna noodle casserole on the table.

It was still there, uneaten and cold, the next morning when Liv got up in search of some pain medication for the headache that had developed in the middle of the night. Guilt added to the pounding in her head. She should have at least acknowledged Rosie last night, thanked her for the food and for letting her neglect her farm duties yesterday.

Liv dragged her fingers through her tangled hair, grimacing when she discovered a massive rat's nest in the far back. God, she needed to get her shit together. This was why she hated crying. Because once she started, she couldn't stop, and what a useless waste of time. She'd lost an entire day of her life crying over him.

And no, she didn't feel better. She felt worse.

She didn't feel cleansed. She felt hungover.

And she didn't feel refreshed or whatever other self-help bullshit emotion she was supposed to feel after a good cry. No. She felt like a dirty Raggedy Ann doll hanging on by a few thin threads after being dragged through a mud puddle and tossed around by a dog.

Because something had broken inside her. Mack had broken something inside her. And maybe that, above all else, was the thing she hated him for.

She threw her hair in a ponytail, splashed some water on her face—scrubbing for a moment at the orange stains on the corners of her mouth. Then she changed into fresh clothes and opened the door to her apartment for the first time in hours.

She paused on the stairs to see whether the world felt different. But nope. She was greeted by the same sounds as any other day. Randy squawked in his tree. The goats bleated. *Move along*, the world seemed to say. Nothing to see here. Just a girl with a broken heart and a lesson learned.

There were only two eggs in the nesting boxes, and a dusting of feed on the ground told her Rosie had already tended to the hens. A surge of determination straightened her spine. This was officially the last day Rosie would have to pick up the slack for her.

She marched into the house, planted her hands on her hips, and got ready to say just that to Rosie. But she didn't get a word out because Rosie turned from the sink, titled her head, and said, "Oh, honey. I promise it will get better."

And, goddammit, the tears started again. Liv let out an *argh* and stomped to the sink. "I am so fucking sick of this."

She splashed more water on her face. Rosie rubbed a slow circle in the center of her back. "Hungry?"

"Is there any tuna noodle casserole left?"

"Got a plate waiting in the fridge for you. Sit down. I'll heat it up."

Liv thought about protesting and saying she could do it herself, but she was out of energy again. Rosie puttered unobtrusively around the kitchen as Liv shoveled hefty forkfuls into her mouth. When her plate was clean, Rosie wordlessly took it away and rinsed it in the sink.

"I made chocolate pie too," Rosie said, her back to Liv.

Guilt clanged again against her temples. "I'm sorry about last night," Liv said.

Rosie looked over her shoulder, confusion tugging her brows together. "What do you mean?"

"I ignored you when you brought me food. And you had to do all my chores."

Rosie snorted and put the plate in the dishwasher. "Honey, you were in no condition to do anything yesterday or last night. You don't need to apologize. Sometimes the best thing a girl can do is spend the day feeling sorry for herself." She turned around and pointed. "Just as long as she gets up the next day and gets back to work."

"I know. I'm sorry. I promise I won't do it again."

"Livvie, I am not talking about the damn chickens."

Liv nodded. "I'm going to start looking for a job again—"

"I'm not talking about that either." Rosie marched back to the island. "I'm talking about Royce."

Liv groaned and shook her head. "I don't even care anymore."

Which wasn't true. But it felt good to pretend it was true. Her capacity for teetering on the edges of emotional cliffs had reached its limit. She needed the comfort of gravity for a while.

"Nonsense," Rosie said. "You're just feeling sorry for yourself."

"I thought you said I deserved to feel sorry for myself."

"That was yesterday. Today I need you to pick up the pieces and carry on."

Shame drew Liv's gaze to her lap. "I feel like I made things worse."

"It feels that way because you poked the bear and the bear attacked. He struck you right where it hurts most, and now you're nursing your wounds and scared to finish the fight."

"Maybe this isn't my fight."

Rosie slammed her palm on the island. "Bullshit!"

Liv jumped in her chair and snapped her head up. She'd never heard Rosie raise her voice like that. Not even at Hop.

Rosie pointed her finger again. "This is every woman's fight, Olivia Papandreas. And I know you didn't ask for it, but this one landed in your lap. Jessica is counting on you. Alexis is counting on you. Every woman on that damn list is counting on you. And *I* am counting on you."

Rosie's expression softened at the last part, and then she rounded the island to stand next to Liv's chair. She reached over and smoothed an escaped knot of hair back from Liv's forehead, a gesture that brought another sheen of tears to her eyes.

"I'm counting on you to finish what my generation started, Livvie. What generations of women have started but couldn't finish."

Liv snorted, grateful for a reason to do so. "Let's not go overboard here. I'm just a pastry chef, Rosie."

"History was built by thousands of women who thought they

were *just* housewives or *just* secretaries or *just* seamstresses until the day they got fed up and decided to fight back."

A memory brought a smile to Liv's lips. "My Gran Gran used to say something like that. *There's no force on Earth as strong as a woman who is good and fed up.*"

"Your grandma was a wise woman."

"Yeah, well, she also used to believe that if all the cows were lying down in the field, it meant rain was coming, so . . ."

"See? Wise woman."

Liv sucked in a shaky breath. "I've made such a mess of things," she said after a moment.

Rosie nodded. "Nothing that can't be fixed."

"I need to apologize to Alexis."

"Yes, you do. We need our female friends. Royce has destroyed enough. Don't let him destroy that too." Rosie nodded crisply. "Now, I have something for you, and this seems like as good a time as any to give it to you because you need a boost of confidence."

Rosie crossed the kitchen and went into the living room. Liv turned and watched as she opened the drawer to her desk and withdrew a thick envelope.

"What's this?" Liv asked as Rosie returned and handed it to her.

"My will."

The air escaped her lungs in one panicked exhale. "I swear to God, Rosie, if you tell me that you're dying right now, I will kill you."

"I'm not dying. I'm going on vacation."

Liv sank into her chair. "Thank God."

"I wanted to get this taken care of before I left."

"Get what taken care of?"

"I'm adding you to the will."

The tiny bit of oxygen Liv had managed to suck back into her lungs once again rushed out. "You can't," she stammered, shaking her head. That emotional cliff was tugging at her again. "You can't."

"It's done. I met with my attorneys last week."

Liv could only form one word. *"Why?"*

"Because I'm old. I want to retire, travel, have more sex with Hop before he can't get it up anymore."

Liv winced.

"And because the day you showed up here was the best day of my life."

Liv gave up and just covered her face with her hands. What was the point of fighting tears at this point? Rosie's hand settled on her shoulder, warm and reassuring. "I gained a daughter that day. A daughter I didn't even know I needed."

Liv wiped her nose with the back of her hand and hiccupped. "I thought the day Neil Young threw a sweaty T-shirt at you from his tour bus was the best day of your life."

"You're right. Your showing up here was the second-best day of my life."

"I don't know what to say," Liv whispered, staring at the envelope on the counter.

"You don't have to say anything." Rosie smoothed her hair again. "Just be the woman I know you are. A woman who makes me proud."

But could she be a woman who made herself proud? Liv stood on shaky legs. Rosie was only the second person in her entire life who had ever said those words to her. She backed away, but in every direction was that fucking cliff. Her arms were helicoptering, and the fear of falling was draining her muscles. "I'm scared," she finally whispered.

"Of what?"

"Disappointing you."

Rosie let out an incredulous noise. "That's the second-dumbest thing you've said today. You couldn't disappoint me if you tried."

Liv looked at her feet. The floor wavered in her watery vision. "Alexis was right about me. I *am* judgmental. I'm so scared of my own weaknesses that I punish other people for theirs. I . . . I don't make it easy for people to trust me. To *love* me."

Rosie made a sympathetic noise. "Whoever made you think that, they don't deserve you."

Liv didn't realize she'd closed her eyes until she felt the warm pressure of Rosie's hands on her cheeks. "Look at me, honey."

Liv obeyed and lifted her gaze. Rosie's eyes were warm, loving, *proud*. "Whatever was broken in that person, it was *their* wound." Rosie's thumb brushed away a tear. "You don't have to carry the scar of it for them anymore. You're allowed to let it go, Liv. All of it. Let yourself be loved and *let it go*."

Liv let Rosie pull her into an embrace and sobbed on her shoulder. How could she just let it go? How did someone just one day decide this was the day they were going to heal? She couldn't. And now she'd lost the only man she'd ever loved.

And she did love him. So, so much. The image of him had haunted her all night. His defeated smallness . . . She'd done that to him. He'd told her the truth, and she'd turned him away because of her own fucking insecurities. How could he possibly forgive her?

Liv pulled away and wiped her face.

Rosie did another one of those *now that that's settled* inhales. "But first you need to take care of yourself. Go brush your hair. Take a hot bath. Drink a glass of wine. I'll bring over some chocolate pie and send Hop to get your car."

Liv's voice broke. "I love you, Rosie."

"I know you do, sweetie. And I love you too." She pointed to the door. "Now go. I got shit to do."

She did what Rosie told her to. She returned to her apartment and brushed her hair. Drank a glass of wine. Took a hot bath. She sank low in the water and let it wash away the fresh tears.

An hour later, she wrapped a towel around her body and walked into her kitchen with the empty wineglass. A book on her table caught her attention.

The Protector.

What the . . . ? Where had that come from?

A note stuck out of the top.

A friend gave me this to read. Thought you might like it.
   —Hop

Liv snorted out a laugh. Hop . . . had given her a romance novel?

There was a postscript beneath his name.

Page 245. Fear is a powerful motivator, but so is love.

Fear is a powerful motivator. Those were the same words Mack—Braden—had said to her. Liv carried the book to the couch and flipped through the pages until she found 245.

Ellie's hands dove into Chase's hair again. "Whatever happened before this minute doesn't matter. We can start over."

"How?" The word—muffled against the hot, fragrant skin of her throat—was a plea from deep down inside him that desperately wanted to believe it was actually possible.

"Look at me." Her hands slid around to his face, gently urging him to lift his head. He did, but only far enough to press his forehead to her cheek.

"We just start over." She tugged his face higher until they were brow to brow. "We forget the past."

"Just like that?"

"No. Not *just like that*. I'm scared and confused and feel completely exposed and vulnerable right now, and those are emotions I've spent a long time trying not to feel. I'm not saying this is going to be easy. I just know that trying to stay away from each other hasn't worked out so well for us. Maybe forgiving each other and starting over will."

Chase clung to her words. He soaked in them, floated on them, felt the weight of guilt and burden rise from his shoulders for the one blissful second when he believed them.

He wanted to stay in this suspended reality where he could be forgiven and where he could deserve her. Where the past, the *truth*, didn't matter. Where he could take what she offered—a second chance, redemption, her. He wanted to be worthy of it—the adoration, the absolution, the forgiveness. He wanted to be the man he saw in her eyes when she looked at him the way she was looking at him now.

And all he had to do was choose.

Honor or selfishness.

Happiness or loneliness.

The choice terrified him, but was there really a choice to be made?

Fear was a powerful motivator. But so was love.

* * *

Several hours later, Liv closed the book and set it on the couch next to her hip. The towel had long since dried around her body, but her hair was cold and clammy beneath the one twisted atop her head.

She had once wrecked her bike as a kid and scraped the skin all up her arm. Her soul felt a lot like that right now. Raw and tender.

Mack had been motivated by fear and love when he lied to her. And she'd thrown both back in his face. Because she'd only been motivated by fear. By weakness. Liv's throat burned with another wave of tears, but she shook them off. She didn't have time for any more crying.

It was almost nine o'clock at night, but she couldn't put this off any longer, nor did she want to. She had apologies to make. She dug through the basket of clean clothes in her bedroom for a pair of yoga pants and a sweatshirt. She dressed quickly, combed out her damp hair, and shoved her feet into tennis shoes.

A half hour later, she found a parking spot in front of Alexis's café.

The OPEN sign was still on, but the café was empty. Liv pushed open the door and heard Alexis yell from the kitchen. "Be right out."

Beefcake peeked out from behind the counter and then shrank away again. Liv imagined him teaming up with Howler to plot their next move. *She's back. You run out just in time to trip her, and then I'll go for the throat.*

A moment later, Alexis came out with a beaming smile—which died on her lips when she saw Liv. "Oh."

The hesitation in her tone sent a chill straight through Liv. There was no easy way to do this. "I'm so sorry, Alexis."

Alexis froze. The only sign of life was a single blink. But then she swallowed, and without a word, she walked past Liv to the door. Liv winced, expecting her friend to toss her out. Instead, Alexis turned the OPEN sign to CLOSED. Her hand hovered over the glass for a second, a slight tremble visible in her fingers.

She turned around again. Her face had lost its color.

Liv sucked in a breath and let it out. "I'm sorry that I wasn't a good enough friend that you felt you could trust me with the truth. I'm sorry that I saw the world in such a black-and-white way that I couldn't see what you were trying to tell me."

Alexis, inexplicably, sighed and waved her hands. "Stop."

Liv shook from the inside out. "O-okay."

Alexis managed a weak half smile. "I owe you an apology too."

"No, you don't."

"I said some unforgivable things to you."

"I needed to hear them."

"No one deserves to hear those things."

Liv took several steps closer to her. "But you were right. I've spent so much of my life ashamed of my own weakness that I've turned it against people, expected them to live up to a standard I couldn't meet myself."

"And I lashed out at you to cover my own shame."

Indignation on Alexis's behalf puffed Liv's chest out. "But you didn't do anything wrong! Royce is a piece of shit who forced you into this position!"

Alexis laughed softly. "I wish I had it in me to fight the way you do."

"Alexis, that's not—"

"You know what, though?" Alexis said, cutting her off. "It's oddly freeing to have someone know. I'm so fucking tired of living with this."

Liv's eyes widened. "You said the F-word."

"I know. It seemed the appropriate time to do it."

"I would agree."

Alexis looked at the ceiling and sucked in a deep breath. She let it out as she lowered her gaze. "I need a drink."

"Girl, same."

Liv followed Alexis into the kitchen, keeping her eyes peeled for Beefcake and Howler. They'd been unsupervised long enough to have acquired weapons. Alexis walked to the far end of the kitchen and withdrew a can of Coke from the fridge. Liv laughed out loud when it was followed by a bottle of whiskey.

"Maybe just the whiskey," she suggested.

Alexis nodded. "Definitely."

Two shots later, they sat on the floor of the kitchen, their backs pressed to the cold stainless-steel counter.

"My mom was sick," Alexis said.

"I know."

"He was offering me all this money, and all I had to do was keep my mouth shut, and suddenly it was like I had a way out. Not just from the harassment or the hell of that job but a way out for my mom. He was offering me enough money to pay off her medical expenses, to give her a real funeral, and—"

She looked around, hands gesturing just wildly enough to reflect the booze in her system.

"To open your own café," Liv finished.

"To live my dream."

"There is no reason to be ashamed of any of that."

"I know that logically. And probably, if I were in your shoes, I'd be telling me the same thing. But it's different when it actually happens to you."

"How long did it go on?"

"It started almost as soon as I got there."

Liv lost her breath. "That was over a year."

"Yep. A year of complete humiliation." Alexis's voice hardened. "A year of learning how to avoid him, how to pretend it didn't matter. A year of believing I had to put up with it to protect my career and everything I'd worked so hard for."

"Did he—I mean, how far did he take it?" Liv didn't know how else to ask the question and felt guilty for even asking it.

"You mean did I sleep with him?"

"It doesn't matter. I shouldn't have asked."

"Yes."

She said it so softly that Liv wasn't even sure what she meant at first. But the look on Alexis's face gave it away.

"You asked why I'm ashamed. That's why. I gave in to him. What does that make me?"

Alexis didn't wait for Liv to answer. She stumbled to her feet, a gag evident in her throat. Liv watched helplessly as Alexis raced to the garbage can and retched.

Liv walked to her friend and hugged her from behind. "It's okay. It's going to be okay."

Alexis braced her hands on the edges of the trash can, panting and sweating. Liv gripped her shoulders and forced her to turn around.

"What does that make you?" she asked, cupping her friend's cheeks the same way Rosie and done to her earlier. "It makes you a survivor."

Tears dripped down Alexis's cheeks. "I slept with him. *Willingly*, Liv."

"It wasn't consensual. Not in a real way. And even if it were, who gives a fuck? He had power over you. He knew you were vulnerable because of your mom. He took advantage of that. Of *you*. And you did the only thing you thought you could to protect yourself and your mom." Liv remembered the book with a small smile. *"Fear is a powerful motivator, but so is love."*

Alexis's face crumbled, and she gave in to her sobs. She bent and pressed her forehead to Liv's shoulder, and Liv held her like that. Rocked her. Rubbed her hands up and down her friend's back until sobs became hiccups and hiccups became shaky breaths. Until it was over.

Alexis pulled back with a groan and turned around, her hands swiping at her cheeks. "God, I hate crying."

"I know. I've done enough of it in the past twenty-four hours to last a lifetime."

"Why?" Alexis sniffed, turning around again.

Oh. Right. She didn't know about Mack. Liv shrugged and brought her up to date.

Alexis's mouth dropped open. "Wow. There's been a lot going on in your life."

"Pretty much."

"And . . . it's over with him?"

A lumped formed in Liv's throat. "I said some unforgivable things to him."

Alexis tilted her head then, and Liv knew something profound and very Alexis-like was about to be stated. "Maybe he needed to hear them."

Liv groaned and rolled her eyes. "I had that coming, didn't I?"

"Yep."

God, what if she'd ruined everything? "He didn't need to hear them, though. He needed me to be understanding, to hold him. And I didn't."

Alexis put a hand on her arm. "Deep breaths."

Liv returned to the counter, poured another shot, and fired it back. Alexis joined her and did the same.

"You know what I really want to do?" Alexis asked as she set her glass down.

"Get sloppy drunk and bitch about men?"

"No. Well, yes. But I'm talking about after that."

"What do you want to do?"

Alexis poured two more shots and handed one to Liv. "Destroy Royce Preston."

Liv clinked their glasses. Because this was one thing she could get right. "Girl, same."

CHAPTER TWENTY-EIGHT

For the first time in his life, Mack wished he were unemployed.

Because after leaving Liv, he'd stumbled home, grabbed an unopened bottle of Jameson, and carried it to bed with no intention of going anywhere near his clubs or a single living person for as long as it took to forget the taste of her, the feel of her, the memory of her.

For three days, he hadn't showered. Barely ate. Ignored every phone call and text. Threw some shit. Broke some shit. But mostly he slept and drank, and when he drank too much, he thought really, really hard about calling and leaving her slurred voice mails, but thank God he didn't because sometimes he even cried.

Because his heart was hemorrhaging in his goddamned chest.

On day four, his bedroom door crashed open. "Oh my God, what the fuck is that smell?"

He rolled over. His friends stood in the doorway with matching expressions of disgust on their faces.

"What do you want?" he growled.

"We're here to save you," Gavin said, "but I think we're going to need gas masks."

"Fuck off."

Gavin held his hand over his nose and mouth. "Seriously, Mack. It smells like a camel exhibit in here. Have you been, like, pissing all over yourself or something?"

Mack grabbed a pillow and threw it. It landed ten feet from them. "Go away."

With a dramatic gag, Gavin stepped over the pillow and a pile of dirty clothes and went into the bathroom. Mack heard the spray of the shower a moment later.

"Hose yourself off, asshole," Gavin said when he walked back out. "Now. And then come downstairs. It's time for a fucking intervention."

The door slammed shut as they left.

Mack stared at the ceiling. Fuck them. He didn't need an intervention. He needed to be left alone to wallow in his misery. He dragged a hand down his scruffy jaw, caught a whiff of his own stench, and realized they were right about at least one thing. He could use a shower.

His stiff muscles protested as he sat up and swung his legs off the bed. He couldn't remember the last time he'd gone this long without at least running. The hot water pounded at knots in his shoulders he'd been too depressed to even notice.

There was a poetic justice to it, of course. The founder of the Bromance Book Club, the man who believed the manuals had all the answers, who thought he knew everything there was to know about love, brought down by a woman.

Except, that wasn't true, was it? He'd brought himself down. He'd violated one of the most important rules: never, ever lie.

There'd been a thousand chances to tell Liv the truth, but he hadn't. Even after she'd confided in him about her painful past, he'd convinced himself he just needed more time to find the right words. He'd ignored everything he'd ever learned from the books, forgotten every hard-fought lesson the heroes had had to learn, and now it was too late.

Mack scrubbed his hands over his face and leaned into the hot water. The scalding downpour became a punishment, a reprimand, a stinging cleanse. It would take a thousand blistering showers to wash away the tattooed imprint of her on his body, and even that wouldn't be enough to scrub his brain or his heart of the memories of what it had been like to finally, fully, fiercely fall in love. The manuals never offered advice on how to survive an *un*happy ever after. He was officially on his own.

Fifteen minutes later he finally emerged from his bedroom and headed downstairs. The Russian met him in the hallway leading to the kitchen. "You need a hug, yes?"

"Not really—*mrph*." The Russian pulled him into an awkward, muscle-bound embrace. His face was smooshed against the Russian's shoulder, and it actually felt kind of good, so he stayed there for a moment and closed his eyes. Hugs were underrated.

"You smell much better," the Russian said, pulling back.

At least he had that going for him.

When Mack walked into the kitchen, he found the guys in various stages of cleaning. Malcolm wore rubber gloves that barely fit over his massive fingers and was scrubbing the sink, which was miraculously clear of the dirty dishes that had slowly piled up.

"This place was a mess, man," Del said without looking up from where he was scraping at something sticky on the counter. "I've never seen it like that before."

"I've had a bad few days."

"No shit," Gavin said. "There was a piece of pizza on the floor that was about to gain independent thought and stage a coup."

"Christ, it's only been four days."

They all stopped and stared.

"What?" he barked.

"It's been *five* days," Gavin said.

His lungs vacated oxygen. Five days? He'd lost an entire day? How the fuck had that happened? Shit. Had Liv tried to call him? When was the last time he'd even checked?

"Where's my phone?" he breathed.

Gavin shrugged. Mack turned and ran back upstairs. He ripped blankets off the bed, threw pillows over his shoulder. Nothing. Where was it? He dropped to the floor and looked under the bed. There. He grabbed it and turned it over. Tried to turn it on. Swore a blue streak when he realized it was dead. He grabbed his charger and ran back downstairs.

Malcolm was pulling something out of the microwave when he returned to the kitchen. The smell of whatever it was sparked a vicious growl in Mack's empty stomach, but he barely glanced at it as he plugged in his phone. His thumbs tapped a nervous beat on the counter as he waited for the white screen of life to appear.

"Come sit down and eat," Malcolm said, walking behind him with a plate.

Mack ignored him as he hit the power button again, but he got the same empty-battery image.

"I'm not going to tell you again," Malcolm said.

Mack's stomach growled again, so he gave in. He sat in a chair along the island, and Malcolm set the plate and a bottle of water in front of him.

Mack leaned forward and stared at his plate. "What is this?"

"Chicken pot pie."

"You found that in my freezer?"

"No, I brought it."

Mack lifted an eyebrow. "Why?"

"You're seriously going to complain about the food I brought? You've been living on bourbon and Cheez-Its for a week."

"Whiskey. Not bourbon."

"Same fucking thing."

"It's not, actually," Gavin said. "All bourbon is whiskey, but not all whiskey is bourbon."

"Christ," Malcolm muttered, tugging on his beard. He pointed at Mack's plate. "My mom used to make me those when I was sick. I thought you could use some comfort food."

Mack tested a couple of bites. His taste buds rejoiced, but his stomach rebelled at the presence of real food. The pot pie turned to rock as soon as it hit his gut. He guzzled the water instead.

Across from him, the guys stood in a straight line, watching expectantly. "I'm alive," he muttered. "You can go now."

Del snorted as if to say, *yeah, right.* "You think we'd leave you alone right now?"

"I want to be alone."

"No, you don't," Gavin said.

"Yes, I do."

"Tough," Malcolm said. "Friends don't leave friends alone."

The Russian pointed at the pot pie. "Is there cheese in that?"

Mack shoved the plate across the counter at him. The Russian picked it up and started eating the pot pie with his hand like a sandwich.

Gavin gaped at him. "Dude, how can you be hungry? We stopped at a fucking drive-through on the way here."

"That was breakfast," the Russian mumbled with his mouth full. "This is lunch."

Malcolm pulled out the chair next to Mack's and sat down. "Tell us what happened."

"You know what happened."

"We only know what happened before you left the chamber gala, not after," Del said.

"And you expect me to believe that he"—Mack nodded at Gavin—"hasn't filled you in on the rest?"

"Thea told me about your father." He paused before adding, "I haven't seen Liv. She's kind of hiding out like you and avoiding everyone."

Mack clenched his hands into fists to ward off the sudden urge to drop his forehead to the counter and cry. If Liv's quiet anger had been painful, Gavin's quiet sympathy was torture. Part of him wished Gavin would hurt him. Hit him. Scream at him.

"Come on, man," Del said quietly. "You know how this works. If you don't tell us what happened, we can't help you fix it."

"There's nothing to fix. It's over."

"Spoken like a true romance hero when all seems lost," Malcolm said.

Mack groaned. "I don't want to talk about stupid book shit anymore."

Then guys exchanged a collective eye roll. "Mack," Malcolm sighed. "You know full well what this is. It's the low point of your story. You can't give up."

"Are you listening to me? This isn't a story. It's my real fucking life, and it sucks. She said it's over, and that's all there is."

"Which is basically what every romance heroine says when the hero fucks up," Del pointed out. "But that's not the end. Come on, man. You know all this."

"All I know is that Liv was right all along." His chest caved in just from saying her name out loud. "I've read too many romance novels, and all it got me is a broken fucking heart."

"Those romance novels have saved all our marriages, man," Del said. "*You* did that for us. You kept us going, kept us reading and hanging on even when we felt exactly like you do now. You really think you can scare us off just because you're finally experiencing the black moment?"

"The *black moment*?" Mack pointed to the back door. "Out. All of you."

They ignored him. "What exactly did she say?" Malcolm prodded.

"Christ," Mack muttered, scrubbing his hands down his face. "What does it matter? It's over."

"What. Happened." Del growled, his frustration evident not only in his voice but in the tense thinness of his lips.

Mack exploded. "Just what I knew would happen! I told her everything! I poured my heart out to her, but the minute she learned the truth about me and my past, she didn't want me anymore." Exhaustion and resignation turned his muscles to mush. His shoulders slumped, and his hands fell uselessly into his lap. "I told her everything, and it wasn't enough."

Malcolm crossed his arms and adopted an intimidating stance. "So that's it? You're not even going to fight for her?"

"There's nothing to fight for. She made it clear that she wants nothing to do with me."

"Bullshit," Del barked. "There has to be more to it than that. Liv wouldn't send you packing over this."

Gavin let out a heavy sigh and sank into one of the chairs at the island. "I don't know, Del. Liv just might. She has a vindictive streak a mile wide."

Mack narrowed his eyes. What kind of bullshit was that?

Gavin leaned on his elbows. "Look, I love my sister-in-law, but she drives me crazy. Sometimes I don't even understand how she and Thea could possibly be related. Thea is kind and nurturing, and Liv is sarcastic and cranky."

Mack's hands curled into fists as his blood pressure spiked.

"I mean, I admire you for trying to get past all her bullshit, Mack. Because that girl . . ." Gavin shook his head and let out a *hoo-boy.* "She makes it awfully hard to love her."

Mack had heard enough and shot to his feet. "Gavin, out of respect for our friendship, I am going to give you exactly one second to take that back before I break your fucking face."

Gavin cocked an eyebrow. "Excuse me?"

"That is the biggest load of bullshit I've ever heard. Liv is the easiest person to love I've ever known. She's funny and smart and kind and brave, and if you spent any time actually getting to know her, you'd see that her sarcasm is just a way to push people away before she gets hurt. It's all a front for a mushy heart that's afraid of being broken. If you can't see that, you don't deserve to have her in your life."

The guys all exchanged another one of those annoying all-knowing looks. Gavin sat back in his chair and tilted his head. "So why exactly aren't you fighting for her, then?"

And that's when Mack realized he'd been played. Sonuvabitch. "You didn't actually mean any of what you just said, did you?"

Gavin grinned. "Not a word."

A blood vessel seemed to burst in Mack's temple. "Get out of my house. All of you."

He spun and stomped to the opposite counter where his phone was still dead and black. Mack planted his hands on the edge of the granite and squeezed until his knuckles turned white, until the flesh of his palms stung.

"Dude, for someone who has spent years lecturing us on how to adapt the manuals to our own lives and relationships, you sure suck at taking your own advice," Malcolm said behind him.

Mack flipped off the room over his shoulder.

There was a scrape of wood against the kitchen tile followed by Gavin's voice. "What did you tell me when I said I couldn't understand Chase's actions in *The Protector*?"

Mack squeezed the counter tighter. "I don't want to talk about the goddamned book."

"You said I was missing the subtext."

"It's a fucking book!"

A fist lightly bounced on his shoulder. "You're missing the subtext of your own actions, Mack," Gavin said.

Mack shrugged him off. "She ended it, Gavin. Not me."

"Did she, though?" Malcolm asked, his feet scuffing across the floor as he, too, approached. "Or did you just walk away without a fight?"

Mack stiffened, his chest tight from a sudden sense of being caged in—not from his friends but from a truth he didn't want to face. "She told me it was over."

"You said yourself that Liv pushes people away to protect herself," Gavin said quietly.

"You knew she would react defensively," said Del, who now joined their small huddle. "That she would put her walls back up."

"You knew that, and yet you did exactly what she expected of you," Malcolm said.

Mack stared at his phone and willed it back to life, but the screen remained dark. Maybe that was for the best, because what if it powered up and he saw zero messages from Liv? Ignorance really was bliss. In so many ways. What he wouldn't give to be ignorant of this feeling, this agonizing pain, this soul-sucking fear that the guys were right.

The vise around his chest tightened again.

"You let Liv push you away instead of staying and fighting for her," Gavin said. "Why?"

Mack closed his eyes. *Fear is a powerful motivator.*

"Come on, man," Del said. "Talk to us."

He couldn't. He couldn't form the words.

"Mack—"

"Because she's better off without me." It came out quietly. Maybe because he was saying it more to himself than to them. Maybe because he simply needed to say it out loud. To acknowledge it. Own it. Live with it. Once and for all.

"Shit," Gavin breathed. "I guess we found the subtext."

"Why would you think that, Mack?" Del asked.

Mack opened his eyes but saw nothing.

"Look at us." That was from Malcolm, quiet and commanding.

Mack shook his head. He couldn't face them right now. They'd take one look in his eyes and see right through him. The *real* him. See him for the fraud that he was. Nothing but a scared fourteen-year-old kid who hid in a closet while his father beat his mother. And then they would reject him too.

"Why would Liv be better off without the man she loves?" Del asked.

"Because she loved an illusion." Shit. What was wrong with his voice? He could barely talk. "She loved a made-up man crafted from the pages of too many romance novels."

"No. You were more real with Liv than we've ever seen you be with a woman," Del said. "She fell in love with the real you."

"Maybe that's what really scares you," Malcolm continued.

"I—" His voice officially failed.

"Mack," Malcolm said softly, his fingers squeezing his shoulder with comforting certainty. "Tell us about your father."

Mack closed his eyes again and tried to swallow, but once again something hard had taken up residence in his throat. "I'm so afraid that part of him lives in me. I think that's why I changed my name."

Jesus. The truth made him dizzy. He gripped the counter harder to stay upright. "I changed my name because I'm terrified that his blood runs through me. What if there's a part of me somewhere that's just like him?"

"Mack," Malcolm said. "You are not your father."

The arrow-sharp precision of Malcolm's words pierced what little steel remained around his bruised, battered heart.

"And you are not what your father did."

Something dripped from Mack's chin. Ah, fuck. He was crying. Goddammit.

"The fact that you started reading romance novels to learn how to be a better man than him shows that you already were a better man than he could ever dream of being."

Gavin came closer. "You've been living with some kind of under-cover identity for so long that you've forgotten who you really are—a good, decent man."

"Fuck," Mack growled. "Fuck!"

Mack pounded his fist on the counter, but then Malcolm

wrapped two giant arms around him from behind. And then Del hugged him, and then Gavin, and suddenly even the Russian was there, and it became a great big manly hug huddle with Mack in the middle.

His friends held him up as all the shit he'd been bottling up since he was fourteen came flying out in a torrent of sobs that he couldn't have stopped if he tried. And they let him cry, let him cling to them.

Malcolm pressed his forehead to the back of Mack's neck. "Let it go, man. Let it go. We got you as long as you need."

He did need them. So much. Because his knees shook, and his legs barely functioned. Mack lost sense of time as his chest released all the built-up pressure of a lifetime of secrets and remorse, pain and regret.

Until the pleasant ding-dong of his doorbell interrupted, followed immediately by an impatient knock.

Great. Who the fuck . . . Wait. Maybe it was Liv. Mack untangled himself from his friends.

"I will get it," the Russian said before Mack could stop him.

He raced back thirty seconds later, eyes bulging with panic. "Code red. Code red."

Code red? What the fuck did that mean?

A diminutive, pissed-off woman appeared in the kitchen.

Oh, fuck. Code-fucking-red.

A collective gulp filled the tense silence as Thea Scott crossed her arms and glared.

"Um, hi, honey," Gavin said. "What are you—"

"Don't *honey* me," Thea snapped.

Gavin shut up.

Thea fired her missile-like stare squarely at Mack. "Now, see, this really pisses me off. I come over here all riled up, ready to call you some really creative names for breaking my sister's heart, maybe even kick you in the balls, and instead you have the audacity to stand there looking like that." She waved her hands at his general state of pathetic loserdom. "How am I supposed to make you feel like shit when you're already there?"

Mack gripped the back of his neck. "Thea—"

"Stop talking."

He snapped his mouth shut.

She slammed her hands on her hips. "I swear to God, you and Liv are going to be the death of me!"

Mack's heart sputtered. "What-what's wrong with Liv? Is she okay?"

"I told you to shut up."

His friends' loyalty had found its limits. They all headed toward the back door, except for Gavin, who hovered like he wasn't sure which would get him in more trouble—staying or going.

Thea threw her arms out to block them from leaving. "No one's going anywhere. You're all to blame for this."

Gavin inched forward cautiously, taking one for the team. "To blame for what?"

Thea pursed her lips. "My sister is about to go after Royce."

CHAPTER TWENTY-NINE

Mack heard a buzzing sound in his ears. "I—what did you say?"

Thea made another frustrated noise. "Hello? The cookbook release? She's going after him."

Today was the day of the cookbook release. Holy shit. He'd been drunk and depressed for so long that he hadn't even added up the days. His mouth went dry. "She's going after him *alone*?"

"No. Jessica and Alexis are helping. And Hop and that weird Geoff guy."

"What the hell is their plan?" Mack couldn't help the tone of his voice. He was worried and feeling super protective about the woman he loved. So sue him.

"Same plan as before, I guess. Except instead of leaking the audio tape, she and Alexis managed to get seven women from the list to agree to come forward. Each woman wrote an essay or something about what happened to them, and Liv had this crazy idea about getting Riya and Geoff to switch out the press kits for all the reporters at the last minute to include those essays." Thea threw her hands in the air again. "I don't know all the details! I just know it's nuts, and I blame you guys!"

Warring emotions made his hands shake. Pride, because holy shit, she'd done it. She'd gotten women to come forward. But panic, because holy shit, she couldn't go in there without him. Without the backup of the guys and, fuck, Noah.

Noah. Mack spun around and grabbed his phone, willing it to life. Noah answered on the second ring. "Wow. You're alive."

"Where's the audio? Is it in any shape or form to be leaked?"

Noah paused. "The audio of Royce? Why? What are you thinking?"

"I'm thinking we need to get our asses over there and do what we said we were going to do."

Mack heard a rustling noise, as if Noah were standing and searching for something. "How much time do we have?" Noah asked.

Mack put Noah on speakerphone and looked at Thea. "How much time do we have?"

She shook her head. "Not much. The event starts in an hour. I couldn't get away until now."

"I can do it," Noah said. "I can get it ready in the van, but we need to move now if we're going to do this."

One by one, the guys shared a look, a smile, and then a nod.

Del walked over and clapped Mack on the back. "Is it grand gesture time?"

His heart pounded with hope and fear. "It's grand gesture time."

It was time to get back the woman he loved.

Liv wasn't going to have any fingernails left after today. The plan was simple, but the risks were high. By the end of the day, either

Royce Preston would have been exposed for the predator he was, or . . .

Or all the women who'd agreed to come forward were going to face his wrath all over again, and Riya would be out of a job, and—

Liv stopped pacing in the driveway outside the garage and dragged her hands down her face.

"Stop worrying," Alexis said, jogging down the stairs from Liv's apartment.

"So much could go wrong."

"And so much could go right."

"What if Riya can't get us in? What if Geoff can't make the switch? What if—"

Alexis palmed Liv's cheeks. "What if two hours from now the entire world knows what Royce did to us? Think about that and only that. I know I am."

Jessica came down the stairs next, her arms heavy with the folders that would be handed out to reporters. Riya had managed to steal one for them so they could match it exactly. Just before the doors opened, Geoff would make the switch.

That was the plan, at least.

Liv grabbed half of the folders, and they carried the load to Hop's car. He was driving, but he'd yet to appear from the house. Every second that ticked by sent her anxiety into another level of hell.

Liv bit another nail. "What is taking him so long?"

"That," Jessica said, pointing.

Liv turned around. There, standing just outside the back door, Hop and Rosie were wrapped in a passionate embrace and a swoony kiss for the ages. Joy for them managed to push through her sorrow over Mack just enough for Liv to smile and enjoy the sight. At least someone got their happy ever after.

"Wow," Jessica sighed. "It's cool that even old people fall in love."

Liv must have made a face that revealed the direction of her thoughts because Alexis once again came to her side. "Are you sure you don't want to call Mack?"

Liv squeezed her eyes shut. Mack. She couldn't think about him right now. She needed to stay focused. "I'm sure."

"It's not too late."

Alexis's words could have had two meanings—that it wasn't too late for Mack to help today or it wasn't too late for them. But Liv didn't ask which one she meant before sliding into the front seat. She had to do this first. And then she would go to him and tell him what a fool she'd been. To tell him she was sorry—so damn sorry—for not being brave enough to hear his side of the story, to accept it, to trust him.

To tell him she loved him.

Him.

Braden Mack or Braden McRae. Whatever his name was, she loved him. She didn't know how it was possible, but it had happened, and she wouldn't survive if she'd destroyed it with her stupid insecurities.

Hop climbed into the driver's seat. "Last chance to back out," he said brusquely.

Alexis and Jessica slid into the back seat and buckled their seatbelts. "Let's do it," Alexis said.

"I'm ready," Jessica added. "He can't get away with this anymore."

Liv reached into the back seat. Alexis and Jessica placed their hands on top of hers.

"I love you two," she said, her voice heavy with an emotion she hadn't expected. "I'm sorry I made such a mess of things at first—"

"Stop apologizing," Alexis said.

"I know I pushed too hard."

Jessica shook her head. "None of this would be happening without you."

Liv felt their support and forgiveness all the way to the tender parts of her soul. She laughed through a sheen of tears.

"Okay," she said. "Let's go."

"Okay," Mack said, snapping his seatbelt. "Let's go."

Mack drove the van with Malcolm in the front seat. The Russian was crammed into the back next to Noah, who worked feverishly to get the tape of Royce ready. Thea, Gavin, and Del followed in Thea's car because they actually had a stupid game tonight after this. Mack would've laughed about it if his heart weren't lodged in his throat.

Mack's phone buzzed just as the small caravan pulled onto the freeway. His heart sputtered with hope that it would be Liv, but it was Gavin. "What?" he barked.

"She just texted Thea. They're almost there. We need to go fast."

Mack hit the accelerator, but the fucking van was a million years old and barely broke sixty-five.

Mack pulled the phone away and relayed the message to Noah. Then he returned to the call. "Thea is sure we shouldn't tell her we're coming?"

"She's sure. Liv needs to—"

"Do it her way," Mack finished. "I know."

He ended the call and tried again to nudge the van up to something close to the speed limit. Cars passed on the left and right. When this was over, he was buying Noah a new fucking van.

Actually, there were a lot of things he was going to do when this was over, and almost all of them involved doing whatever it took to get Liv back.

The skyline appeared after several tense moments.

"Mack, we got a problem," Noah said from the back just as he took the exit.

Not the words Mack wanted to hear. "What kind of problem?"

"I can't edit it down."

"What does that mean?"

"The part about you. I can't cut it out in time. If we hack into their audio, I can't guarantee that I'll be able to turn it off before—"

Mack squeezed the steering wheel.

Before all of Nashville's elite learned the truth about him.

What would that feel like? To be free of the shame? To wake up every morning without the crushing weight of his past? What would life be like if he could finally free himself of the suffocating illusion that was *Braden-Fucking-Mack*?

Here was his chance.

And he was taking it. "I don't care."

"You're sure?" Malcolm asked quietly.

"I'm sure," he said, certainty adding an edge to his voice. "I'm done being undercover in my own fucking life."

He just prayed he wasn't too late.

They were going to be late.

An entire block around Savoy was blocked off for the event, because of course it was. If Royce had to shut down the whole city to bask in his undeserved glory, he'd do it. Traffic slowed to a stop three blocks from the parking garage where they planned to meet

Geoff. Hop let out a string of curse words that made Jessica's mouth drop open; apparently she didn't know that even old people could swear too.

"Text him and let him know," Alexis said.

Liv hammered out a message to Geoff and bit her lip waiting for a response. It wasn't good.

If I'm not inside in fifteen minutes, we're toast.

Liv turned around in her seat. "Hand me the folders."

"What?" Alexis said. "Why?"

"I'm getting out here. You guys park and meet me there."

Alexis shook her head as Hop cursed again. This time at her. "No way," Alexis said. "We do this together."

"We *are* doing it together, but Geoff needs these now."

Hop must've realized there was no other way, so he braked hard. "Go fast."

Alexis shoved the folders through the opening between the front seats. Liv gathered them up and threw open her door. Dodging traffic, she jogged to the sidewalk, which was teeming with tourists.

Liv clutched the folders to her chest and started to run.

Three blocks. She just had to make it three blocks. And then she could prove this was all worth it.

"You didn't check the fucking traffic?"

Mack jerked his eyes from the road to Malcolm, who almost never swore. "I've been a little busy," Mack snapped.

Traffic around Savoy was a nightmare of stop-and-go, but mostly stop.

The van hadn't moved in three full minutes. Mack dragged a hand down his jaw. "I have to get to Liv."

"Put it in park," Malcolm ordered.

Mack did a double take. "What? Why?"

"Because I'm going to drive. You just get out and go."

Mack shoved the ancient gear stick into park. He threw open his door and jumped out as Malcolm slid behind the wheel. He wove through the cars stopped in both directions but heard the creak of the van door behind him. He turned just in time to see the Russian leap out.

"What are you doing?" Mack yelled.

The Russian vaulted over the hood of a car and came to a stop on the sidewalk. "Because it's grand gesture," he said.

Mack grinned and patted his shoulder. "And we always run for grand gesture."

Three blocks. He just had to make it three blocks. And then he could prove to her he was worth it.

Oh God, Liv hated running. Like, hated it. All those people who ran for pleasure and did marathons and stuff, she'd never understand them. Never. Because every slap of her shoes against the pavement was torture, especially since she couldn't move her arms.

But it would be worth it. Geoff would switch the folders. Reporters would read the truth about Royce. And then she would run any distance, any length of time, to get to Braden and tell him everything she should have said long before now.

One. More. Block.

Liv skidded around the corner. The parking ramp was in sight.

Finally. Sweat ran down her back. Her heart pounded in her ears, eclipsed only by her labored breaths.

"LIV!"

She skidded and spun. She had to be hallucinating from lack of oxygen, because that sounded like—

It was. There *he* was. Running toward her. Arms pumping, legs sprinting, leaping small curbs in a single bound.

He slid to a stop a foot away from her.

And the only thing she could think to do was grin and say, "Braden-Fucking-McRae."

Of all the things Liv could've said when she saw him, that was by far the best.

Mack didn't think. Not when he ate the distance between them. Not when he cupped her face and kissed her until neither could breathe. Not when he tugged her against his chest.

"God, Liv. I'm so sorry."

She pulled away. "What are you doing here?"

"Thea told us. I'm so proud of you."

She shook her head and squeezed an armful of folders to her chest. "I have so much I need to say to you, but there's no time. I have to get these to Geoff."

Mack reached for them. "Give them to me. Where we are going?"

"The parking ramp. Fourth floor."

He followed her pointing finger and then wrapped her hand inside his free one. "Let's go."

Behind them, his footsteps slapping the sidewalk in time with theirs, the Russian let out a whoop.

"I love grand gesture!"

* * *

"Where have you been?" Geoff ducked out from behind a concrete column, sweat circles darkening the underarms of his shirt.

Liv bent at the waist and panted. "Traffic."

"Here," Mack said, shoving the folders at him.

Geoff took them and spun. "Meet Riya at the kitchen door in five minutes."

He ran toward the staircase and disappeared from view.

"We have the recording," Mack said, out of breath. "Noah is going to hack into the audio and play Royce's confession."

"Mack, I—"

He cradled her face between his hands. "I know. I know. Let's just do this thing, and then we can say all the things we need to say."

They linked hands again and ran the same direction as Geoff.

"Where is everyone else?" Liv panted.

"Noah will stay in the van. I don't know about Malcolm."

The Russian held open the heavy door to the stairway. "Hurry," he said, ushering them through.

They jogged down the stairs two at a time, their heavy footfalls and heavier breathing the only sounds in the concrete walls. The Russian ran ahead and turned a corner to the ground level.

He grunted suddenly and let out a Russian curse.

Liv and Mack locked eyes before bolting down the last few steps. "What's wrong," Mack barked as they rounded the corner.

The Russian was crouched over someone on the ground. Oh, shit.

"Geoff!" Liv dropped to her knees. Geoff was on his side, eyes closed.

"He is out cold," the Russian said. "Like hockey player knocked into the glass."

"What happened?" Mack patted Geoff's face. "Come on, man. Wake up."

"The folders are gone," Liv whispered.

A sinister voice responded behind them. "These folders?"

Liv jumped and spun around.

And face-planted into a massive chest that smelled like salami.

She lifted her gaze to find ice-blue eyes glaring down.

CHAPTER THIRTY

"I knew you'd try to pull something," Sam sneered, holding the folders aloft in his massive hand. "What are these?"

"The truth," Liv spit out, her voice echoing inside the concrete cavern.

Mack wrapped his arm around Liv's waist and pulled her against his chest. Geoff groaned on the cold, dirty ground and rolled onto his back.

"What did you do to him?" Liv asked.

Sam shrugged. "Just a bump on the head. He'll wake up sooner or later."

"It won't matter how long you keep us in here," Mack said. "Even if you stop us from getting those folders to the reporters, we have Royce's confession on tape."

Sam blinked. It was almost imperceptible, but it was there. *Fear.* He covered it with bluster. "You're lying."

"Nope," Liv said. "And with Geoff's help and Jessica's, you're going down too. You've been covering for him and doing his dirty work for years."

Liv's phone rang in her pocket. Sam glared. "Don't answer it."

"It's all coming out, Sam," Liv said. "It's over. Just accept it and let us go."

Now Mack's phone rang. Everyone was looking for them.

"Now or never, Sam," Mack said.

Sweat beaded on Sam's brow. "I'm not going down for him."

"That's between you and the authorities. We just want to stop him. Either help us or don't, but Royce is going down. Today."

Sam spun and started to pace, panic fueling his steps. Mack met the Russian's eyes. "Vlad?"

The Russian raised his eyebrows. "Yes?"

"Break his balls."

Sam's eyes registered the threat only a split second before a massive Russian fist met his face. Sam crumpled, the folders slipping from his hands. Liv squatted to gather them up, pausing just long enough to check on Sam. "Is he okay?"

The Russian hoisted Geoff over his shoulder. "He will be fine. Let's go."

"I don't want you to get in trouble for hitting him," Liv said, glancing over her shoulder as Mack grabbed her hand.

"Let me worry about that," the Russian said. Or Vlad, as Mack called him. He actually had a name.

They ran into the alley behind the restaurant, their feet crunching broken asphalt as they ran toward the kitchen door. Riya stood just outside in her Savoy uniform and chef's coat, biting her nails and pacing. When she spotted them, she nearly deflated in relief. But then she saw the Russian with Geoff over his shoulder. "Oh my God, what happened to him?"

"Sam hit him."

Geoff's voice rose above Vlad's shoulder. "What's happening? Why am I upside down?"

"Here," Liv said, shoving the folders at Riya. "Go."

Riya shook her head, and time stood still as Liv registered the look on her friend's face. "No," Liv breathed. "We're too late?"

"They've already started letting people in. We can't switch the folders now."

No. Dammit, no! Liv dragged her hands through her hair. Mack punched his fist into his other hand and cursed.

"We still have the recording," he said. "Let me call Noah."

Liv sucked in a breath. She needed to think. Regroup. "Where are Jessica and Alexis?"

Riya swallowed hard. "They tried to call you."

Dread filled Liv's stomach. "Where are they?"

"Inside. They're going to just confront him in front of everyone."

"Breathe." Mack rubbed Liv's back. She sat on the bench inside the employee locker room, bent at the waist and sucking air. Riya had hidden them in there before running out to take her place among the staff, but fifteen minutes had gone by with no news, no updates. Gavin and Thea had called ten minutes ago and said they couldn't get in. Neither could Malcolm. He was stuck in the van with Noah.

Liv was going to throw up.

Geoff was laid out on the other bench, his head in the Russian's lap. Vlad held an ice pack to Geoff's temple. "No concussion," Vlad said. "I know these things."

"I should be out there," Liv said. "I'm the one who dragged them into this."

"Royce dragged them into this," Mack said.

"I can't just hide in here!"

The door flew open. Riya burst in, a wild look on her face.

Liv shot to her feet. "What's happening?"

"They stood on chairs and yelled that he's a serial sexual harasser, and all hell broke loose!"

Riya punched a few buttons on the audio unit on the wall that controlled speakers throughout the restaurant. The locker room was suddenly alive with the sounds of yelling, gasping, and the blustery denials of Royce.

"These women are disgruntled former employees! I had to fire them! Do not listen to them."

Liv gripped Mack's hand as Alexis's voice rose above the cacophony. "Royce Preston blackmailed me into an unwanted sexual affair—"

"Shut up!" Royce bellowed. "Don't listen to these women!'

"—for more than a year!" Alexis finished.

"Does that woman even look like my type?" Royce sneered.

"We have seven more women who have come forward," Jessica yelled.

Liv's hands flew to her mouth. "Oh my God," she breathed. "Listen to them."

"We have written statements for every reporter in the room," Alexis said.

"I want these women arrested!" Royce screamed over the noise. "I will sue your asses for slander. Sam! Where the hell is Sam?"

Liv sank against Mack's chest, her back pressed against the strong beat of his heart.

Chaos was a concert through the speakers—a clash of blustery denials and reporters' questions and, above it all, the confident, strong voices of two women who'd had enough and were taking back their lives.

The door burst open again.

Royce stalked in. A belligerent bison, huffing and puffing. He shook from the top of his toupee to the toes of his Berluti loafers. His face was the color of a stewed tomato. *"Olivia."*

Mack's arm snaked around her waist.

"I knew you were behind this." He advanced with threatening intent, but Vlad shot to his feet, sending Geoff sideways onto the floor.

Vlad jumped in Royce's way. "You will not move," he said flatly.

Royce gulped and backed up.

"It's over, Royce," Liv said. "You're done."

Royce shook his finger at her. "You won't get away with this. I will sue your asses. All of you. You really think anyone is going to believe you over me, you insignificant little bitch?"

Mack dialed Noah and, with his eyes locked on Royce, gave a simple instruction. "Play it."

The speakers throughout the restaurant scratched with static, and then a clear, strong voice came through.

"What do I have to give you to get you to back off?"

Liv smiled. "I was recording our conversation, Royce."

Royce's face drained of color, the first sign of any recognition that he was good and truly done.

"A signed statement."

"A signed statement saying what?"

Liv laughed at the sound of her own voice—so much calmer than she'd felt that night. And far calmer than she felt right now.

"That you didn't see a goddamned thing."

"Is that how you do it? How you keep your dirty little secret? You intimidate women until they sign statements saying it never happened, they never saw anything, you never touched them?"

"Do you really think I don't know how to do this after all this time?"

The last line skipped and repeated. Skipped and repeated. Over and over. A nightmarish echo. A confession that spelled the end.

Mack laughed and dropped his forehead to Liv's hair. "Noah," he murmured.

Royce found his bluster one last time. "Aren't you forgetting something? I confessed something about you, too, that night, *Mack.* I will make sure everyone knows *your* dirty little secret."

Mack lifted his head, spread his hand wide across Liv's stomach, and held her tight. "I don't care, Royce. I'm done hiding."

Liv turned in his arm and looked up. "Are you sure?"

Mack smoothed a curl behind her ear. "I want to start fresh. You deserve that."

Once again, the door flew open. Royce's publicist ran in. "We need to go out through the back, Royce," the man said, a greenish tint to his face. "It's chaos out there. The reporters are going to swarm you."

Vlad planted a hand in Royce's chest. "You will not move."

"Let him go, Vlad," Liv said. "There's nowhere he can go to escape from this now."

The publicist cast a wary and perhaps apologetic glance at Liv before wrapping his fingers around Royce's elbow and pulling him out.

Liv was only peripherally aware of things happening after that. Geoff rose from the floor with a groan. The Russian ran to his aid. Riya said she needed to go check on Jessica and Alexis.

Liv saw and heard only one thing clearly.

Mack.

He pulled her into his arms. "Are you okay?"

She pressed her cheek to his chest. "I am now."

His arms suddenly tightened, and he dropped his face to her shoulder. "Tell me I haven't lost you, Liv."

Liv pulled back and once again looked up at him. "Do you think maybe we can say those things to each other now?"

Mack swallowed hard and cupped her cheeks with his hands. "I'm so sorry I left that night at your sister's. I should have stayed and held you, but I failed you because I was a fucking coward—"

She covered his mouth with her hand. "Shut up."

He blinked but obeyed.

"I'm the one who failed that night." She slid her hand to his jaw. Her voice took on the tremor that reflected how she really felt. Nervous. Scared. So damn sorry. "I used the bullshit about your name as an excuse because I was scared. Because I knew I was on the verge of falling in love with you, and that's never happened to me before."

He broke into one of those grins, the kind that told her everything was going to be okay. "Well, hell, darling. Maybe we should just give it a try."

Her heart pounded. "Give what a try?"

"Don't you think it's high time you and I fell in love?"

Something broke in her chest that spread warmth and joy and safety. Happiness coursed through her as she rose on tiptoes to brush her lips across his. "Hey, Braden?"

He dipped for another kiss. "Hmmm?"

"I already *have* fallen in love with you."

"Good," he laughed quietly, his breath warm against her lips. "Because so have I."

His brow came to rest on hers, his hands cradling her face as if he never wanted to let her go. "Hey, Braden?" she whispered.

"Hmm?"

"Kiss me, you idiot."

He did. Oh, how he did. He devoured her mouth, poured his heart into every nudge of his lips, every caress of his hands, every murmured promise and vow. Liv tangled her fingers in his hair and held on to him. She was never letting him go.

A loud scuffle of shoes at the door drew them apart just enough to turn and look.

Gavin, Del, and Malcolm skidded into the room followed by Thea. "Oh my God! We couldn't get in!" Thea said. "What did we miss?"

They all stopped at the same time and stared, taking in Mack's hands on Liv's back, her hands in his hair, the freshly kissed plumpness of their lips.

"Oh," Thea squeaked. "Oh, thank God."

Del dug into his pocket and pulled out his wallet. He strode forward and shoved a wad of bills at Mack.

"What's this?" Liv asked, eyebrow raised.

"Congratulations," Del said. "You finally have a girlfriend."

Liv backed up, hands on her hips. "Excuse me? You had another bet about me?"

Mack shoved the money in his pocket, drew her back, and silenced her crankiness with his lips. For once, she didn't mind.

A discreet cough a moment later drew them apart again. A man Liv didn't recognize had entered the room. With his plain white shirt and khaki twills, he had reporter written all over him.

"Jessica and Alexis said you were the one who started all this," the man said.

Liv turned around. "We just helped."

The man shook his head, looking from face to face, recognition dawning as he saw Gavin, Del, and even Vlad.

"I don't get it. You guys are all, like, famous. What do you have to do with this? I mean, who *are* you guys?"

Liv watched as the guys did that silent conversation thing—raised eyebrows, shrugs, nods.

Mack grinned down at Liv. She laughed and burrowed her face in his chest.

"Who are we?" Mack said, standing all. "We're the Bromance-Fucking-Book-Club."

The reporter raised his eyebrows. "The what now?"

Mack grabbed Liv's hand. "They'll explain it," he said, nodding at the guys. "Now, if you'll excuse us, we have a happy ever after to start."

EPILOGUE

Six months later

"Prosecutors announced today that disgraced reality-TV chef Royce Preston has accepted a plea deal for charges of endangerment, embezzlement, and tax evasion. Preston is expected to receive a sentence of sixteen to twenty years in federal prison . . ."

Liv turned down the volume of the TV in her garage apartment and flopped down on the couch next to Braden. "No charges for sexual harassment."

Braden lifted his arm so Liv could snuggle against him. "He deserves a lot more than twenty years."

"It was nice of Gretchen to take on the cases of all the women. I can't believe they need legal protection, but at least she's doing it pro bono."

"I'm just glad it's over," Braden said, pressing his forehead to her temple. "I'm ready to focus on other things finally."

"Like the new restaurant?"

"And my hot new pastry chef."

"Seems risky," Liv said, turning to straddle his lap. "Hiring your girlfriend? Could be really complicated."

"I'm willing to take the risk." Braden's hands snuck inside her shirt. "Especially if she's not my girlfriend."

Liv scrunched her face up. "This is a really weird way to break up with me, Mack."

"I was thinking more along the lines of going into business with my wife."

Liv froze. "What did you say?"

"I'm asking you to marry me," he said, his hands spanning her waist, his heart in his eyes. "I want to come home to you every night and work with you every day. I want you to lean on me on the couch and tell me about your day. I want to make love every night and fight and make love some more."

She gazed down at him and felt her chest clench at the expression in his eyes. How did this happen? How had she found this man? She covered his lips with hers. His kiss was hungry, probing. She let him plunder her mouth, but she finally grasped his head and held him steady. He obeyed, and then his fingers were at the button of her jeans, his hands tugging impatiently to ease the denim from her hips. She slid off him and reclined on the couch, the need suddenly fueling an inferno inside her.

They made love and promises, and when they were done, he tugged her close to his chest. "You wanna snuggle?"

She pressed her cheek the warm valley over his heart. "Yes."

"Yes, you want to snuggle? Or yes, you'll marry me?"

"Both."

It was actually a while before they got to the snuggling part, because after she said yes, he did things that made her say it a whole bunch of times naked. She collapsed, spent and satisfied, on top of him, and he pulled a blanket over their bodies.

"I love your chest."

He kissed her head. "It's yours."

Liv made a fist and held it out for him to bump. "Partners?"

He brought her fist to his lips. "Forever."

Don't miss

THE *Bromance* BOOK CLUB

Out now from

HEADLINE
ETERNAL